Charlotte's Nemesis

by

Violet Moore

Cover Art by Tamara Copeland

Charlotte's Nemesis

Copyright © by Violet Moore

Library and Archives Canada
ISBN: 978-1-928100-06-5 paperback
Inspirational Fiction; abandonment; unconditional love

First Printing October 2015

Published by T.I.G. (The Inkster Group)
theinkstergroup@live.ca

The Inkster Group
TIG theinkstergroup@live.ca

This book is
Dedicated to

Elena Wiebe

How do I say thank you…
Your gift of healing the body through deep massage
Has freed me from the debilitating pain
to write and write!

iv

Acknowledgements

Bobbi Junior, how grateful I am for your patient editing, the love and encouragement that permeates from your very being

Rick Junior, your cheering from the stands blesses my heart

Dot Midling, I hear ya – all the way from Florida! Bless you

Pastor Mac, the spiritual truths you've shared keep on bearing fruit, long after they've left your lips

Pearl McKay and **Jenny Hiebert,** my diligent beta readers are the best encouragers to keep on writing

Grandson Jon – thx for the suggestion to add goons to the plot

To the truck drivers who are generous in offering folks a lift when they see the need and care enough about them to share the good news of the gospel of Jesus Christ; with special thanks to **Richard Stasynec, Jerry Rogers,** and **Sacha Kaboha,** for sharing helpful background information.

Last but not least, **Larry,** without you and TIG, my writing would still be in notebooks, and I *don't mean electronic.*

Chapter One

1977 March 10th

Fierce love filled the seventeen year old girl's whole being as she held the tiny bundle close to her heart. "You're all mine," she cooed. Loving fingers gently traced the outline of his perfect bow-shaped mouth. "No one can take you away from me." She kissed the little mouth. "And I'll *never* kick you out of the house to fend for yourself. That's a promise."

Tired, she leaned back against the snow white pillows keeping a firm grasp on the baby. Her eyelids flickered shut and hid the dark chocolate colored eyes. A head full of long dark tresses framed her face, beautiful even when free of makeup.

Moments later her eyes popped open. She let her gaze sweep around the sterile hospital room. She shivered. "There's no one who cares about us. Too bad I don't have any idea which man could be your father; the one who paid for the rent; or the one who bought me nice clothes; or… And your grandparents…ha, they wouldn't come even if they knew they now have a precious grandson. Too bad your great-grandparents aren't around anymore. They would love to see you."

The baby stirred in her arms. A warm feeling filled her and melted away the despair as her eyes focused on the little boy. Only hours old but already he had a special hold on her heart. "It's just you and me, my little one," she whispered as she caressed his dimpled chin.

Her eyes narrowed and focused on a distant point as she vowed, "I will do my best to give you a better life than I had."

She shifted him so they were face to face. One of her nicely-manicured hands held his tiny head and the other one supported his little bum. She gazed with love-filled eyes at his perfect features.

"Marcus." She rolled the name off her tongue. "Yes, Marcus. I like it. It's a manly name, a strong name for my precious little boy."

She pulled him up against her shoulder and patted his back as she gently rocked back and forth. Her eyes focused once more on the empty walls and the empty beds in the room – *just like my empty life.*

She shook her head to clear away the depressing image and hugged the baby closer to her heart. "But not empty anymore. Now I have you, my little Marcus. We belong to each other. No one is going to make you go from one miserable home to another like I had to. Where I got beat up, ridiculed and constantly reminded that I wasn't wanted. No siree!" she whispered fiercely. Then she kissed the cute little nose that rested on her shoulder. She kissed each of the closed eyelids and rested her cheek on the top of his head as she snuggled with him. "We have each other and that's all we need."

***

Four days later she left the hospital, her baby boy wrapped snuggly in a slightly used blanket. The diaper bag, donated by the local Women's Auxiliary, was slung over one shoulder. It bounced against her slender hip as she made her way carefully down the icy steps; mindful of the fact that the newborn depended on her and her alone. No one waited out front to drive them home. She didn't even have bus fare, so walking the eight blocks was not a choice.

Gratitude filled her heart as she slid a hand over the contour of the bag. It held two sleepers and a dozen diapers besides a bar of baby soap, baby shampoo and a pink bottle of lotion. "My boy will smell so nice." She smiled but kept her eyes on the snow covered path leading to the sidewalk. "There's just the two of us. We've got no one to help us with all that a newborn needs, so we're really happy for every little bit, aren't we?"

Talking to the baby helped to distract her from the shaky feeling that threatened to buckle her legs.

The cold March wind tore around every corner, no lull in it to grant a small reprieve. Weary and shivering, she forced herself to keep putting one foot in front of the other. Her teeth chattered. She pulled the baby closer to her breast.

Half way home there was a narrow inset in front of the Real Estate Offices. She stepped into the niche, hoping to be out of the wind so she could rest for a few moments. The bricks dug into her back as she leaned against them. But even there the fierce wind found her. It blew stronger than ever and drove her out of the pseudo shelter. Still weak after giving birth, she had no strength to resist the wind as it pulled and pushed at her, until she feared the little one would be snatched right out of her arms.

The young mother was exhausted by the time she spotted their apartment building up ahead. It looked beautiful to her at the moment, in spite of the fact that the brownish red brick was old and crumbling and that the windows were too dirty to reflect the sunshine when it did shine. The front steps sagged in the middle and creaked loudly with each step she took.

Fierce determination gave her the needed strength to climb the stairs to the second floor. With shaking hand she managed to unlock the door. Stale air hit her nostrils as the door opened but she didn't care. She'd made it home.

Inside, she laid the baby on the narrow bed and dropped the diaper bag at its foot end. The young mother didn't wait to remove her jacket. She crawled in beside Marcus and pulled the well-worn quilt over both of them. Curled around him for warmth, she felt his soft breath fan across her cheek. She was amazed at the strong feelings that swept over her. "How can I love you so much and you're not even a week old," she whispered just before she dozed off.

***

The baby stirred. It startled her wide awake. She propped herself up on one elbow and watched as he stretched and twisted his little body. A tiny fist pushed out of the blanket. The young mother gently folded her hand around his. She smiled. It felt nice and warm.

After she nursed him, she lifted him up onto her shoulder to burp him. Leaning her back against the wall she cuddled Marcus, enjoying the moment. When he started to squirm she bounced him up and down, gently patting his back until he settled down again.

Her gaze roamed around the room. A small fridge with a shelf above it for the microwave was stacked in one corner. Beside the door sat a dresser. The drawers could only be opened when the door was shut. Next to the dresser sat the crib that she'd found beside a dumpster. At the local Thrift Store she'd paid three dollars for a small mattress. She still remembered what a struggle it had been to get it home. Afraid to ask lest they would deny her request, she'd snitched a rope hanging from a shelf in the hardware department. The rope had given her the leverage needed to keep the mattress from sliding off her back as she staggered along the sidewalk. She smiled at the sight it must have been, having to stop every so often to massage her swollen belly.

She continued her inventory of the room. The narrow bed on which she sat filled the wall across from the door. She reached out one hand and rested it on the small table next to the pillow end of her bed. Half of its surface was taken up with a cardboard box placed on its side. It held her dishes. "It's not much but it's mine." Her dry chuckle made the baby stir. It was time to put Marcus into his crib.

Most of the paint had peeled off of its slats. But that wouldn't hinder it from keeping her baby safe. She lowered him down onto the lumpy mattress and picked up the blue quilt hanging over the crib's side. As she tucked it around her boy she admired the yellow duckling placed in the middle of a bunch of dark blue flowers. *Someone went to a lot of work on that applique. And it looks hardly used. Maybe her baby didn't live. Why else would the mother give it away?*

The quilt had been tucked into one of the bags of stuff along the wall at the Soup Kitchen. One of the servers had told her to take whatever she needed. *I'm so glad that lady from the Salvation Army told me about the free food on Main Street. Beggars can't be choosers, and I'll do anything for my baby, beg, borrow, or steal. And I'm not too proud to take free handouts.*

After she settled Marcus in the crib, it took only a few moments to unpack. The donated items barely covered the bottom of the top drawer. She had no money to buy more diapers. Breastfeeding the little one would eliminate the cost of bottles and formula, but it also meant that she needed to eat proper food. "Well, the folks at the soup kitchen seemed to care about me. So I won't have to worry too much about food for me. I'll get at least a few good meals each week."

Maybe they'll know where I could get some more diapers. Or maybe there are some well used towels in those bags. I could use them for diapers. They'd be easy to wash and would dry quickly.

6

She turned and took all of two steps to reach the table. Taking a mug from the cardboard box she walked to the door. Before she stepped out into the hallway she glanced over her shoulder at the baby. He was still sleeping soundly.

She hurried to the shared bathroom at the end of the hall. It took only a moment to fill the cup with water. Back in her room, she heated it in the microwave. A teaspoon of instant coffee, also kept in the box on the table, was added to the cup. The powdered crystals swirled around in the clear liquid and changed it into a deep brown color as she stirred. *Now if only I had a bit of cream.*

She heaved a sigh of relief as she lowered her tired body onto the bed. She pulled her feet up and leaned back against the wall behind her. Eyes closed, she savored a sip of the fragrant beverage. But just as she began to relax, the baby decided it was time to wake up.

The blue quilt fell away from his face as two little clenched fists waved in the air. She smiled and set her cup on the table. How could she be upset that there was no time for her to rest? He was too precious.

Chapter Two

Time Goes On

The days were long and the nights longer. She began to pace, frustrated that the room was so small there were only two or three steps in any one direction. She felt like the walls were closing in on her.

Marcus was such a good baby, which left her with nothing to do while he slept. The quiet in the room, broken only by the baby's gentle breathing almost drove her crazy.

She tried to ignore the loneliness, the lack of finances, and most of all the constant craving. She just had to get out of the apartment. It was the craving that finally dragged her out of the room. After a whole week of fighting she couldn't resist it any longer.

She caved in on Monday. Haste made her clumsy as she pulled on her jacket and wrapped the baby his blanket. Careful not to slip on the icy steps she set off for her old haunts.

Marcus began to squirm at being confined. She pushed the top flap of the blanket to the side, "Whatsa matter baby? You wanna look around, don't you? I'm taking you for a walk, see?" she cooed. His beautiful dark eyes stared up at her. She tucked a stray wisp of hair back under the blanket and smiled at him.

"Let's go introduce you to the nice man at the pub. He'll want to see you, yes he will. You'll see. He really cares about us. He's always ready to listen and sometimes he even slips me a free drink. That's so nice of him, isn't it?"

Marcus' mother continued to talk to him as she hurried along the street. It didn't take long to arrive at her destination. After proudly showing off her baby boy, just as she'd expected, a number of drinks were offered to her.

It was getting too hot in the room. The baby squirmed in her arms until they ached. She made her way to a secluded corner and used her jacket to make a bed for Marcus. He gave a big stretch as if pleased not to be held so tight anymore, rolled to his side and closed his eyes. He slept without making a sound until the next feeding time.

"Gotta go look after the kid," she called to the bartender. She blushed as he kissed his fingertips and blew the kiss her way. Tickled with the special attention, her feet almost flew as she hurried home to take care of Marcus' needs.

It was easy to fall asleep this time, contented with the attention at the pub and all those free drinks.

***

At first it was easy to take the baby along. And she didn't mind the rush to get home to look after him. He was such a precious baby.

But the time wasted on going back and forth began to wear on her. She didn't want to miss out on any of the special attentions from the patrons at the pub. As the baby gained weight, it became harder to carry him. Her own strength was slow in returning. Not enough nourishing food and too much alcohol, she grew skinnier as he gained weight.

Bit by bit resentment set in, not at the baby, but at not having time for herself. *I know what I can do. I'll just slip into the ladies' bathroom when he's hungry. That way I won't have to miss out on the fun while I wait for him to finish his nap. And it will save me a trip out in the cold.*

***

He started to roll over at three months. She had to be so careful about where she put him down. He strained at her arms whenever she carried him, especially when the bright sunshine beat down on them as they walked along the street. Even though he couldn't walk yet, he wanted to be free of any restraint.

For a while his mother was able to contain him at the pub. She grabbed a few cushions off the padded chairs and made a play area in one corner. But by late September he began to crawl. The little corner could no longer contain him. To solve this problem and still allow her some freedom to focus on other folks, she tied a long scarf to one of his legs and the other end around her wrist. That way she knew when it was time to pull him back so he could start all over.

***

By the middle of November Marcus began to walk around the room by holding on to the bed and the dresser. His giggles of delight made her smile. But his mother knew that her situation would have to change soon.

It was no longer a good idea to take him along to the bar. Men were interested in providing for her, but only until they realized that Marcus was included.

And she had to spend most of her time making sure that he didn't trip the waiters or spill someone's drink. At first it had been funny but no one laughed about it anymore.

Another problem was that Marcus wouldn't give in and fall asleep like he used to. The constant noise distracted him from all her efforts of trying to get him to settle down. Loud bursts of laughter would startle him wide awake if by any chance she had been able to lull him to sleep. Each time she pulled up the blanket, Marcus cried out and kicked his legs until it fell away.

Her agitation at the situation grew. Frustration caused her to beg cigarettes and drinks from different patrons; patrons who had previously been most generous. Now her cheeks turned red with humiliation at their begrudging responses.

Apparently she had depended on the good natured folks for too long. If only she had enough money so that she could return the favor. But the Family Allowance was her only income and it was spent before it arrived.

Her rent was two months overdue and the landlord had threatened to break her fingers. The evil laugh that followed the threat made her worry about what else he might do. But most of all she worried about Marcus. She needed to protect him from that vulgar man.

Things at her hangout continued to go downhill. The bartender no longer winked at her and definitely did not slip her any free drinks. Tired out from lugging Marcus around, plus the worry of her hopeless situation, she knew it was time to leave.

Saturday evening when she stepped out of the pub, gentle snowflakes wafted down from the sky. They fell on her eyelashes and turned Marcus' toque a pretty white. But all too soon their softness turned into stinging pellets of sleet. She tried to shield his face with her hand. Marcus resisted. He arched his back and cried out. He pushed at her chest to get away from her. He turned his face to the sky and was startled into a moment of quiet when the snow pellets pinged against his cheeks.

His mother could hardly hang on to him as she trudged wearily along the sidewalk. Marcus was getting far too heavy to carry, especially like now when he squirmed and fretted. He wanted to see the snow but didn't like the pain.

Her back felt like it was on fire by the time they arrived at home. She gave a sigh of relief as she let him slide out of her arms onto the top step. But Marcus wasn't happy about that. He began to whimper and threw himself against her legs, wanting to be picked up again.

She pulled out the key and unlocked the front door. "Shush, my big boy," she whispered. "You don't want to wake up our landlord, do you? He'll be really angry if we wake him up this late." She picked up Marcus and covered his face with kisses to calm him before she stepped into the hallway.

Relieved to be in his own bed, he fell asleep almost as soon as she tucked the quilt around him. The discouraged young mother fell onto her own bed and cried herself to sleep.

Chapter Three

The sun peeked in the window and warmed one side of her face. She rolled over onto her back and stretched. Slowly she opened her eyes and let them gaze around the room. The moment she saw Marcus still curled up in his crib, all her worries flooded back into her mind. She knew. It was time.

The calendar showed that it was Monday, December 10th, 1977. Another rent payment was due on the 15th. This would be the third month of trying to think up an excuse why she couldn't pay.

She sat up and slid her legs over the edge of the bed so she could lean over to look out the window. She heaved a big sigh. The landlord's truck was still in the driveway. *He's probably waiting around to see if he can catch me at home. Good thing we didn't wake him up last night.*

Happy that Marcus was still asleep, she forced herself to sit quietly and think out a plan of action. Her pillow case would make a handy tote. She removed it from the pillow as she listened for noise from downstairs.

Careful not to make a sound, she stood up and pulled the dresser drawer open. She set out an extra outfit to put on Marcus and rolled up the rest of his clothes. Stuffed into the bottom of the bag, it only filled half of it. She wrapped her few pieces of jewelry in a couple of her blouses and added them along with her makeup kit to the pillowcase.

Another glance out the window revealed that the truck was still there. And no sound could be heard of any movement downstairs. *Maybe he's still asleep because of working a late shift. Hope we don't have to wait until evening. There's no way I'll be able to keep Marcus quiet once he wakes up.*

She decided to wear a double layer of clothes. It was easier than adding extra weight to the pillow case. The rest of their things would have to stay behind.

Now all she could do was wait and hope that the landlord would leave before Marcus woke up. Tears threatened to spill over. That must not happen. She stood in the middle of the room and pressed her fingers against closed eyelids. A few deep breaths beat them back where they belonged.

There was no clock to tick away the minutes as she waited; waited for the landlord to leave; hoping he'd leave before her little boy awoke; hoping they could find another place before dark.

There were two slices of bread left. She covered them with peanut butter and placed them back into the bread bag. The jar of water that she kept beside her bed would help to wash it down. She'd wait until they were away from the area and then find a park where they could eat their breakfast, or would it be lunch?

Everything done that she could, the anxious mother sat on the bed. She clasped her hands in her lap and rocked back and forth as she bided her time.

Her body tensed at the sound of a door closing somewhere below. The landlord must be leaving for work. She stood up and stepped to one side of the window. It was him.

When she saw the truck turn at the intersection she pivoted and smiled as she took a deep breath. It was time to wake Marcus.

"Hey, baby," she touched his rosy cheek. "Good boy for sleeping so long. Are you ready to go for a long walk?" She gazed at her wee boy as he stretched and slowly opened his eyes.

She nuzzled his cheek as she picked him up out of the crib. In his drowsy state it took only a few moments to dress Marcus in the extra outfit.

She placed him on her hip. The pillow case was tucked under her other arm, resting the bottom of the bulging bag on her hip to ease its weight and to keep it from slipping out of her hand. All that was left to do was to pull the room key from her pocket and toss it on the table. Her gaze took in one last look at the place that had been home for over a year.

"The longest I've lived anywhere." She didn't quite manage a laugh, "Even counting the years with my parents before they kicked me out and went to join their hippie friends."

A dry sob stuck in her throat as she pulled the outside door closed behind her. The bright sunlight almost blinded her as it reflected off the newly fallen snow. "If only my life had such a bright look about it," she sighed. "Guess we'll have to change our name now, find a new place to hang out and hope that no one will recognize us; especially not that nasty landlord."

When she had turned a few corners, she let Marcus slide down her side until his feet touched the ground. She held onto his hand and let him toddle along beside her. They wouldn't get anywhere fast that way, but she didn't have a clue as to where they would end up so nothing mattered at the moment.

"This isn't any easier than carrying you, my dear boy," she murmured as she pulled up on one little arm to steady him for the tenth time. "But at least it helps to keep us both warm."

The lumps in the snow covered sidewalk kept tripping Marcus. One little foot slid out and hit against his mother's shoe. "Careful, son," she chuckled, "Or we'll both end up in the slush."

It got very quiet. His mother had stopped. Marcus looked up at her. He tried to pull away but she hung on to his arm.

"I'm too tired to walk any farther. But look at that Marcus, a church. Church people are supposed to help the poor. Let's go see if that's really true."

They made their way across the street only to find out that the front door was locked; so was the side door even though someone had taken the time to clean the snow off the sidewalk. Exhausted, she put down the pillow case and arched her back to work out the ache. With a heavy sigh, she sat down on the cold cement steps and rubbed at her temples.

Marcus was delighted with the stop. It meant his mom quit tugging on his hand. She pulled out their peanut butter sandwich and broke off small pieces and popped them in his mouth. When the bread was all gone he took a few steps on the snow covered lawn and fell down. It surprised him but he didn't cry. He sat up and turned to look at his mother. Her head was buried in her hands. He patted the snow beside him and swished his hand back and forth. He looked up when he heard a motor. It was a shiny red car and it came into the yard. It stopped close to the front step where his mother sat.

Marcus sat perfectly still and watched. A tall thin man got out of the car. He was dressed in black and had a white collar around his neck. The man walked over to his mother and spoke to her. She looked up, tears running down her face. Marcus tried to stand up to go to his mother, but his feet kept sliding out from under him. He gave up and crawled over as quickly as he could. He grabbed onto her leg to pull himself up beside her. "Mama?"

"Ssh, ssh, It's okay sweetie. This kind gentleman says there is a nice place not far from here where we can stay." She put her arm around Marcus and pulled him close as she talked some more with the man.

Marcus watched; fascinated by the glitter of jewelry on her wrist as every once in a while his mother dabbed at the tears in her eyes. She smiled and nodded her head in response to whatever the man had said. Then she said, "That would be nice," and stood up. Marcus tumbled back when he lost his grip on her leg.

Before he could hit the ground, the man caught him and lifted him up into his arms. Marcus stretched toward his mother but the man turned and walked to the car.

The next thing he knew Marcus found himself buckled into the back seat of that red car and his mother was in the seat in front of him. Houses flew by too fast for his eyes to see them. It made him dizzy.

The car stopped and the man came around to open the front door for his mother before he pulled Marcus out of the back seat. It was scary to be so high up. He buried his face in the man's jacket. He could feel the rumble of the man's voice as he was carried to the front door of a bungalow. A wonderful smell filled the air. It was the smell of baking bread. Pretty red and green decorations, attached around the big front window, fluttered in the wind. Marcus reached for them but quickly jerked his hand back when the door opened with a sharp click. It startled him.

A tiny gray-haired woman stepped into the doorway. One hand rested on the door frame as she looked up at the tall man holding Marcus. There was a question in her eyes. But she hesitated only a moment before she stepped aside and said with a smile, "Come in." She looked at all three of them in turn as she waited for the Pastor's explanation. Then her eyes settled on Marcus who was squirming to get down. She reached out to help him but Marcus cried and flung himself toward his mother.

A box full of toys waited for him beside the couch. But they would have to wait because his mother dragged him down the hallway to follow the woman.

In the bedroom he saw the crib. A sheet covered the mattress and it had green and yellow tractors all over it. He crawled over to the crib and pulled himself up. He touched one

of the tractors and tried to make the sound of a motor. Soon
the saliva dripped down his chin.

Marcus turned when he heard the door shut. He watched
his mother as she tossed her bag on the big bed. He giggled
when she slid down on the floor beside him and whispered in
his ear. She tickled him and kissed him all over his face until
he squirmed to get away. As soon as he was free, he waddled
over to the closet door, falling twice. He pulled himself up and
put both hands behind his back. He laughed and held out a
hand in front of him when she got on her knees and crawled
toward him.

When the game was over they walked back down the hall
and ended up in the kitchen. The woman reached down and
said, "Here you are," as she handed him a cookie. She also
said, "I hope you'll like it here." Marcus chomped away
happily and didn't notice his mother shrug a shoulder instead
of answering the woman.

Marcus liked this new home. There was lots of floor space
for him to explore. And there was another cookie every time
he scooted into the kitchen. The woman smiled at him a lot
and picked him up to give him hugs. He didn't mind because it
let him see that jar on the counter, the one filled with cookies.

Marcus wasn't used to carpeted floors. When he reached
the living room where the rug began, he tripped and fell. He
looked up but no one was watching. Then he got up on hands
and knees. His little bum went up in the air before his upper
body straightened out. He brushed his hands together and
giggled, satisfied with his accomplishment.

The little woman laughed and reached to pick him up. She
threw him high in the air before she brought him close again
and squeezed him tight. She gave him a little shake and said,
"You sure don't let anything stop you, my little cutie." She
gave him another squeeze and set him back down. With a
gentle swat on his backside she sent him off on another trip

around the house. "I can tell already that you will be a determined young man."

But she didn't smile so much when his mother was around. Marcus often heard her sigh. If she was holding him when she sighed, he would reach out a chubby hand and touch her face, as if to give comfort.

Chapter Four

It was Christmas Eve. Gentle snowflakes drifted past the front room window. Marcus leaned against the sill and watched, mesmerized by the ever changing pattern as the wind swirled them about. He giggled and reached out a hand to catch a big flake close to his face, but his hand thudded against the glass. His mouth opened in surprise but he was instantly distracted as the snowflake twirled away from the window to join its buddies.

"Come, Marcus," said the woman, her hand stretched out to him. "Let me get your coat on while your mommy fixes her hair. Then we'll be all ready to go to the Christmas Eve service."

Marcus, eager to go outside, willingly put his hand in hers. They waited a good while before his mother appeared. He couldn't understand why she had such a frown on her face. They were going outside and she was always going out, even when she didn't take him with her.

Silence reigned in the car as they drove down the street. Marcus didn't mind. There were so many pretty colored lights on all the buildings. The lights on the trees in the yards twinkled as snowflakes drifted down and tried to cover them.

Inside the church there were more beautiful lights. An usher helped them find a place to sit in one of the many crowded pews. Soon after they were seated the lights were dimmed and many children came out of the side door and stood on the platform. Marcus sat entranced as they sang about baby Jesus in a manger. The little bells that they shook along with their singing kept his eyes wide open.

Just as Marcus began to wilt the bright lights came back on. He was wide awake again. After everyone around him sang Silent Night, candy bags were handed out to the children. Marcus clutched his bag with both hands, reluctant to let go while the woman buckled him into his car seat. His mother turned in the front seat and smiled at him, "It's okay, Baby. It's all yours and no one will take it away from you. Just wait until we get home, okay."

Marcus didn't really think about what was inside the bag, he just liked the crinkly sound that it made and it was his.

When they got back home there was a big box by the front door. Marcus slapped his hand on it and laughed as the soft snow on top of it flew up into his face.

Inside, his mother seemed to be in a hurry to get him out of his coat and into bed, but the little woman interrupted.

"Do you mind very much if we open our gifts tonight? Then everyone can sleep in tomorrow morning." She looked at Marcus' mother and waited.

At nine months Marcus wasn't sure what it was all about, but he sensed tension in the air and began to whimper.

His mother picked him up and held him close as she whispered, "It's okay, Baby. She just wants to give you a present. You'll like that, won't you?"

Marcus didn't know about presents, but he liked the woman who had cookies and his whimper turned into a smile.

"All right then," the woman let out her breath like she was glad it got settled so easily.

Marcus was plunked down on the floor in front of the couch. His mother sat down beside him and tried to keep him from crawling away as they waited.

The woman read from her Bible, what she called the Christmas story. His mother sniffed a couple of times, pulled herself up onto the couch, but stayed seated. Marcus rested his head against her knee and watched the lights on the tree.

"Time for gifts," chuckled the little woman. "Here's one for you, Marcus." She handed him a package.

His mother got him started on tearing off the paper. She didn't have to help for long. Marcus thought this was the best game ever as he ripped long strips in the wrapping paper. But he stopped when he saw wheels peek out of the package. He reached out and touched one of the wheels. He slid his hand across it and spun it round and round. His mother decided that he needed to be rescued.

"Here, son, like this." She ripped the rest of the paper off to expose a Tonka Truck.

Marcus giggled and got up on his knees to drive the truck around the couch and around the big chair and back to the front of the couch through the torn paper. Both his mother and the little woman laughed and clapped their hands.

There were more packages for Marcus to open. He knew what to do now and soon he had a ball that almost fit in the box of his truck and a soft snowy white teddy bear to hug. It had numbers on one foot that said 1977. He hugged it and rested his head against it.

The little woman came over to Marcus' mother and put a hand on her shoulder. "I hope you'll like it," she said as she placed a pretty package in her lap.

Marcus watched as his mother tore into her package.

"You got me a real cashmere sweater!" she exclaimed as she held up the soft teal-colored sweater in front of herself. "And it's the right size!"

The little woman didn't say anything. She just nodded her head and smiled.

Marcus wasn't really interested when the big unwrapped cardboard box was pulled into the house. But he hugged his teddy bear and listened to his mother's oohs and ahs as she emptied the big box. There were a bunch of diapers, a diaper bag and little boy clothes in blue. When she pulled out a grown-up outfit and wrinkled her nose at it, Marcus started to giggle. His mother joined him. That made him giggle some more.

The little woman interrupted their giggles and said, "The folks at church thought that with your son growing so fast, these might come in handy."

Marcus' mother stilled her laughter and agreed, "They got that right. And I'm not too proud to take things for my son." Then she turned and tossed the outfit meant for her on the back of the couch. "You can give that back to them. It's not my style."

Marcus didn't like the sad look on the little woman's face. He turned to his mother and reached up with one arm. The other arm held his teddy bear in a vise-like grip.

His mother chuckled as she picked him up and tucked his head onto her shoulder. He gladly nestled against her. She patted his back and crooned, "Is Mother's little boy all tired out? You've had such a busy day, haven't you?"

All the way to the bedroom she hugged him and kissed his cheek as she called him her good boy.

Chapter Five

March 10^{th,} 1978, early in the morning before any sound of stirring came from down the hall, Marcus' mother woke him up. Not to celebrate his first birthday. No, that fact had taken a back seat in her mind. She thought she had a more urgent matter to deal with.

"Marcus," she whispered, "Wake up baby, but be quiet. We've got to quit this joint. I can't stand another minute of the heavy sighs of disapproval. Who does she think she is to give her the right to judge me?"

His mother changed his diaper and pulled up his pajama bottoms with a jerk. "Just 'cause I go out in the evening, and leave you in your crib doesn't make me a bad momma. Honest!"

His mother's whispers got louder and louder. She sounded angry. "I never leave you alone. The old lady's in the house, isn't she?" Mother's hands moved faster with each word. It scared Marcus. His lower lip quivered and the tears gathered in his eyes.

She must have noticed because she softened her voice and brushed the hair off his forehead, "Mother's not angry at you, Baby. No she's not. You're my good little boy." She picked him up and cuddled him close, patting his back. "You're mother's precious son. I could never be angry with you."

Marcus settled into the curve of his mother's body and was well on the way to falling asleep again. But it was not to be.

He almost fell out of her arms when she bent over to pick up the already stuffed diaper bag. She swung the long strap up over one shoulder and moved Marcus to settle him on her hip. Unable to carry another thing, she left all of his toys.

Careful to be quiet, she opened the door to their room and walked swiftly down the carpeted hallway. The deadbolt on the front door made a loud screech as it slid back. She stood still, not breathing. When no sounds came from the back of the house, she stepped out and pulled the door shut behind her.

She hurried down the shoveled sidewalk and past a few corners before she slid the heavy one year old down to the ground. "There you go, Baby. You can walk for a little ways. It's such a beautiful day we're not going to take the bus downtown. This nice man I met yesterday, he got a place for us so he can come over to visit us. Isn't that going to be nice?"

Her smile turned into a frown and her sweet voice changed into a grouch as she complained, "That old woman didn't want me to bring any of my friends into her house. It's not exactly the Christian thing to do, if you ask me," his mother huffed.

She stopped abruptly and put down the bulging bag. She pulled out her purse and grabbed a cigarette package. "You don't mind if mother has a smoke, do you?" She cackled as she lit one. "That old girl would have a fit if she knew where we're going."

Fascinated, Marcus watched the smoke curl up over her head. Then he watched her mouth as she talked. He liked it when she stayed with him, he didn't care what she had to say.

"The nice man said that we won't have to pay a cent. Isn't that sweet of him?" She flicked the ashes off the end of her cigarette and picked at imaginary fluff on her jeans.

Marcus lost interest. He turned and toddled to the edge of the sidewalk. He tumbled headfirst over the curb and into the street. Before he could stand up, a car honked its horn and startled him. His big brown eyes stared up at the car but he didn't cry. He heard the driver yell at his mother and she shouted back. Then car tires squealed and kicked up dirt into Marcus' face as the driver took off. His mother came and knelt in front of him. She helped him up and brushed at the dirt on his pants while she berated that driver. Then she licked her finger and made a curl in his hair and called Marcus her sweetheart.

That settled, they continued their walk to the new home. His mother tugged on his hand until it hurt as she tried to hurry him along the sidewalk. His feet were wet, he was tired and hungry. Marcus started to whimper, he wanted to go back home and play with his toys.

Instead, his mother stopped suddenly in front of a huge house. She gasped as she stared at it. There were a few black holes in the light brown bricks that covered the front of the five story building. The cement steps were crumbling away at the edges. The windows looked like they had years of dirt encrusted on them.

She opened the outer door and helped Marcus into the hallway. It was long and dark. The dark yellow rug had holes in it. Marcus began to follow some muddy footprints that led to the stairs. He had one knee on the first step and both hands on the second one when his mother's voice stopped him.

"What is that god-awful smell?" she exclaimed loudly. "I thought he said it was a nice place. This place smells worse than hell!"

Marcus' unblinking eyes filled with tears. He stared at her and his bottom lip quivered. Her loud voice frightened him.

She came quickly and knelt down beside him, "I'm sorry, Baby. It's okay, Markie. Please don't cry. We can always fix our own room up. We can make it smell all nice and clean no matter what the rest of the place smells like. Sure we can. Okay, baby? Here, let me dry your tears." She dabbed at his face with the edge of her blouse.

She picked Marcus up and climbed the stairs to the second floor. The same color of rug covered the hallway, but with less mud. The door to Room 207 squeaked loudly when they pushed it open. Marcus' mother cringed, "That hurts my ears!" she declared as she moved her jaw up and down, "I hope the landlord can fix that."

Inside the room there was a single bed covered with a stained comforter. A grimy crib with a lumpy looking mattress stood at the foot of the bed. When they moved in for a closer look there was no bedding for it. A dresser and some hooks on the wall above it completed the furnishings. No table or chairs were in sight. There wasn't any space to put anything else.

The window shade hung at a crazy angle and covered only the top half. His mother shrugged a shoulder and said, "Guess it won't matter seeing as we're on the second floor."

She brushed her hand across the top of the dingy dresser before she placed the diaper bag on top of it. Then she shook out the comforter and punched the pillow a couple of times. "Guess us beggars can't be choosers." She made a sound. Marcus wasn't sure if it was a laugh or not.

"Come, son. Let's go check out the bathroom down the hall. I wonder how many people we have to share with."

The toilet bowl looked like it hadn't been cleaned in months. Strands of black hair covered the counter and were stuck in the crud around the base of the taps. A ring of gray soap scum circled the tub.

His mother fumed all the way back to their room. "One of the first things we're going to get is a big bowl for sponge baths. We're never going to bathe in that tub!

"Just wait until I see that man. He's going to get an ear full!"

She waited a couple of weeks, but the 'nice man' never showed up.

Chapter Six

1979 March 10th   Saturday

"You are getting to be such a big boy!" his mother exclaimed. It was Marcus' second birthday.

She had purchased a cupcake for him at the bakery on the corner. She'd snitched a candle off of a cake at the pub last night. Some guy's wife had brought it in to celebrate his birthday.

Now she stuck the partially burnt candle into the cupcake and lit it. Singing happy birthday to Marcus she let him blow it out. He didn't need any help. There was no gift, but at two years of age, Marcus didn't expect anything. His eyes sparkled as he grabbed the candle and bit into it.

"No, no, Baby," said his mother as she stuck her finger into his mouth and pulled out the wax. "Don't eat the candle. Here, eat the cupcake."

Marcus hesitated only until he got a taste of it. Then he gobbled it all up. The chocolate icing covered his face from ear to ear before he was done.

Maybe it was all the sugar he'd eaten or else he was over-stimulated by the extra attention, but he just wouldn't settle down for bed that night. His mother paced around the narrow room as she waited. She kept singing a soft lullaby over and over. At last his even breathing filled the room. Quickly she grabbed her jacket and stepped out into the hall. She pulled the door shut and locked it.

The loud click woke Marcus up. He whispered, "Mother?" When she didn't answer he sat up and called again, louder. By this time he was wide awake. He couldn't sleep. He didn't want to sleep. He stood up and shook the bars of the crib and called again. He rubbed his eyes as the tears came. When she still didn't come back into the room he sank down to a crouch. Two eyes, bright with tears, peered between the bars but couldn't see anything. His hands slid slowly down to the mattress. He rested on his heels and stared into the dark until his body slumped over when he couldn't hold on any longer. His little thumb found its way into his mouth. Sniffles and a few hiccups were the only sound in the room.

Much later when his mother tiptoed up to the door of their room in the early hours of Sunday morning, she held her breath as she unlocked the door. No sound came from the other side. "Good, he's still asleep," she muttered.

Inside, she walked over to the crib. He was fast asleep but she could see some tears on his cheek. "Oh my poor baby, did you have a bad dream?"

Seeing as he was still asleep and she was exhausted, she stumbled over to the bed and plopped down hard. She pulled her feet up onto the mattress and her bleary eyes slid shut. A tired sigh escaped as she pulled the comforter up over her shoulder. "Hope he sleeps for a couple more hours," she murmured as the early dawn filtered light into the room through the thin curtain.

***

Her need for food and liquor drove her to sell her body. She felt it was her only means of income. No one would hire her if they knew she left her little one at home alone. She didn't want to take the risk of someone finding out and taking him away from her. He was all she had.

They'd moved four times that year. Of course, the promise of not having to pay a cent had not come true. The only option she had was to promise to pay 'next week' and then try to find a new place. Of course, without a job, the paycheck never came and after a couple of warnings, she had to disappear again.

Little Marcus left alone for hours at a time, learned how to amuse himself. When he sat quietly with his head resting against the bed, the cockroaches came out of hiding. He tried to catch them. "It's too fast," the almost 3 year old giggled.

The day Mother brought home a little car was a happy day for Marcus. He drove it 'round and 'round the room, under the table and up the table legs. Then he made it jump up onto the top and drove it back and forth, the full length of the table. The turning wheels fascinated him. When he pushed it really fast it looked like a streak of light.

Such hard work made him tired and hungry. He drove the car down the table leg and raced it across the floor. He put on the brakes beside his crib. A grin covered his face as he placed it under his blankie for safe-keeping. Then he turned and ran back to his mother.

She stood motionless, staring out the fifth floor window. At this place they were so high up that they could look over the top of most of the trees. He leaned against her and looked up at her face. He waited. She didn't take her eyes off the window, so he tugged on her pant leg. There was still no response. "Mother," he raised his voice and tugged again. "Moth-er, I'm hungry."

His voice finally caught her attention. She tore her eyes from the window and focused on him. "Sure you are, Baby. So am I. Let's go and see what we can find."

Marcus slid his arms into the jacket she held out to him. He stood patiently while she buttoned it up to his chin. Then he reached for her hand and they walked out the door, down the stairs and out onto the street. Soon they were at a noisy place.

His mother found a booth and hoisted Marcus up onto the seat while her eyes swept over the room as if she was searching for something, or someone.

Marcus just wanted food. He stood up on the bench and leaned towards her. "Moth-er, I'm hung-ry."

"Just a minute, Baby, just a minute," she whispered, her eyes roving over the place instead of looking at him.

He reached up and patted her face. She was still distracted so he put up both hands and pulled her face down to look at him. When he could see both her eyes he whispered, "Markie is hungry."

She sat him back down on the bench and patted his leg, "You stay here, Baby. I'll be right back."

"I not a baby, I a big boy." He frowned in concentration as he sat as tall as he could.

"Sure you are." She patted his rosy cheek, "And my big boy is going to be a good boy and wait. Mother will be right back."

Marcus watched her walk across the room. She stopped to talk to a man who smiled at her until she pointed back at Marcus. The smile turned into a frown and the man shook his head. It happened a few more times.

Marcus got tired of waiting and slid off the bench. He made his way over to the next table and reached up to help himself to a French fry that hung over the edge of a plate. The couple looked at him and laughed. They offered him another fry. He grabbed it and shoved it into his mouth.

"You must be hungry," said the woman. "You want to sit on my lap and have some more?"

Without a word, he walked around her and got up on the chair beside her. She mustn't have minded because she pushed the plate in front of him and squirted some more ketchup onto the edge of the plate.

Marcus had finished the rest of the fries and half of a cheese burger before his mother returned. She was hanging onto a man's arm and giggling. *She must be happy* thought Marcus. He turned his attention back to the food on the plate in front of him.

His mother thanked the couple for being kind to her boy and told him, "Marcus, come. This nice man wants to buy us some lunch and then he'll walk us home."

Marcus frowned at that 'nice man'. He already had some food and he didn't like to share his mother with anyone.

***

1980 May 25th Wednesday

She reached down and caressed Marcus' curly dark hair, "Sweetie, Mother has to go out for a little while."

His lower lip quivered as his solemn dark eyes focused on her face for a moment. Then he turned his attention back to his toy car.

She knelt down beside him, "I can't believe that you're three years old already; my precious, handsome boy." She kissed his forehead, "You're old enough to understand, right? Mother needs to go get some food for us."

Marcus was on his hands and knees on the floor. He did not look up again, even when he heard the door close and the click of the lock.

He drove his Matchbox car back and forth on the bare floor, through the sunbeam that changed the floor into two different colors. It felt warm on top of his hand.

Marcus already knew that he would have to amuse himself until she returned. He also knew that when his mother came back she would kiss him and hug him. Sometimes she cried and said how sorry she was for being gone so long. Other times she handed him a bag with a hamburger and some French fries. Then she fell across her bed and slept.

How long he would have to wait today, he did not know. Marcus played until his arm was tired. He rolled up his blankie and rested his head on it. He lay perfectly still with one hand stretched out to touch his car. Slowly his eyes blinked shut against his will. Soon he was fast asleep.

It must have been many hours later when the sound of a key unlocking the door woke him up. The sun was gone and the only light in the room came from the street light shining through the top half of the window. He sat up and watched his mother step into the room with a bag in her hand. She stopped short when she caught sight of him sitting on the floor.

"Marcus! Baby, you should have crawled into the bed."

She put the bag on the floor and bent down to pick him up. His legs dangled below her knees. Her breath tickled his neck when she said, "Look how big you are! You'll soon be taller than your mother."

She sat down on the floor and pulled him onto her lap. "I had to wait for the stores to open, honest sweetie."

She licked her index finger and wiped away a tear stain from his cheek.

"See, Baby!" she said as she pulled the bag closer. "I've got bread for toast and some peanut butter. Won't that be a nice breakfast?"

The young boy nodded and stood up. He grabbed the bag, plunked it on the table and scrambled onto the chair. He was so hungry he tore the tab off the end of the bag and pulled out a slice of bread. He didn't wait for his mother to make toast. Holding the bread with both hands, he chewed his way through to the middle.

His mother got up from the floor and went over to the bed and fell across it. She was fast asleep long before he had eaten his fill. The peanut butter lid was too hard to open, so he had another slice of plain bread. Finally his tummy was full.

Marcus went and stood beside the bed. He watched in fascination as his mother's chest rose and fell with each shallow breathe she took. Then he grabbed the blanket with both hands and pulled himself up onto the bed. He fell asleep snuggled close to her warm body.

***

Early that evening his mother began to pace again. She wrung her hands, sighed and paced some more. Marcus knew what that meant. She would be going out.

He ran to her and threw his arms around her legs. He looked up at her; his beautiful brown eyes were filled with tears. "Don't go, Mother," he begged. "Please stay with me,"

She shrugged a shoulder and shook her head, "I have to go, Baby. Be a good boy Marcus and I'll bring you a new toy."

He lowered his eyes – she promised a lot of things but he didn't believe her anymore. She had promised before, many times. But she always came home empty-handed with a hundred excuses why she couldn't bring the promised toy.

***

One day, late in the month of December, his mother came in the door with a couple of small boxes. Snowflakes glistened on the side of the box and on his mother's hair. He reached out a finger to touch the snow. It melted on his fingertip. He giggled and looked up at his mother. He wanted her to enjoy the snow with him but she didn't have time. She was busy pulling stuff out of the drawers.

Marcus knew this meant they'd be moving again. It must be close to the first of the month. It appeared that moving was easier than finding money to pay the rent. He didn't mind. It

34

meant that his mother would be spending more time with him for a little while.

Marcus looked at the boxes and went to stand beside his crib. This one had a nice mattress. "Are we going to carry it?" he asked.

His mother's cheeks colored guiltily, "We're not. It's too heavy. Besides, you've grown too big for it. We'll just leave it here for another little boy."

Marcus was fascinated as he watched her toss her head and saw her beautiful dark hair flare out and fly over her shoulder. He heard her harsh laugh.

She said, "Besides, if we tried to take it out the door, then the landlord would know that we're moving. He would demand the rent money before he'd let us go." She spread out her hands, palms up, "And that is money we don't have."

She picked out some of the jewelry that her men friends had given her and placed it in her purse. With a string tied around each box to make it easier to carry, they headed out the door. Marcus got to carry his mother's purse. He felt very proud to be able to help.

Their first stop was at the pawnshop. A bell clanged as they stepped inside. His mother placed the two boxes on the floor just inside the door. "Here, sit on this box," she said to Marcus. She turned and walked over to the counter. After some loud words with the man behind it, she came back to Marcus. "What a rip off! A real cheapskate! Outright robbery, that's what it is!" She fumed as she handed him the purse and picked up the boxes. "Let's get out of here before I smash something."

Marcus wasn't sure what she was mad about. He was just glad that she wasn't mad at him. He knew it couldn't be him because once they were out the door she smiled at him.

After they had walked in silence for a block she said, "At least we have enough money for bus fare and the first month's rent at our next place."

Chapter Seven

1981 January

This move took them to different province, to the town of Steinbach. As they got off the bus his mother said, "I hear that the people are really nice here. I hope that's true."

They made their way to a place that his mother called Family Services. There was a kind lady who helped them with food vouchers and knew of a furnished apartment that was for rent. She made a phone call.

Marcus slouched on the hard plastic chair as he waited. Try as he might, he couldn't stay upright on that rounded seat. Pretty soon he gave up and slid off the chair onto the floor. He pulled the little car out of his pocket and drove it up and down his leg. Then he crawled on his belly underneath the row of chairs. He pushed the car along in front of him.

He heard the lady make another phone call. He peered at her from under one of the chairs. He saw her stand up to get her coat. She smiled at his mother and said, "The place was vacated yesterday, so you can move right in."

She drove them to a house on Reimer Avenue. Parking her Minivan on the street in front of the house, she removed a set of keys attached to a clip board and handed them to Marcus' mother.

Marcus hurried out of the car and was half way up the steps before his mother even made it out of the car. He shivered, partly from being excited to see their new home and also because he didn't have a winter coat. The wind blew skiffs of snow across the yard, up his sleeves and into his face. It was so cold he tucked his chin against his chest as he huddled beside the door, waiting for his mother to catch up.

Inside they found a short hallway with two doors. When they opened the door to their apartment his mother laughed out loud. "This is a very nice place. It smells so clean!"

After a quick walk through to make sure everything was in good order, the nice lady headed for the door. She turned to shake hands with his mother and said, "I'll leave you to get settled in. If you need anything else, just give me a call."

Marcus liked how the tile on the floor gleamed in the bright sunlight. The fridge and stove were so clean that they reflected the overhead light. There was a table and two chairs in the middle of the kitchen. They could both sit down to eat.

"There's enough room to put a couch and TV in here, opposite the window," laughed his mother. "We'll have to talk to that woman and see if she can help us with that."

They continued to explore their new home. Marcus followed close beside his mother as they walked into the bedroom.

"Look at all this space!" she exclaimed as she spun in a circle, her arms stretched wide. "There's enough room to put a bed for you along that wall."

Marcus looked to where his mother was pointing, an empty space between the dresser and a closet. The door to the large closet stood open. He tugged at his mother's arm, "I could sleep in there." His big brown eyes sparkled at the idea.

"We'll see, Baby," she said as she mussed his dark wavy hair. "But until we find a bed for you we can share this one. It's big enough."

Marcus liked how happy his mother's voice sounded. She continued to smile as they walked through the suite and admired all the space.

"This is the best place we've ever had; two rooms and a bathroom all to ourselves." She grabbed Marcus by the hands and danced him around the room. When she let go of his hands, Marcus giggled and continued to spin around until he got dizzy and fell down.

***

Christmas had been lost in the flurry of their move. Now January and February flew by as they were busy getting settled in. With the help of the nice lady, they got a couch, a TV and a mattress for Marcus. He laughed and clapped his hands when Mother slid the top end of his mattress into the closet. He didn't care that there were a few clothes hanging above his head. It felt like he was in his own room.

Once again his birthday came and went without a celebration. "I'm sorry, Baby, there are so many things to do with moving into a new place. I just haven't had the time or the money. Even though the lady gave us some extra cash, it's all gone."

"It's okay, mother. I've got my neat bed in the closet and maybe my car would be jealous if I got other toys."

"Sure baby. But I'll see if I can get you some cake and a candle."

Marcus' eyes sparkled in anticipation. Later in his bed he told his car, "Maybe it'll really happen this time."

***

A couple of days after his fourth birthday, Marcus waited at home for his mother. It was dusk. The street lights began to pop on but did little to brighten the inside of the house. He stood at the front window in the darkened room and watched patiently with the hope of seeing his mother's face.

The sidewalk, busy with people rushing along, faded away as he focused on his reflection in the window pane. Snot mixed with tears reflected as a silvery trail.

Fascinated, he stared at the reflection in the window. He couldn't see his dark curly hair. It blended in with the darkness behind him. But his eyes twinkled when he moved his head back and forth. He bared his perfectly even row of teeth at the reflection and growled. It distracted him for a little while. Then his tummy growled and reminded him that he was hungry. The toast that his mother had given him at lunch was barely a memory.

Last week one of the wheels of his Matchbox car got bent over. Now it wobbled as he pushed it along the window sill. He drove it up the window pane. It made a loud screech. He drove it off the window and nestled it in the palm of one hand. He caressed its smooth white roof with his thumb before he put it in his pocket. It was such a nice car.

A big sigh filled the room. He wished his mother would stay at home or take him with her. He ran out of ideas to amuse himself in the long lonely hours. A lone tear slid down his cold cheek. His little pink tongue reached out to catch the teardrop before it fell on the sill. *Mother, where are you? When are you coming home?*

The clock on the wall ticked away in the quiet room. He sniffled and wiped a sleeve across his nose. He took one last look, just in case she was coming down the street. There was no one at all on the sidewalk so he headed to the couch. His tattered blankie trailed along the floor behind him. He curled up into a little ball on the grey couch and stuck his thumb in his mouth. The blanket tucked over the side of his head was too short to cover him, but it helped him to forget how cold the house was. Soon he was fast asleep dreaming of being held in his mother's arms.

His head popped up at the sound of a key in the door. He turned onto his belly and leaned on his elbows with his face propped in his hands as he waited for her.

His mom stumbled into the room. He watched her kick off a three inch stiletto. She swore as her ankle twisted and she fell heavily against the wall. A paper bag slipped out of her hands and dropped to the floor. At the smell of fries and burgers, Marcus jumped off the couch and hollered, "I'm hungry."

His startled mother lashed out, "Marcus! You scared the crap out of me!" Her manicured hand flew to her breast. "What are you doing up - and in the dark?" She collapsed into the nearest chair and held her head as she muttered, "Supper's in the bag."

Marcus plunked down cross-legged onto the floor and pulled the bag close. The top of it ripped as he reached in to pull out a burger. Eagerly he tore off the wrapper and grasped the cheeseburger with both hands. He took a big bite and rested his elbows on his knees as he chewed. A couple more bites and then he reached for some fries.

His mom watched him for a few minutes and then called out, "C-mere son, let me wipe that ketchup from your face."

Marcus stared up at his mom but didn't bother to move. He kept on with the business at hand – to fill his empty tummy.

"Sorry baby, I would have been home sooner but I missed my ride." She threw her head back against the wall. "Who'm I kiddin'? I just didn't want to come home to another long lonely night. Too bad we don't know who your pa is. We could make him take care of us. Other guys don't want to be burdened with someone else's kid."

Marcus stared at his mother as he continued with his meal. He'd heard it all before.

Her head still rested against the wall. She peered down at him through half-closed eyelids. "What'm I gonna do with you, Marcus? I can't even take care of myself."

A car pulled into the driveway next door. He saw his mother turn her eyes to the window but she didn't bother to get up. Marcus got up, still clutching his burger and walked over to the window to check it out.

"Is that the old girl from next door?" asked his mother.

Marcus nodded and continued to chew. His elbows fit nicely on the window sill. He tucked one foot behind an ankle as he continued to chew. He watched intently as the lights turned on in the neighbor's front room. Then the door closed and the swatch of light across the sidewalk disappeared.

The burger was finished. He went to look for more food in the bag. Marcus pulled out the bottle of chocolate milk and took it over to his mother. Her fingers fumbled with the lid but she got it open. Then she almost dropped it as she handed it back to him.

Careful not to spill any of it, the four year old went back to his food and sat down on the floor. Contentedly he reached for more French fries and ate until the bag was empty.

Chapter Eight

1982 September

Five year old Marcus loved kindergarten. "Can we go now?" He stood at the door with one hand on the doorknob; the other hand pushed his backpack farther behind him. His eyes sparkled at his mother.

"Dancing by the door isn't going to get you there any faster, son. You just have to wait until I'm ready."

"I like my teacher. She gives us papers and crayons. She is proud of my drawings."

The first few weeks were wonderful. Mother walked him to school and she was waiting for him when the last bell rang. Marcus skipped along beside her, babbling about his school work.

Soon his joy dimmed. Mother came later and later. When she finally showed up, she always rushed over to him and gave him a big hug and said, "Sorry, Baby, I couldn't help it." Sometimes her breath smelt funny when she kissed him.

Marcus lost interest in school as worry about his mother increased. The papers in front of him remained blank. When Teacher began to ask too many questions, he hung his head and refused to answer.

One day when the teacher was ready to go home, he was still waiting for his mother. Marcus didn't mind waiting patiently on the swing for her. She would come eventually.

But Teacher wasn't happy. He could tell by the look on her face as she stood in the doorway and looked up and down the street. All the other kids had gone home.

She came and stood beside Marcus. "Where's your mother?"

He lifted one shoulder slightly but did not make eye contact.

"When will she be here?" Teacher glanced at her wristwatch.

Marcus hiked up the other shoulder, "Don't know," he mumbled.

Teacher crouched down to look him in the eye.

He squirmed, uncomfortable with her nearness.

She smiled at him, "Do you want to come and wait inside? Maybe we can find a cookie."

He shook his head. He'd love the cookie, but was too embarrassed. He didn't want Teacher to know how few cookies he had ever had and how very much he wanted one.

Teacher stood up and held out her hand, to urge him to come with her.

Marcus was saved by the sound of rapid heels clicking along the sidewalk. He looked up and saw his mother. "There's my mother," he yelled and ran toward her.

His mother caught him and ruffled his hair. She asked, "Sorry for being late, Baby. Was that teacher giving you a hard time, son?"

He loved it when she called him son. Today he didn't even pretend to duck when she touched his hair. He was just so glad that she had come when she did.

***

The phone rang as they stepped into their apartment. His mother was on the phone for a long time. She kept saying, "Yes, I know. No, I wouldn't want that." In between times she sniffled and shrugged her shoulders. When she said, "Marcus wouldn't do that! He's a good boy. There must be some misunderstanding..." his ears perked up and he sat without moving. This did not sound good.

Mother always said that no Family Service people would ever get their hands on her boy. And that's why I should always behave...so I don't give them any reason to come snooping around...I wonder what happened. He barely moved as he listened to his mother's voice. But he couldn't hear enough to figure out what the problem was.

When the call was over she hung up the phone and went to look in the fridge for something to eat. She didn't say anything at all to Marcus.

"Was that my teacher?" he asked in a trembling voice.

She just nodded and continued to rummage in the fridge.

Marcus decided that it mustn't have been very important after all. But he knew he was going to have to do something about that teacher's interest in him. *She's going to get me in trouble and then those Family Service people are going to come and take me away.* He'd have to figure out a plan.

When school let out, he began to walk a short distance down the sidewalk towards home, and then he retraced his steps to hide behind the big garbage bins. With heart pumping wildly, he hoped his teacher wouldn't notice.

One time he decided to cross the street to wait for his mother. He could play on the boulevard. But that was too difficult because he had to watch so carefully not to miss his mother while keeping an eye out for the teacher. It was no fun and the cars driving by kept throwing dirt up in his face.

His mother showed up later and later. "Now that you're in school all day, I can work at the Hair Salon." She fluffed her hand through her hair. "Seeing as I'm the new girl they make me stay and clean up."

Marcus worried when his mother began to bring a man with her. One night when she tucked him into bed he said, "Mother, I don't like that man. I'm scared of him."

She gave a half snort, half laugh, "What's to be scared of?" She gave Marcus a pat on the cheek, "Besides he's loaded. That means he'll buy us anything we want."

"But I don't want anything, Mother. And I don't care when you come late to pick me up; at least not very much." He gave a big sigh, "But I wish you'd just come by yourself."

Things got worse. His mother gave all her attention to that man. When they walked home from school she hung onto the man's arm like Marcus wasn't even with her. When they got home she'd hand him a piece of bread and propel him into the bedroom and say, "Be a good boy and play with your car."

His arm hanging at his side, the bread clutched in his hand, he stood and looked at her with sorrowful eyes. She'd blow him a kiss and close the door. When it clicked he knew he was locked in.

This wasn't how it was supposed to be. It began to happen more and more often. Some days he didn't even get a piece of bread. He sat, hungry and alone. The leaves on the tree outside the window waved at him. Marcus wished he could wait out there instead of locked in here.

He hated it when he wet himself because his mother wouldn't open the door to let him use the bathroom. As often as not he cried himself to sleep while he waited.

One day he threw himself on his mattress in the closet and covered his head with his pillow. He tried to block out the noise and the yelling from the other room – later he heard his mom sobbing but she wouldn't answer him or come to unlock the door, no matter how loud he hollered.

Marcus got into trouble at school. He hit one kid for saying bad things about his mother. When the other kids teased him about his stinky clothes, he walked around with his hands clenched into tight fists. He would fight anyone of them. He didn't care if they were bigger than him.

Teacher blamed him for the fights in the school yard, whether he was guilty or not. He glared at her as he twisted away from her when she tried to put her hand on his shoulder.

One day after being harassed to tears he left school early. Somehow he found his way home. He wiped the tears from his cheeks and quickened his steps when he spotted the building. His mother was surprised to see him in the hallway when she opened the door to take out the garbage.

"Marcus! What are you doing home so early?"

"It was time to leave," he said as he walked into the apartment behind her.

"I didn't know that school was letting out early," she said with a puzzled look on her face. "If I'd known, I would have come earlier."

"It's okay, mother. You don't have to come get me anymore. I'm a big boy now and can come home all by myself." He stretched as tall as he could.

His mother shook her head and smoothed the hair off his forehead. "You're my big boy. How did you get all grow'd up without me noticing?"

Marcus began to leave school at different times. On days his mother wasn't at home, he couldn't get into their apartment because he didn't have a key. But the hallway was warm. It was a lot better than having to watch for his mother or to have that teacher spying on him. On nicer days there were trees to climb and flower beds to dig in with a stick. So far no one had bothered to question him or to scold him for being in the yard when he should have been at school.

What a happy day it was when a stray cat wandered into the yard and plopped down in the dirt right in front of Marcus. The cat was all white except for a bit of black on her face. "You are so soft, and so warm," whispered Marcus as he ran his fingers through her warm fur. "I wish I had some milk to share with you, but I guess we both have to wait for mother. Maybe she'll have some food for us. Nice kitty."

The cat let him pick her up. The purring rumbled against his chest and made him giggle.

Chapter Nine

1982 October

It was the first week of the month. Teacher was telling the class a story. It was something about how a year earlier a Spider had fallen out of orbit while being tested. Whatever that meant... Marcus didn't like spiders, they made webs that stuck to his face and then he couldn't get the sticky stuff off. He sighed audibly and turned to stare out the window. *I wish I didn't have to sit in this stupid desk. If only I could go outside and play on the structure. I don't care about spiders in the sky. They're bad enough when they fall off the ceiling.* Marcus opened and closed his hand on the ray of sunshine that warmed a spot on his desk. He sighed loudly as his eyes followed the sun beam. *And that cat's waiting for me to come home and play.*

His eyes turned back to the front of the room. The teacher was pointing to a photo stuck on the blackboard. He tried to pay attention, really he did, but his empty tummy kept talking to him even though it wasn't lunch time yet. Mother had forgotten to shop for groceries again. There'd been nothing in the cupboard or fridge to pack for lunch.

Marcus waited until the teacher's back was turned. Quietly he slipped out of his desk and disappeared through the open door. He held his breath until he was out in the hallway and down the front steps. Once on the sidewalk he ran as fast as his little legs could carry him.

Halfway home he stopped to catch his breath. There were a few moms with little kids in a playground. He spotted an empty swing and made his way over to it. Grabbing the chains on each side, he hoisted himself up onto the seat. He kicked his legs until he got the swing to sway gently back and forth.

A few minutes later his breathing was slowed down to normal. He looked around. No one seemed to notice him or care that he was there.

Two boys, a little younger than him, were racing to the steps leading up to the highest platform on the structure. It looked like fun. Marcus jumped off his swing and hurried after them. The two boys never made it up the steps. They crashed into each other. This made them giggle so hard that they fell down and rolled on the ground. Marcus sent a smile their way as he eagerly climbed up the steps and whooshed down the curved slide.

When the two boys quit giggling, they joined Marcus. Without saying a word, they hurried up the steps behind him. It was fun to take turns. No one argued about wanting to go first.

A rumble from his tummy reminded Marcus again that his toast from breakfast had been a long time ago. He took one last slide and trotted across the grass to the sidewalk.

At home Marcus hurried up the outside steps and down the hall. Before he could reach up for the door handle it flew open. Surprised, Marcus just had time to see an angry face on a very big stranger before he was grabbed by the arm and jerked inside. The door was slammed shut with a huge booted foot and Marcus was thrown against the table. His big brown eyes filled with fear were glued to that angry face.

The man pulled off his belt, "I'm going to teach you a lesson, you little brat. You're not going to worry your mother again, ever."

Before Marcus could look at his mother for an explanation the man began to beat on him. It stung like fire wherever the belt landed. He danced this way and that way to try and protect himself. He covered his face with both hands but the belt never missed.

Vaguely he heard his mother sobbing in protest, "Stop it! You're not allowed to hurt my boy! Please stop, you're going to kill my baby."

All she got for that was an elbow in the face that sent her flying backwards against the kitchen counter.

Marcus watched with fear and trembling as she crumpled to the floor. He rushed over and fell on his knees beside her. "Mother?" he whimpered. She didn't move.

A vise-like grip around his upper arm caught him and jerked him up, away from his mother and forced him across the room.

Marcus' eyes flew up to look at the man. It was an ugly face, contorted with rage. Marcus was flung into the bedroom with such force that he skidded across the floor. He automatically put up one hand to protect his face as he slammed into the opposite wall.

"Don't you ever miss school again!" the deep voice thundered. "You're going to kill your mother, making her worry so much." The door slammed shut and was locked.

The beating left Marcus trembling; hurting all over his body but he did not utter a sound. His mind swirled with thoughts as his heart pounded against his aching ribs. *Why does mother let that man in our house when he's so mean? How did he know I left school? Teacher must have called to get me in trouble. She probably told him to beat me.*

He swiped the back of his hand across his nose and wiped the snot on his pants. *Well, she's never going to know what happened, 'cause I'll never tell.*

Slowly he crawled over to his mattress and curled up into a ball. His simmering angry thoughts slowly lessened until he finally drifted off to sleep. His only comfort was his thumb and his blankie.

***

Marcus woke up with a start. The pain shooting up his shoulder as soon as he moved reminded him of what had happened. He listened but it was awfully quiet in the front room. *I have to check on Mother to see if she's okay. I wonder if that bad man is still here. I hope she never lets him come back.*

Every move he made hurt. It hurt bad. He managed to sit up. Then he got onto his knees and was able to stand up without too loud of a groan. The welts on his body felt like they were on fire. He didn't want to sit back down, everything hurt too much. But he had a dreadful need to go to the bathroom.

He went to turn the door handle but it was still locked. He stood with his ear to the door. He couldn't hear anything. "Mother?" he called softly. Then he called louder, "Mother! I have to go pee."

His mother didn't answer, no matter how loud he called. He banged on the door. "Mother! Moth-err! Please! I gotta go to the bathroom." He threw back his head and hollered as loud as he could. No answer came. He resorted to pleading, "Please let me out. I won't do it again. I promise."

When still no sound came from the other room, Marcus was filled with terror. It was too quiet. *Is Mother still in there? Did she go away and leave me alone again? I wish she didn't lock the door when she goes away.* He went to the window and looked out. It wasn't dark yet.

He returned to listen at the door. *At least that bad man can't be here anymore. It's too quiet.* He had to go pee so bad his tummy hurt. He went back to the window and squeezed his legs together as he leaned against the window sill.

Tears running down his cheeks, he looked at the hedge behind the house. He saw his little friend, the cat, waiting on the lowest branch. It was meowing for him to come outside. It gave him an idea.

Marcus grunted as he tugged a box close to the window. He climbed up on it and pushed at the top board of the window. Slowly it moved. Soon it was open wide enough for him to get out. He started feet first, on his tummy, over the sill. Lower and lower but his feet didn't touch the ground. The cat meowed again as if to cheer him along.

"Okay, kitty, here I come." He dropped to the ground and tumbled backwards into the bushes. The cat jumped over the hedge and took off in a streak. Marcus emerged from the shrubs spitting leaves. Every part of his body hurt more than ever but he didn't care. He was free. He took care of his bathroom needs in the shrubs. Then he inched along the hedge until he reached the edge of the yard. He looked up and down the street. There was no sight of the cat, or anyone else for that matter.

He ambled down the street, keeping an eye out for his friend, but the cat was nowhere to be seen. "Here, kitty, kitty," did not bring a response. Finally Marcus gave up.

Just down the street he saw Extra Foods. "They've got food in there,' he declared. Off he trotted. A large family entered the grocery store with Marcus right on their heels. No one took notice of the little boy as he meandered up and down the aisles behind the family. When they stopped at the meat counter, he went around them and headed straight to the bakery section. He picked up a small bag of buns. "I think some cheese would be nice with these," he said as he made a U-turn and headed to the back of the store. It was a long walk before he found the dairy section. He stood on tippy toes to grab a small package of cheese but he couldn't quite reach it.

A kind lady smiled down at him and said, "Here, let me help you. You must be a good helper for your mother."

Glad for the help, he reached up eagerly to take the cheese. His 'Thanks' was uttered very quietly.

In the next case he saw all sizes of milk containers. "I can't carry that big one but if I put the cheese in my pocket I could take a small one. Then kitty and I can share it."

Satisfied with his plan he made his way back to the front of the store. The little five year old boy got lost among all those adults. Next thing he knew he was back on the street. He didn't even think about the fact that he hadn't paid for his groceries.

Eager to get back home and maybe to the cat, he trotted along the sidewalk. The milk carton got heavy. He put it down and moved the buns into his other hand. "That's better," he sighed. "And I can see our front yard from here."

He was just going to put the food down so he could use both hands to open the outside door when someone pushed it open from the inside. Marcus stepped into the hallway and remembered to say thank you. The door to their apartment was partly opened. He could see his mother lying face down on the couch with a pillow over her head. He pushed at the door with his elbow and quietly stepped over to the table. He put his groceries on a chair.

Is mother okay, he wondered. He went and pushed the door shut. The noise did not wake her. He tiptoed over to her side and stood perfectly still. Marcus stared at her back. When he saw her shoulders move as she breathed he relaxed. *She's still sleeping.* Glad to see her take another breath, he turned back to the food.

He got a knife from the drawer and began to enjoy his hard earned supper. When he was full, he put the leftovers in the fridge and went back to stand beside the couch. His mother still hadn't moved. *She must be really tired.* His shoulders heaved as he wondered what he should do. It was time to go to bed. The bedroom door was still locked. He looked over his shoulder at his mother. What should he do? He needed to get back in there. Then he remembered how he'd seen his mother push against the door knob and turn. It took him a few tries but he finally got it open.

He went in and shut the door behind him. After he closed the window he sat cross-legged on his mattress. With his elbows resting on his knees, his face cupped in both hands, he pondered his situation. "I need to put a box on the outside, so I won't fall into the bushes next time."

Next morning Marcus woke up and looked over to the big bed. It had not been slept in. He went into the front room with his blankie trailing behind him. Mother was still lying face down on the couch. Marcus went and shook her. "Are you awake, Mother? Mother?"

She groaned. "Shush, not so loud. My head hurts. In fact, everything hurts."

"Is it time to go to school?" he asked.

"I don't know. What time is it?"

Marcus looked at the clock on the stove but it was blinking. He shrugged and walked to the fridge. He knew he'd find cheese, milk and a bun. After a quick breakfast he headed out the door. Last night he had fallen asleep in his school clothes, so he didn't need to get dressed this morning.

Marcus was excited. He had learned how to look after himself. "Now I won't care when Mother locks me in the bedroom. I know she only wants to keep me safe but she doesn't know how scary it is when I have to go to the toilet, or when I get hungry." He glanced at the shrubs growing beside the sidewalk and smiled. "And I can get food whenever I'm hungry and even some milk for my kitty."

For the next few days he stayed out of his mother's way as much as possible. She didn't seem to notice him anyway. Most days she just sat and drooped over a cup of coffee. Other times she lay on the couch with an arm covering her face.

Marcus enjoyed that winter. He stole a wool toque and some mitts to keep warm when he played with his kitten. *Maybe I should steal a sled, but where would I keep it? And*

besides, Kitty might not want to enjoy it with me. He didn't go
without milk, peanut butter or bread again.

***

Marcus loved his mother very much. He wished she didn't
go away with those men and leave him alone. But it was even
worse when she let them come in the house. He wished she
would be happy with just the two of them.

He hated it when the kids at school said bad things about
her. He felt embarrassed. Then he was angry because he
didn't understand how he could help her. He couldn't do
anything about it. He had tried fighting but that only made
things worse.

Besides he knew that what they said was true. He'd seen
his mother come home with bruises on her arms and sometimes
on her beautiful face. How he wished that he could protect her
from all those mean men.

*If only I was big enough, so I could find some money for
her. Then she wouldn't have to be nice to strangers to get
money for us.*

Chapter Ten

"Soon you'll be six years old!" exclaimed his mother. They had just finished supper. Marcus was leaning against her, glad that she was home tonight. She had cooked macaroni and cheese, his favorite meal.

His mother ran her long fingers through his curls. "We'll have a big party and you can invite all your friends."

Marcus frowned, "I don't want a big party. I just want you and me. No friends for me and no friends for you."

"But Baby! A party has to have lots of people."

"No, it doesn't. I don't got no friends and your friends hurt me."

"Oh, no, honey. What makes you say that?"

He glared at her, "You know."

She hung her head. Then she laughed sheepishly, "Perhaps you're right. We'll make it just you and me and we can have lots of presents instead. Will that be okay?"

He nodded but didn't say anything. Marcus did not let himself hope, even though he really wanted to believe that there would be a present this time. Something always came up to delay the promised gift.

But Marcus began to hope. A sparkle returned to his eyes. His mother had not gone out once in over a week. Every morning she walked him to school, and was waiting across the street when school was done for the day.

He surprised Teacher when he handed in a page with all the designs colored. He had even printed his name at the top like she always asked. He had not done so before. She smiled at him and made a big fuss over it.

Marcus pulled back as memory flooded in about the beating he'd received because she told on him. He was almost sorry about completing the paper. But then he remembered that his mother was probably waiting outside for him. He turned and ran out the door. Maybe, just maybe, there would be a present to open for his birthday this time.

Excitement made him jump out of bed. He kept getting the wrong foot in the pant leg and had to start all over. Tomorrow was his 6th birthday and it looked like this time his mother would remember her promise.

She deliberately mussed his hair as she helped him adjust his backpack. "Are you sure you don't need me to walk you to school today?" she asked. "You're still five years old."

"Nope. I can do it by myself 'cause I'll be six tomorrow," he declared as he stretched as tall as he could.

His mother laughed and swatted his backside as she helped him out the door. "Go on then, my big boy. See you later, alligator."

He giggled, "After a while, crocodile."

When he turned to look back before stepping out the door, she blew him a kiss off her fingertips.

Little Marcus felt ten feet tall. He talked to himself as he walked along the sidewalk. "I hope there will be a race track for my car. Maybe even another car so they can race each other and see which one goes the fastest. Maybe mother will give me my present tonight. Then I won't have to wait a whole 'nother day."

The walk to school wasn't nearly long enough. He wished he had a friend to talk over the possibilities. It was almost too exciting to keep all the maybes to himself.

During the last hour Marcus could hardly sit still. He wanted to leave early. But he couldn't, not today. Mother just might be coming to pick him up even though he had declared that he wasn't a baby anymore.

Tomorrow was going to be such a special day.

He looked up in dismay when Teacher called him up to the front just before it was time to dismiss the class. *Not now...*

Chapter Eleven

Teacher actually had a smile on her face as Marcus made his way up to the front. There was an old lady dressed in faded blue jeans standing beside Teacher's desk. The woman was watching him carefully as he approached, like she had a question for him.

Marcus glanced warily at her and then swung his eyes back to Teacher. He frowned. *I don't want to miss Mother in case she comes. What if she'll think I've gone home already and she doesn't wait for me?*

Only half listening to Teacher, he missed the first part of what she said. But he definitely heard the last part. His mother wasn't coming.

Surprise followed by deep disappointment flickered across his face. The frown deepened. His eyes shot daggers at the old lady as if it was her fault.

The old lady ignored his frown. She gave him a warm smile and said, "Hi, I'm your neighbor. My name is Edith. Your mom had to make a special trip to the city this morning and she asked me to pick you up."

Tears threatened to embarrass him. He chose to be angry instead. He clenched his fists and shook his head. "No! Mother wouldn't do that to me. Not today!" The words shouted in his head but came out a mere whisper in the room.

Then he relaxed a bit. *Maybe she had to go to the city to get my present.*

Edith yearned over the boy as she watched him struggle with the situation that had obviously caught him unawares. She thought back to the morning. She'd seen him leave for school when she'd come home from working the midnight shift at Bethesda Hospital. She'd only been in the house for a few minutes when there'd been a knock at the door. She had opened the door to a dark haired woman.

"I'm your neighbor." She'd motioned toward the house next door. Her long fingernails were painted a delicate pearl pink. "I saw you drive in," she'd continued as she tucked a strand of long dark hair behind her ear. "I have a big favor to ask. Could you pick up my son, Marcus, after school today?" Her dark brown eyes wouldn't connect with Edith's for more than a second at a time. They darted back and forth like a humming bird at a feeding station.

I wonder what is distracting this woman... What is she hiding Edith had wondered. She'd squinted and tuned back in to listen to what the woman was saying.

"I have to go to the city to buy a present for my boy. It's his birthday tomorrow. He's going to be six years old!" She'd stepped back ready to leave. Again, without making eye contact she'd added, "I won't make it back before school is out."

Edith had nodded, "Yes, I can do that." She'd hid the smile that wanted to pop out at the other woman's odd behavior. Instead she'd asked, "Which school does he go to?"

The woman's reply had come smoothly, "Oh, he's attending Elmdale." She'd pulled a wallet out of her purse and fluttered through a number of pictures. "Here's a recent photo. It looks just like my sweet boy." Love-filled eyes had smiled at the picture before she'd handed it over to Edith.

A quick glance had shown the face of a very handsome little boy. But the face was marred by a sullen, almost angry expression.

"He always waits for me at the front doors." The woman's eyes had darted up the street and then down to her feet before she said, "Thank you." She'd turned away, then swiveled back and held out an unfolded piece of paper. "Here's a note for him so he'll know it's okay to come home with you."

Edith had taken the note without reading it. Instead she had watched the woman walk away with a jaunty step as if free from any care in the world. She'd looked very smart in a tailored jacket and a slightly flared skirt with matching three inch spiked heels.

The large bag slung over her shoulder had thumped against her side in time with her eager steps. Edith's first thought had been, *she must love to shop to need such a big bag.*

Immediately another thought had sprung out of nowhere. Could it have been an overnight case? Then Edith had given her the benefit of the doubt. *No way. The big bag is probably to make it easier to bring back her purchases.*

Edith had closed the door and placed the note on the counter beside her purse. Her list of tasks for the day had been short, only one load of laundry and supper to prepare. She added baking cookies to the list.

"And I'd better plan supper for two, just in case." Edith had decided with a laugh. "I wonder if I still know how to cook for more than one." She had continued to muse. "George used to find it funny when I complained about leftovers. It was easy for him to say, 'just cook less'. But no matter how hard I tried, by the time I was done the portions had always doubled. Now that I've finally got the knack of cooking for one after five years of being a widow, I'm going to spoil my record."

Edith reigned in her thoughts when she became aware of being glared at.

Marcus stood quietly and watched the woman's face. She had a funny look while Teacher was explaining the situation. Her expression looked just like his mother's did when she was thinking about something else instead of listening to him while he tried to talk to her.

Now the woman gave her head a shake and smiled at him. "Sorry," she said as she held out a piece of paper. "This is a note from your mother so you'll know that she wants you to come home with me and that she had to go to the City."

At his questioning look, Teacher nodded in agreement.

Marcus was angry. Not only had his mother not shown up, now these two adults were lined up against him as well.

Belligerently he followed the woman to a beat up old vehicle. *It's better to be angry so I won't cry* Marcus decided as he tossed his backpack onto the back seat with a thud. He slid in beside it and glowered as he slammed the door shut. With both Teacher and this old lady hovering over him at the moment, he had no other choice.

"Your mom had to go to the city," the woman repeated her earlier words. "She said that she'd be back too late to pick you up from school."

He refused to tell her that his mother hadn't planned to come pick him up today. He kept his mouth shut tight and his eyes out the window as the woman asked a lot of questions about school and how he liked their town. Thank goodness she finally lapsed into silence. The drive home was most uncomfortable for him. *If only I could run someplace and hide till Mother comes back.*

Marcus raised hopeful eyes when they pulled into the neighbor's driveway. He got out of the car. The slight hope in his heart disappeared when he saw no light in their apartment window. His mother wasn't back.

Edith's kind voice broke into his thoughts. "Please come inside, out of the cold," she said as she held the door open. "Would you like some milk and a cookie? I baked some sugar cookies this morning."

He shook his head no and followed her inside. He remained standing by the door, a dark look in his eyes as he frowned.

He snatched his arm away from her when the woman had to move him over a bit to shut the door behind him. She seemed to ignore his reaction.

"Do you have any homework?" she asked in a gentle voice.

The woman seemed desperate to make him talk but he wasn't going to give her the time of day, no siree. *I don't even want to be here. There's no way I'm going to act nice about it.*

When she stood there and looked at him with raised eyebrows he spat out, "Never!" It was the only word he spoke until bedtime.

She shrugged and suggested that he might as well be comfortable while he waited for his mom. After she'd gone into the kitchen, he shuffled into the living room and plunked down on the navy blue couch with a big sigh. He kept his backpack beside him, ready for a quick departure.

Without moving his head, Marcus let his eyes roam around the room. It was very different from home. He had to admit, although grudgingly, that everything was nice and tidy.

The woman came and sat down in an easy chair and turned on the television set. Marcus looked at it with unseeing eyes and wouldn't let his body relax.

He heard her sigh and he glanced sideways at her through narrowed eyes. She shook her head and murmured, "Oh, the poor boy. What a shame to have so much pain and anger in one so young."

He hated to be pitied. It made him feel ashamed but he didn't know what for. His thoughts kept busy. *Where's Mother? She couldn't have forgotten her promise. It's my birthday!* The possibility made him sniffle.

Immediately the woman was in his face. "I'm sorry that I don't have any games for you to amuse yourself with, but I do have cable TV," she suggested hopefully.

Marcus did not even raise his eyes to meet hers. He heard her sigh again and watched out of the corner of his eyes as she headed down the hall. It sounded like she had gone to look after a load of laundry.

At supper time she called him to come eat. On his way to the table he let his eyes flicker next door. There were no lights to soften the darkened windows at his place.

As the evening wore on the woman kept talking to him. He refused to answer. A few times he looked at her but his drooping lips were sealed. She drove him crazy with all that nattering. His mother hardly said a word all evening, well, on the evenings that she stayed at home. Marcus only wanted to talk to his mother.

Seeing as he wasn't interested in the TV the woman changed the channel to what must be her favorite program, something called CSI.

Marcus sat with hunched shoulders, his hands folded in his lap. His eyes wandered back and forth between the TV screen and the window. He jumped when Edith spoke aloud. The show was over and the credits rolled across the screen.

"What can be keeping your mother?" The woman looked at her wristwatch. "It is past 9 o'clock and it's a school night."

Marcus still remained silent – not so much as a lift of his head. How could he answer the woman when he didn't know where his mother had gone or when she'd be back? He continued to stare at nothing, just waited. His shoulders ached and his eyes burned but he didn't move.

"Marcus, how about you lie down on the spare bed till your mother comes? That way you can rest while you wait."

He looked up at Edith in horror.

She had the nerve to giggle as she said, "I'm not asking you to wear my flannel nightgown."

Thank goodness she excused herself. He could hear her plump-up the pillows. He stared down the back hall. Despair filled his little heart. When he heard her steps come back to the living room, he quickly lowered his eyes.

She said, "Come, Marcus. Come lie down and I promise to wake you the moment your mother returns."

"She won't be back tonight." Resignation laced his words.

"What do you mean, Marcus?"

"She's done this before," he growled, "stayed away a long time."

The woman's gasp and her words, 'I'm so sorry to hear that,' made Marcus angry; mostly because her kindness brought tears to his eyes. He did not want to cry in front of this strange person, even if she was trying to be kind. He didn't need anyone to pity him.

The woman had rigid shoulders as she turned away and her voice seemed tense as she said, "I don't have any pajamas that would fit you..."

He interrupted her, "I never had any pajamas." He glared at her back in case she dared to voice more pity for him.

But all she said was, "Come."

Marcus followed her down the hall. As he entered the bedroom he noticed a large bed with a dark blue quilt on it. There were two fluffy pillows propped against the headboard. They matched the quilt. A cedar chest stood at the foot of the bed. He plunked his backpack on top of it. A tall dresser sat against the wall opposite the window. The closet door had been removed. Instead of clothes or hangers, Marcus saw a number of shelves filled with books.

He stood beside the cedar chest until the woman left the room. When she left, he jumped up on the bed. There was a bit of a squeak. His eyes lit up but he didn't quite loose the frown. *It's cool to have a bed to jump on.* But sadness that the bed came without his mother destroyed most of the fun. He moved to the edge and let his legs hang down.

"Do you want a night snack before you lie down?" she called from down the hallway.

Her words startled him. The young lad started to shake his head but thought better of it. He watched her as she stepped into the room.

Her raised eyebrows echoed her question, "Maybe a couple of cookies and a glass of milk?"

He nodded.

When she left the room he walked over to the window. It looked into the same backyards as he was used to. His eyes searched the hedge for his cat. He thought he saw something move out there but the woman was coming back. He rushed back to the bed and sat down on the edge of it.

Edith entered with a plate and a tall glass of milk. Marcus' eyes widened as he noticed three large sugar cookies covered with sprinkles and chocolate chips. He grabbed one before the plate touched the side table.

"If you need anything else, just call me."

He gave a slight dip of his head and hoped she saw it. He didn't want to talk to her at all because his throat felt so tight.

Marcus kept a little bit of milk in the glass, just in case there would be an opportunity to give it to the cat. He went over and tried to open the window but it wouldn't budge. He looked up and noticed that there was a toggle on the top of the frame. He couldn't reach it and there was no chair in the room. He'd have to see if he could sneak a chair into the room, just to unlock the window. He would leave it unlocked and put the chair back. Then he could open the window when he spotted the cat. *Maybe I can let it in to share my snack. Then I'll put it right back outside.*

He tiptoed over to the door and opened it carefully. There was no chair in sight. *Oh well, no sense getting the old lady in a huff over it.* He returned to the window to finish the last of the cookies.

His eyes grew tired as he stood and peered into the darkness outside the window. Finally he shuffled back to the bed and plopped down on it. He lay on his back and stared at the ceiling. Just before he fell asleep he turned onto his side and curled up into a ball.

Some minutes later he stirred when he felt the comforter being pulled up over his body. "Mother," he mumbled without opening his eyes.

"Ssh, Ssh," came a gentle whisper in the darkened room. Marcus burrowed deeper under the blanket and gave a contented sigh.

Chapter Twelve

1983   March 10th   Thursday

"It's my day off today," said Edith at the breakfast table. Marcus shrugged a shoulder to acknowledge her comment but didn't reply. His knife clattered against the glass plate. He quickly glanced at the woman in case the sudden noise might have bothered her. But she must not have noticed because she was concentrating on her coffee mug.

Marcus eyed Edith through the fringes of his long dark eyelashes. *She doesn't look too bad for an old woman...nice pony tail. But she's not as pretty as my mother...definitely not in those blue jeans and that old T-shirt. It's pretty neat that she made pancakes for me; especially today.*

A big sigh erupted before he could stop it. He frowned because Edith looked up at him and his thoughts spiraled downward.

She probably just wants to be nice to me so I'll like her. Well I won't. She's not my mother! Besides, my mother would probably have made pancakes for me too, seeing as it's my birthday.

That reminded him of another promise - his birthday party. *Not much hope of having a party now with just Mother and me. I wonder how long before she comes back this time.* His lower lip quivered and he put down his fork. He wasn't hungry anymore.

68

Later when Edith dropped him off at school she smiled at
him and said, "Have a nice day, Marcus. I'll watch for your
mother's return. If I don't see her, I'll come pick you up after
school, okay?"

He paused, half way out of the car, but didn't say anything,
just shrugged a shoulder and completed his exit. When he
heard the car pull away, he turned and watched it drive down
the street. *Mother probably won't be back, and the old lady
doesn't even know that it's my birthday.* Shoulders hunched
over, he turned and ambled towards the front steps. *Why can't
it be my mother that takes me to school and makes me a special
breakfast?*

*When are you coming back, Mother? What about the party
that you promised me?*

Marcus straightened up. "I don't care. I can look after
myself. And when I'm big, I'll have all the parties I want." He
sucked in his breath and quickly looked around him. Good
thing no one seemed to have heard him. They were all in such
a hurry to get to their classroom that they didn't worry about
what anyone else was doing.

***

Marcus didn't realize that Edith was headed to Winnipeg
after she dropped him off at school. It would have only added
to his fears of another person failing him – of not being
trustworthy.

At Walmart, it didn't take long for Edith to pick out
several outfits, a couple of PJ's, kid's toothpaste and
toothbrush with a Mickey Mouse design on it. She had so
much fun she almost wished that she had waited until Marcus
could come too. But it seemed that he needed these things
immediately, whether his mother returned or not.

The trip back to Steinbach was shortened by the busy
thoughts racing around in Edith's mind. *Wonder when his*

mom will return...or if, as Marcus mentioned, she's planning to be gone for a while. What do I do in the meantime? Do I go to Family Services for advice?

Back home, there was no response to her knock at any of the doors in the neighboring apartment house. Edith shook her head. It was time to head back to the school. With a few minutes to spare, she leaned back against the headrest with eyes closed. *Lord, give me wisdom in dealing with this child, especially with the sad news that his mom hasn't returned. May I know when to interfere and when to leave things be.*

She saw him come out of the school and head east on the sidewalk. She rolled down the window and called out to him,

"Marcus!" He stopped but didn't turn around. For just a minute she thought he was going to run.

He sighed and his shoulders drooped the minute he heard Edith's voice. He turned and shuffled back up the sidewalk as slowly as possible. *Seeing as she's here, that means Mother isn't back yet.* A tear slid down his cheek. He swiped at it with the back of his hand. *Nobody needs to see me cry, ever!*

They went to McDonalds for an early supper. Edith could not tell if Marcus was pleased by this or not, but he did eat the whole Big Mac Meal. *Such a skinny little fella, I sure would like to fatten him up a bit.* She had forgotten the mother's words about it being Marcus' birthday.

"Marcus, you have such a nice head of dark hair. That wave is very handsome. Do you usually wear it that long or is it time for a haircut?"

Marcus pushed a hand through the hair drooping over his face, moving it behind his ear. He muttered, "Whatever. It don't make no difference." And he ate another handful of French fries.

The old lady smiled at him and said, "If your mother isn't back by then, we'll look after it on the weekend."

Hope flared up and died just as quickly. He slouched back. His mother had never dropped him off at someone's house before. It felt bad, real bad, like she meant to be gone for a long while this time.

On the way home Edith asked, "Marcus, where are your grandparents? Do they live far away?" She watched his face in the rear view mirror. It was so sad she wanted to cry. And tears did come when he replied in a very quiet voice.

"They didn't want us."

Back at the house the old lady grabbed a couple of bags from the trunk and held them out to Marcus. "Here, I hope these will fit you."

His eyes lit up! Then just as quickly they dulled. This wasn't from his mother. He took the bags and with a mere grunt he headed for the front door. He couldn't bring himself to thank that woman. He grouched, *it should be from my mother.*

He hurried down the hall to the spare room and threw the bags on the end of the bed. He flopped down beside them and swiped angrily at the tears that refused to be stopped. Tired and disappointed, he lay down and curled up into a ball. *Mother, where are you? It's my birthday today and we were supposed to have a party, just you and me. But you're not here. When are you coming home?*

The questions roiled around in his mind, but not a word was uttered out loud. He pulled up a part of the blanket to cover himself and held onto the corner. It wasn't his blankie, but it would have to do. He fell asleep telling himself that he was a big boy now and didn't need it anymore.

Chapter Thirteen

1983 March 21st Monday

About a week later Edith told Marcus that she'd have to go to Family Services. "I don't know what else to do." She had a frustrated look in her eyes. "We'll see what help they can offer in finding your mother."

Marcus took a quick breath, opened his mouth, and shut it again. What could he say? Mother had promised that Family Services would never take him away. But she wasn't here to protect him. What could he do about it? He reined in his thoughts to listen as the woman was still talking.

"I just want to take care of you and do everything I can to make sure it's best for you."

She reached out as if to touch him, but thankfully she dropped her hand before it reached him. The wistful look in her eyes made Marcus want to trust her. But she was a stranger and now she was going to give him to Family Services.

Oh if only my mother was here. She'd put her arms around me and kiss me until I told her to stop it already. Then she'd tell me that everything's going to be okay. Marcus sighed sadly because she wasn't here to look after him.

Edith moved a bit closer but still kept her distance, for which Marcus was thankful. "I'm going to see if they can help us find your mother, to make sure she's okay," said Edith.

Again momentary hope flared up in his heart. Marcus stared at the woman's face. He didn't even blink; just gave a slight nod of his head. The brief moment of hope that had flared in his mind died just as quickly as it had sprung up. He knew his mother wouldn't come home until she wanted to. He dropped his head and shuffled off to the bedroom to get his backpack. It was time to head off to school.

All day he worried. What was going to happen to him in the meantime? Could Family Services come and take him away? What would happen if they did? How would his mother ever find him when she returned?

***

Six year old Marcus came out of the school doors and saw Edith sitting on the top step. She was chewing on a long piece of straw or maybe it was one of those tall weeds that he'd seen in the ditch. Her shoulders were hunched and she looked sad.

Hesitantly he approached from the side and sat down beside her. She jerked and twisted sideways. Her mouth agape in a gasp, he couldn't help but give a bit of a grin.

She grinned back at him, "You sure startled me!"

He nodded. His face turned somber as he waited to see why she was so sad. He didn't have to wait long.

"Marcus," the sad look disappeared and turned into an angry look. She took a deep breath. "Marcus, I got mad today."

He cringed and dropped his eyes to look at the steps below his feet. The woman put an arm around his shoulders and he jerked back. He couldn't help it. If she was mad at him, he needed to be ready to run.

She withdrew her arm, "I'm sorry, Marcus. I didn't mean to frighten you." She gave him an apologetic smile. "And no, I'm not mad at you. I'm furious with the system. I keep forgetting that they are understaffed and that they must be frustrated with how their hands are tied every time they turn around."

Marcus gave her a sideways glance. *She's not mad at me...* He watched her and listened as she continued, "I don't know what is supposed to happen now. Apparently they don't either. With your mom gone and your stuff just sitting there in your apartment..." she glanced at him and paused.

Marcus watched in fascination as her expression changed from being sort of nervous to an angry look. Then she raised her eyebrows like she had a question. He waited to see what would come next when she pressed her lips together and nodded her head.

"By hook or by crook, we're going to get in there," she said as she turned to look him full in the face. "We're going to go get some of your stuff."

His eyes lit up, "Really?"

"Yes!" she exclaimed as she stood up, "And I have a plan. Come on, Marcus, we have to go see someone about a key."

Marcus could feel her excitement in the air and for once he followed her without balking.

The old car also seemed to sense their excitement as well. Instead of it's usual resistance, it started on the first try. Marcus' excitement built with the sound of the turn signal. They merged smoothly into the traffic on the main road. A few short blocks later Edith pulled over to the curb and parked in front of a Real Estate Office.

Just as she had expected, they happened to have a master key for the apartment. The moment they understood why she needed it, they handed it over. After that it was a simple matter of driving home.

Marcus' heart beat fast as he walked quietly beside Edith. They crossed the narrow patch of grass that separated the two driveways. He was fearful and yet excited about what it would be like. What would they find? Would his mother be there? Maybe they'd get caught by the police and have to go to jail.

He sucked in his breath. What if someone had entered the apartment and taken all their stuff away?

Dread broke out in full bloom as reality set in when they stepped through the door into the apartment. It was dark. His mother wasn't there.

The stuffy smell from being closed up for so long hit their noses. Things didn't feel any better when the lights were turned on. Marcus wanted to shrink into his jacket and disappear. It felt too eerie, not a bit like home.

"What would you like to take with you, Marcus?"

The voice right beside him scared the wits out of him. His insides jumped but he managed to hide it well. The woman mustn't know how scared he was.

He looked up at her. "Aren't we supposed to ask my mother first?"

The woman's blue eyes looked sad. She opened her mouth and closed it again. It looked like she was supposed to tell him something important but couldn't do it. Marcus watched her carefully.

Then she threw back her shoulders and said, "I believe your mother would want you to take anything that you would like; anything that makes you think of her."

Mutely he nodded and headed for the bedroom. His blankie was still lying on the pillow, just as he'd left it 'such a long time ago'. He picked it up and buried his face in it. Then he hid it under his jacket, away from prying eyes.

He reached over and picked up the one picture on the night table. It was of his mother sitting on a porch swing. She looked so happy. He knew it was his great grandparents' place in a different country. He thought of the stories his mother had told him. He wished he was in the picture too. When he'd asked why they didn't go live there, his mother had told him that they couldn't because her grandparents were in heaven and the house was gone.

Anger swept over Marcus. He didn't know who he was angry at but his insides boiled and he threw the picture down. The glass shattered with a loud crash. He stared at the mess. Hot tear drops fell and hit the back of his clenched hands. He scrubbed at them but it was no use, more spots appeared faster than he could erase them.

At a sound behind him, he turned and sent a hard angry glare toward the woman as she appeared in the doorway. It angered him even more when she shook her head and said, "I'm so sorry, son."

"I'm not your son!" he shouted, "And I never will be. You're just an old woman who lives next door."

He pushed her aside as he shoved past her. The hand she put out to stop him was slapped away. He didn't wait to see what she would do. He rushed out of the room, out of the apartment and down the front steps.

Out on the sidewalk he ran as fast and as far as he could. Finally out of breath, he stopped. He couldn't go another step. Marcus ended up behind a car dealer lot. There was a black pick-up truck parked in the farthest corner. He hurried toward it and managed to heave himself up and over the side. He curled up behind the cab, pulled out his blankie from under his jacket and let his angry thoughts flow. His lips clenched and so did his fists.

Why don't you come back, Mother? Why can't we be at home, just you and me so your friends won't beat me up!

And why is that woman trying to take your place? At that thought he clenched his teeth tighter and his lower lip pooched out. *It's not fair! I don't want her to try to be nice to me! I'll never say her name and I don't want to go to that old school!*

Marcus sobbed until there were no more tears. When his intermittent sniffles were the only thing that broke the stillness around him, he grabbed the corner of his blankie and his thumb found its way into his mouth.

***

The next thing Marcus knew, someone was calling his name. He realized that she must have been calling him for some time.

"Please, Marcus, come out from wherever you're hiding. Come and have a nice warm supper. Please, honey. Come back."

Without remembering that he was trying to hide, he sat up. There she was, walking along the street. He must have made a noise because she turned and looked right at him.

"There you are, precious. Let's get you back to the house, where it's nice and warm."

Marcus didn't want to, but he had no other choice. He clambered over the side and dropped to the ground. At least she didn't try to take his hand as he shuffled along beside her.

At the house she opened the fridge and pulled out a plate of macaroni and cheese. It took only a minute in the microwave to warm it up. It tasted so good but he didn't tell her. He couldn't. Her being nice to him didn't change the fact that he didn't want to be here.

Oh, if only he could go home and find his mother there. His bottom lip quivered as he scooped up another spoon of pasta.

When he went to his room he found some of his things lying on top of the bed. He looked up and saw more things sitting on top of the dresser. When he looked at the open closet, there were his clothes hanging in it.

He stepped toward the dresser. Could it be? Yes it was! It was his toy car! He clasped it in his hand and sat down on the floor. His back leaning against the dresser, he drove the car up and down his leg.

After a while he turned and looked at the stuff on the bed. It looked like that woman had brought everything, even his mother's things. "Looks like she thinks Mother will never come back." Hope crept into his voice, "Or she brought them for when Mother does come." He gave a quick glance at the door. "Good thing I remembered to close the door," he muttered.

That brought back memories. "The only time my door at home was closed was when Mother locked me in." His shoulders heaved with a heavy sigh, "I guess she didn't want me around, or maybe she didn't want those guys to hit me."

A warm feeling filled him as he thought about his mother. Great sadness followed on the heels of the warm glow and he threw himself face down on the rug beside the bed.

***

Edith sat in the front room and yearned over the little boy. He was filled with such pain. And the worst of it was that he didn't know yet that his mother had no plans of returning. *I don't know when will be the best time to tell him, but whenever it is, I'm not looking forward to it.*

Listening to the young boy walk around in the spare room made Edith think of his obvious anger back at the apartment. When they had entered she'd wanted to hold her nose. The air was so stale. The place was a mess with stuff thrown everywhere by someone in a hurry. The couch had a blanket on it. When Edith moved it, it reeked of stale perfume and was so dirty that she'd left it. Entering the bedroom behind Marcus she'd been appalled. There was a crib mattress on the floor, stuck part way into the closet. Marcus had pounced on a little blue blanket, obviously his favorite. The unmade bed had a blue and green striped quilt hanging off the end. Its mattress looked lumpy and most uncomfortable. The dresser was covered with bottles of perfume and cheap jewelry. The closet held a few empty hangers. It didn't have a door, although the hinges still hung crookedly from the door frame. A small clothes hamper, overflowing with dirty laundry filled the space at the foot of the bed.

The crash had made her want to rush over and put her arms around the young lad, but she already knew it would not be appreciated. Any words of compassion from her would only have sent him into a deeper frenzy. Her heart still ached at the intense anger she'd seen in his beautiful eyes.

When he'd run out the door, her first impulse had been to chase after him. But she'd held back thinking how hard it must be for him and that the best thing probably was to give him some space. Such a little tyke, he wouldn't run too far.

Even though the mother wasn't planning to return, Edith had felt an urge to tidy up the place. While waiting to see if Marcus would return, she'd straightened the quilt and moved the clothes hamper beside the front door to take home.

In the kitchen she'd pocketed the lone matchbox car that sat on the window sill. She'd looked around but spotted no other toys.

She had watched out the window as she'd rinsed the few dishes in the sink and wiped the table, praying that the young boy would return. A quick look into the fridge had revealed that it was practically empty; a couple of beer bottles and a small container of milk turned thick. The freezer part was empty except for thick frost on its sides.

Poor Marcus, poor little mother. I'll have to come back later and give everything a good cleaning. Edith pitied them for having lived with so little. She wished that she'd known. But they hadn't lived there very long, and with her shift work she'd rarely caught a glimpse of them.

Now as she sat and listened to the sounds down the hall, she was glad that she'd brought the stuff before she went to search for him. Edith clasped her hands over her heart as her eyes filled with tears. His hope of his mother's return had a very slim chance of ever happening. It was too final; signing the boy over to Family Services. No, it wasn't likely that she'd ever return.

Edith grieved for the boy. "Oh Lord, he's only six," she whispered, "All alone in the world; left with a stranger without a word of explanation. How could she? I wonder what happened to his dad."

When no more noise came from the room down the hall Edith relaxed and reached for the TV remote. "I guess he's finally fallen asleep." Sadly she shook her head, trying to grasp the idea of a young boy with only one little car to play with. On that thought Edith sat up straighter, "Well, that's something I can fix." Then she sighed and slouched back against the couch, "But only if he'll accept them from me."

Chapter Fourteen

1983 April 2nd

The apartment next door had been re-let. Edith had tried to explain that it was because his mother was not coming back. That she had signed papers so others would care for Marcus. He had refused to listen to her. He shouted that she'd promised to NEVER do that.

Now a little three year old girl had moved into the place where he and his mother were supposed to live.

The girl lived with her mom and grandma. She was a precocious child who loved to talk. Most folks were delighted with her chatter, but not Marcus. She bugged him constantly. Whenever he stepped out the door she'd call out, "Wanna play?"

Why doesn't that kid just give up wondered Marcus? He would growl at her, "Don't bug me." If she continued to ask he shouted, "Just go away." Then he added softly, "Far away; as far away as possible."

One day he'd had enough. He stared at her and said, "Don't you hear your mother calling you?"

She stood quietly for a moment, her eyes squinting at him, "No, her's not!" was the vehement response. "Her can't 'cause her went shoppin' for gwocies."

Marcus frowned at Edith when she came out and stood on the top step. She called out over the fence, "Hey, Missie, would you like a cookie?"

The dumb kid couldn't wait to get off the table she was standing on and hurried around the hedge. Marcus made sure he had grabbed a couple of cookies and was in his room with the door shut before she made it to the front steps.

He could hear her babble away at Edith. "What'd she invite that kid into the house for? I got no place for my own." He muttered around a cookie.

His mouth stopped chewing when there was a knock on his door. "Go away, I don't want to play with you," he shouted.

"It's me, Marcus. I just brought you some milk to go with your cookies," called Edith from the other side of the door.

He wanted to tell her to keep it. He was still angry at her for inviting that kid in but a glass of milk would be very nice. He opened the door and reached out to take it.

He had to give her that much, the old lady always knocked and waited for him to open the door. But it also made him angry. He didn't need anybody. He could hardly wait until he was big enough to look after himself.

He took the glass without looking at her. When he began to close the door she whispered, "thank you."

What's she thankful for? That I opened the door? Oh, right. She wants me to say it. Well I won't! I didn't ask for it, so I won't.

***

Marcus' attitude seemed to go from bad to worse. He dug his heels in and resisted any suggestion Edith made.

At church she shared her need for a sitter. Up till now, her boss had been most gracious in planning Edith's shifts around school hours, giving her evenings and weekends to be with Marcus. It was time for things to return to normal scheduling.

A rather plump little lady, who Edith saw regularly across the auditorium, came over after the Praise and Prayer time and slid into the pew beside her.

"Hi, my name is Abby and I volunteer for recess monitor at Marcus' school. I know he has some behavior problems, especially toward some of the teachers. But I haven't had a run-in with him so far. I will gladly help you with Marcus.

"Our own children are all grown up and live far away. It will be nice to have a youngster around. Drop the boy off any time, night or day. My husband and I are both retired so our schedule is very flexible."

"Thank you so much. Just promise that you'll let me know if it ever becomes too hard." Edith gave a sad smile as she looked at the kind wrinkled face in front of her. "He is so full of anger and fear that half the time he doesn't know what to do with himself." Edith straightened her shoulders and took a deep breath before she continued. "Sometimes he even breaks things. But the worst thing is when he blatantly defies me by walking away and slamming his door shut."

Edith wiped a tear, "I don't know what it will take to help that poor boy learn to trust someone."

"We live on a five acre lot, on the edge of town," said Abby. "And there's a small creek at the back of it. He'll have lots of room to run off his anger." She smiled, "And he can give our dog some much needed exercise."

***

After the first time, Marcus didn't complain about going to Abby's. The old couple made him think of the photo of his great grandparents. They didn't fuss like Edith but they still made him feel safe. They showed him were they kept the games and books and then let him be. Sometimes when they watched TV, they sat with heads resting on the back of their easy chairs and snored. It made Marcus giggle softly. He didn't want to wake them.

There was always snacking food available and they never nagged him about his homework. It was kind of cool how the old man had him doing arithmetic before Marcus realized that he was learning useful things. One Saturday they started a woodworking project. It was a birdhouse. Marcus had to do subtractions and additions to get the boards to fit. He smiled to himself, proud when the old man praised him that he'd been able to do it. Nice as it all was, Marcus couldn't quite bring himself to thank the man.

Marcus liked it when the old lady sat down beside him and picked up a book from the end table. She opened it and read to him. Her finger pointed to the words. Marcus liked that because he could follow along. She didn't mind reading it more than once. Soon he had memorized it and added his voice to hers as she read.

Marcus was pleased the next day at school. When Teacher pulled out a book for the class to read, it was the very same one that the old lady had read with him. *It's weird that she likes school books."*

When it was his turn to read the next sentence, as was usual, Teacher prompted him with the first two words. He remembered that part of the story and rattled off the rest of the sentence. But he wasn't stupid. He kept his eyes on the page so the teacher would think he was actually reading.

He blushed at her praise but he did not admit that he was reading from memory. Nor could he acknowledge that her kind words made his heart feel warm. He knew that in no time at all she would find something else to scold him about. *She has to yell at me 'cause my mother isn't around for her to complain to about me.*

Marcus found a friend, a very special friend. It was the old couple's dog named Spiffer. The old man said that he was a Pocket Beagle. His long floppy ears almost dragged on the ground. They'd fly up like wings when he jumped up at Marcus. His long tongue hung out of the side of his mouth and drool sprayed everywhere in his excitement at seeing Marcus.

The two romped all over the backyard. Marcus threw a Frisbee and Spiffer dashed after it, his nose close to the ground as if he could follow its scent. Then he grabbed it with his teeth and eagerly returned to drop it at Marcus' feet. Spiffer was a happy, loving, inquisitive dog but not yappy. That's why he startled Marcus the first time he made a sudden half-howl right beside him. Spiffer had caught sight of a squirrel and dashed off after it. Marcus ran after the dog and laughed out loud. The dog with its ears flapping and bouncing tore around the yard until he chased the squirrel up a tree.

Then the boy and the dog flopped down on the ground under the tree. The dog panted, his long tongue hanging out while Marcus ran his hand back and forth across the dog's belly.

Hungry after all that exercise, Marcus got up to get a dog biscuit for Spiffer and a bite for himself. He knew that Abby liked it when he asked for another cookie. She smiled at him and gave his shoulder a soft pat. Then she turned back to continue whatever he had interrupted. It made his heart feel warm.

But Marcus really missed his mother. One day he felt so sad that not even Spiffer could distract him. He just sat cross-legged under a tree and hung his head. Spiffer crept close and yawned. The yawn ended with a squeak. He placed his paw on Marcus' leg and looked up with his big brown eyes. He swallowed, and squeaked again, as if pleading for Marcus to understand that he sympathized. Marcus couldn't resist. He leaned over and buried his face in the dog's neck. He whispered, "I know she's never coming back...but I don't want to believe it. Why would she leave when she knows how bad it feels?"

Abby found them fast asleep. She hated to wake the boy but Edith had arrived to take him home.

Chapter Fifteen

Back at Edith's it was hard for Marcus. Every time he looked out the window, the sight of the apartment he'd shared with his mother reminded him of his loss, his rejection. The pain swept over him and he took it out on Edith.

He was slow to respond to her call; he resisted all her efforts to take care of him. The only reason he wasn't late for school was because Edith basically dragged him there.

At his belligerent statement that his mother always let him go on his own, to both of their relief, she finally agreed. She might not have been quite so willing to let him set his own pace if she'd realized how often he left school early and wandered the streets or hung out at the nearest park.

In the middle of the month of June, Marcus heard Edith on the phone. "Are you sure? It would certainly make things easier."

Was she talking about him? What would be easier? He started to worry. Was that those Family Services people on the phone? Were they planning to come and take him away?

He went and threw himself on his bed. He stared across the room toward the window and tried to remember what his mother used to say about them; scary things about how mean they were to her; made her work hard and slapped her when she wasn't looking. He trembled and curled up into a ball.

"I should've been nicer to the old lady. Then she wouldn't want to send me away." He rolled onto his back and stared at the ceiling. "What if they decide to send me far away? Then if Mother comes back she won't be able to find me." Angrily he swiped at the tears that were determined to leak out of his eyes.

There was a knock on his door. He stiffened. If he pretended to be asleep maybe she'd go away. Maybe the whole problem would disappear. But she didn't go away.

"Marcus," she called in a soft voice. "Marcus, I have good news for you."

Ha, there was no such thing as good news for the likes of him.

"Please open the door, honey. That was Abby on the phone. I think you will like what I have to tell you."

Marcus got off the bed and took his time getting to the door. He opened it a few inches and glowered at her.

She wasn't intimidated at all. Instead she smiled and said, "That was Abby on the phone. She called to say that when school is done for the year you can go over there every day, even when I'm not at work. Isn't that good news?"

Marcus sucked in his breath. "All summer?"

Edith nodded. Her blonde ponytail bobbed and her blue eyes had a glad twinkle in them. "I know you love their dog."

"Spiffer," Marcus burst out eagerly and then quickly slouched back into his sullen attitude.

"Yes. Abby said that their dog will be happy for a buddy. He gets lonesome with just an old couple around the place."

Marcus could not restrain the thread of joy that leapt into his heart. He nodded and said, "The dog likes me."

"I'm glad you'll have someone to love."

The woman's words shut out his brief moment of joy by reminding him that he was all alone in the world.

Summer Holidays

Marcus and Spiffer roamed the fields out behind the house. He liked to pretend that Mother was waiting at home for him. And he'd take the dog home, so she could see what a nice dog Spiffer was.

When he got tired or hungry Abby always had something good for him to eat. It didn't matter what time of day it was. Red Kool-Aid was the best drink on a hot day. Sometimes Abby told him to open his hand. Then she tapped a few red crystals onto his palm so he could lick them. They were sweet and sour at the same time. He tried not to shudder when his taste buds kicked in but he couldn't help it. Abby would wait and watch. Then she gave a hearty laugh. Marcus liked it when she laughed. Her tummy jiggled and her mouth was wide open. Sometimes he even had to chuckle with her. Abby must have liked it when he joined her because he'd always end up with an extra cookie or two.

"I'm going to walk down to the creek. Want to come along?" asked Abby one hot afternoon. She was wearing cut-off jeans and a t-shirt, not her usual outfit. She didn't seem to mind that it made her look funny.

Marcus nodded and called for Spiffer, who lolled under the deck to keep cool. When the dog didn't move, Marcus slapped his thigh and said, "Don't you want to go for a walk?" As soon as Spiffer heard the word 'walk' he jumped up and rushed over with his tail wagging furiously.

"Are we going to play in the water?" asked Marcus with a hopeful look in his eyes as he glanced at her cut-offs.

She smiled at him, "If you won't tell. Some folks think an old lady like me shouldn't waste her time playing in the creek."

Marcus liked the feeling of conspiracy. When she stopped in the middle of the trail and waited, he shook his head and said, "I promise I won't tell."

"Then let's be on our way."

At the creek they removed their shoes and socks. Abby showed him how to tuck his socks into the toes of his shoes, so Spiffer wouldn't decide they were a chew-toy.

The grass tickled his feet as he tip-toed to the edge of the creek. Abby waded right in. Marcus stopped and touched the tip of one toe in first. The water was cool to his touch. Before he could decide if he dared step in or not, Spiffer jumped against his back and Marcus fell in head first. He came up sputtering and gasping. He heard Abby holler, "Spiffer, shame on you!"

When Marcus could breathe again, he decided the water was pretty nice. He ran a short distance and laughed as the water splashed up into his face. Soon the dog joined him.

Abby also got soaked from their antics and went to sit in the sun to dry off. When both the boy and the dog were tuckered out, they crawled up on the bank and flopped down on the grass beside her.

Abby rubbed the dog's tummy and smiled at the young boy. "This reminds me of when my brothers and I were young. Whenever our mom couldn't find us, she knew where we'd be." Abby chuckled to herself.

Marcus waited for her to continue.

"Our dad rigged up a pole close to the back door. On it he hung an old tin pot and a stick tied to a string. When our mom needed someone to help her or she wanted to let us know that dinner was ready, all she had to do was bang that pot."

Abby looked over at Marcus. The glad look from her memory was visible in her eyes. She continued, "Summer was the best time of the year for me as a kid."

Marcus nodded his agreement. "I think this is the best too; being out here with no shoes on and playing in the creek with Spiffer."

Chapter Sixteen

On July 1st Abby dropped Marcus off at Edith's place in time for supper. He trudged up the steps and glanced over at the building next door. Even though he knew it wasn't his home anymore, he always hoped that he'd see his mother on the steps, calling him home.

Instead, it was the little girl's face that smiled at him and waved from the window. He turned away and clenched his fists. "That's my place. It should be my mother watching for me."

Marcus came straight to the table but without a smile when Edith told him that supper was ready.

"Guess what?" she started talking before he had hardly seated himself. "A little baby girl arrived at the hospital during the night. She's the tiniest mite you ever did see."

Marcus could feel her eyes on him, but what did he care about a baby and a girl at that.

"She's kind of like you, Marcus. Her mom had to go away too."

He shrugged. It was almost four months since his mother had disappeared. He knew that she wasn't planning to ever come back even though he wished she would. What good did it do to talk about it?

The woman kept on talking. "I sure hope the dad or someone else shows up to take care of that sweet baby.

I wonder where my dad is. Mother never said a word about him. Maybe he died...

His head snapped up when he heard Edith say something about 'she died'. He stared open-mouthed and his heart thumped wildly.

"What is it, Marcus?" the woman asked in a kind voice.

"Who..oo.. who is dead?" he stuttered.

"Why, the little baby's mother, that's who. I'm sorry, Marcus, if I frightened you."

His shoulders heaved and he picked up his fork, only to push his food back and forth on the plate. The fork dropped out of his hand and made such a clatter it startled him.

"I'm really sorry, Marcus. Did you think I was talking about your mother?"

He shrugged but couldn't answer around the lump in his throat. He got up and headed to his room. He heard the woman's sigh follow him but he couldn't think about her problems.

He held in his sobs until the door closed behind him. He went and dropped onto the bed. He reached for his blankie and buried his face in it. Marcus let himself cry for a few moments. Suddenly he sat up, his back rigid as he angrily swiped away the tears. He walked over to the dresser and opened the bottom drawer. He stuffed the blankie in there and slammed it shut.

He wasn't a baby anymore. No one cared what happened to him. From now on he had to be strong. He picked up two of the biggest books that were on the shelf in his closet. Using them as weights, he began to 'pump iron'. "I'll run all the way to school and do push-ups. Then I'll get to be big and strong and no one will tell me what to do!"

Chapter Seventeen

Marcus started Grade One on Sept 6th, 1983. It was a beautiful autumn day following the Labor Day weekend. His feet shuffled through the golden leaves that littered the sidewalk. He was glad that Edith realized that he didn't want to be fussed over. He was a big boy and could walk by himself. When he had told her that he didn't want a ride to school he had expected her to argue. But she'd been cool about it. She just said, "It's good to see you growing up, Marcus, and doing things for yourself."

And he was glad that she didn't say anything about how his mother would be so proud of him. He didn't want anyone mentioning his mother; for no reason whatsoever!

First Grade didn't seem to be much different from Kindergarten. Except the teacher demanded more attention. Marcus found that difficult. The trees outside the window kept distracting him. Their yellow, green and brown leaves were dancing in the breeze. He just knew that Spiffer was nosing about and chasing the ones that fell toward the ground. If only he could be chasing the dog.

When the final bell of the day rang, Marcus was ready for it. His backpack was stuffed with a bunch of notes and a book that he was supposed to read with his parent. Ha, a lot Teacher knew. Not! There was no way he would let Edith read to him. Maybe he could take it to Abby's place. They didn't make such a big fuss over him at their house. They just let him be.

Marcus crashed his body against one of the doors. It felt good to feel it fling open for him. To his dismay he spotted Edith immediately. She was getting out of her car with a big smile on her face.

What's she doing here? I thought she agreed that I'm big enough to get home by myself.

"Come see who's in the back seat." Edith walked around the old tin lizzie and opened the back door. There was a funny looking car seat in the back, right beside where he usually sat when he was riding in her car.

He gave it a quick glance before he settled back and pulled out the seat belt. A sound like someone breathing stopped his hand with the belt half way across his lap. A closer look and he realized that this must be the baby that Edith had been talking about. Her next words affirmed his guess.

"This is little Charlotte. Remember? The baby who's mom died. Charlotte is going to live with us."

What does a baby without a mother look like? Marcus was curious to see, but then his mother had left him, hadn't she? And he didn't look any different. At least he didn't think so.

He sat back and fastened the seatbelt. He didn't care, even though he knew that Edith was hoping he would. *There's no way I'm going to care about that baby. I've got enough problems already. It will probably cry and make my head hurt.*

He frowned. His lower lip pooched out and he kept his eyes focused out the window. *What kind of a name is Charlotte for a baby? It sounds like a Grama name.*

When he thought Edith wasn't looking, he risked a glance out of the corner of his eye. He couldn't see anything. The pink blanket covered the face on his side. He lifted a hand to reach in and move the blanket. Just in time he caught himself. His hand dropped into his lap. *I don't have time to worry about a baby.* He slouched back again and forced himself to watch the buildings slip by as they drove along. If he stared at one spot long enough, everything became blurry. It was kind of cool.

His heart almost stopped beating when there was a big sigh beside him. His head spun around just in time to see the blanket move. One little fist pushed up into the air. He watched, fascinated as the tiny fingers separated and stretched out. *Is the baby waving at me? No way. It doesn't even know I'm here because its face is still covered up.*

Marcus glanced up and saw Edith's hopeful eyes in the rear view mirror, watching him. He scowled at her and turned sideways to look out the window again. He couldn't wait to get back to the house. He opened his door the minute he heard the locks click. He raced up the driveway without bothering to shut the car door behind him. He heard a sigh and wondered why. *I don't know what the old lady's problem is. She needs the door open to get the baby. I'm just being helpful.*

***

The days following Charlotte's arrival merged one into another, baby crying, needing bottle, needing diaper change. Then it started all over again. Questions like, "Marcus can you pat her back while I warm her bottle?" he knew were meant to involve him in the care of the infant but it irked him.

She's the one who wanted the baby, not me, he grouched as he thought about going to the baby. But most of the time Edith had done what was needed before he could decide.

Marcus was glad that he could escape for those few hours he was supposed to be at school. He hated the sorrowful looks from Edith. It made him feel bad. He didn't want to care about anybody or anything.

I just want my mother to come home. Why can't things be like they used to be? Well, all except those mean friends of hers. I don't need them.

Seeing as that wasn't to be, he let his rage boil over at Edith. In his room he often stood and looked at his little car on top of the dresser. He had to admit that Edith had bought him a lot of other toys, and very nice toys too. Like that race car track he had always wanted. And at least a dozen cars to race on it, but whenever he looked at the car from his mother he felt guilty if he played with the other toys. Sometimes he deliberately turned his back and tried to forget about it. But it was always there; always ready to remind him of being alone since his mother left.

Marcus chose not to think about how often he'd been left alone before his mother abandoned him into Edith's care.

Many nights he cried himself to sleep after admitting to himself that his mother was never coming back. Next morning he would wake up filled with resentment, more surly and stubborn than ever.

***

The baby grew. After those first few weeks she seldom cried. Before she could sit up by herself she already smiled whenever Marcus came in sight. If the woman's back was turned he would venture closer to peek into the playpen. It intrigued him when the baby was awake. She would kick her legs and wave her arms. And that smile did funny things to his heart. He wanted to reach in and touch her, but before he could let himself do it he'd hear Edith move. Quickly he backed off and headed out of the room.

Sometimes in school, when he was bored, he wondered what the little baby was doing. Yesterday she had grabbed onto his sleeve when he walked past her. It was a tiny tug but he remembered.

I guess she's too little to know that her mother is gone. Otherwise she wouldn't be smiling all the time.

When Charlotte began to crawl around the house, Marcus made sure that he closed his door before he left for school.

"I don't want that kid crawling into my room and messing with my stuff," he told Edith when he saw her looking at him with raised eyebrows.

Each day he resisted the baby's pull on his heart. Whenever Charlotte crawled in his direction, he deliberately turned away or went to his room, muttering something about being bugged.

School days were a burden to be endured. Marcus' mind was busy as he dragged his feet along the sidewalk. *As a kid you've got no say in whether you go to school or not. The only reason I go is because I don't want to have to go to a foster home.*

Most evenings Marcus hid in his room. He wanted to stay out of Edith's way and he didn't want to get sucked in by the kid. In loneliness he sat, his mind filled with self-pity and anger. "I remember what mother said about when she was little," he told his little car. "Foster people just want the money they get for looking after you. They don't give a fig about you." Marcus glanced towards the door of his room. He didn't want Edith to hear when he talked out loud. *She cares too much! I don't like it when she tries to be my mother. I guess she acts like that 'cause she's a neighbor. At least I'm not in a foster home.*

As the days and weeks slipped by, his school teacher was ready to pull her hair out. No matter what she tried, or how patient she was with him, Marcus refused to co-operate. He was determined to misunderstand.

He soon noticed that when he was defiant, the other kids laughed. This encouraged him to show off and dare to rebel even more.

He refused to do his bookwork because it meant giving in. But he did like to learn about things. Even while he was goofing off, he listened when the teacher explained things to the rest of the class. Then when he was by himself, he thought about what she had said.

He relished the look of surprise on Teacher's face when she asked a question of the class and he promptly answered it. He couldn't understand why the rest sat there and looked stupid. Didn't they remember Teacher's words?

His answers showed that he understood the subject matter better than most of the other students. He felt a sense of self-justification when he saw the teacher's surprise. *Does she think I'm dumb? Anyone could learn that stuff if they bothered to listen.*

Chapter Eighteen

Marcus had been at Edith's house for over two years. He heard her pause by his bedroom door. He'd forgotten to close it and was busy 'pumping iron' in preparation for when he was old enough to be out on his own.

She stood in the doorway and nattered on about if only he was as serious about training in godliness … Whatever that meant ... She said that physical exercise was good, but it was all so temporary; that spiritual training would help him now and for eternity.

Marcus, imprisoned by his anger, knew from past experience that if he remained quiet, sooner or later she'd give up and leave him alone. He wasn't about to find a Bible and look up First Timothy chapter four and verse seven as she suggested.

Instead he gave her a mutinous glare and a guttural hmff. That was the only comment he had for her. It had happened often enough that she'd learned when to leave him alone and move on.

He frowned as he listened to her steps in the hall. Her sad face at his negative response stayed with him. It made him feel angry and gave him a bad feeling, but not bad enough to apologize. She also made him feel guilty. He didn't like that feeling but it gave him an excuse to justify his bad attitude.

Next thing he heard was Edith and Charlotte having fun. They had no right to feel so happy, especially when he tried so hard to destroy their pleasure. It just wasn't fair.

That woman had the audacity to wipe out the unkind aura that he worked so hard to create. They ought to feel just as miserable as he did.

He moved over to the door and peeked through the crack at the back of it. Instead of being put out, Edith reached down, grabbed Charlotte and tossed her up in the air. Giggles in the hallway filled two glad hearts. But not his…

***

The little kid is always smiling. What's she got to be so happy about? She's a reject, just like me. It's not fair. It made Marcus so angry that he tripped her and pushed her on purpose when Edith wasn't looking, just to see if he could wipe that smile off her face. When he did manage to make her cry, he rushed to his room and watched through the crack in the back of his partly opened door. He smirked and whispered, "Go ahead crybaby. That woman's not your real mother. You're just like me – abandoned."

Marcus kept his eye glued to the crack and thought, *Good thing the kid can't tattle yet.*

He snickered to himself as he avoided the squeaky part of the floor and flopped down on the bed. It creaked as he rolled over onto his belly and rested his head on his crossed arms. Before he knew it tears filled his eyes. Angrily he swiped his shirt sleeve across his face. "I'm not a four year old anymore. Tears are for babies; for weaklings."

The stubborn tears refused to be stopped completely, no matter how hard eight year old Marcus sniffled and swiped. "Why does everything bad happen to me? Where is my mother? Why doesn't she come home?"

**

Marcus hated having to go to church even more than going to school. The people had such sad faces when they looked at him. And worst of all they patted him on the head and told him to be a good boy.

Edith dragged him to his classroom but he was never there when she went to pick him up. Instead he'd be waiting out front on the sidewalk. He mumbled unintelligible responses to her questions about Sunday school in the hope that it would distract her. *What the old lady doesn't know won't hurt her. No need to tell her that a swing in the park is a lot more fun than sitting in a stuffy room full of snot-nosed kids.*

When he turned nine he refused altogether. "Bad enough I have to go to regular school," he had huffed with his arms crossed over his chest.

Edith backed off. She did not force him again but continued to invite him.

"Marcus, it would be very nice if you joined Charlotte and me for Sunday school," she said on a beautiful sunny morning.

He didn't look at her, just shook his head.

Her gentle sigh made him feel mean. He frowned and turned his back to her.

She didn't nag at him. All she said was, "In case you need them, the emergency numbers are on the fridge, including Colette's number."

He muttered, "Like I would call that old crab. She hates my guts. She'd rather see me dead than help me with anything."

"Oh no, Marcus," responded Edith, "I'm sure she'd come if you needed her. Her bark is worse than her bite."

"Oh yeah?" he fired back at her. He threw a devilish smirk over his shoulder as he watched Edith back off. Her sagging shoulders said it all.

That witch, Colette, thinks only about herself. She'd probably laugh instead of help if I was hurt. I'm surprised she hasn't tried to get me into trouble yet, but she's too busy thinking about herself.

Marcus' thoughts made his lower lip push out. Still he felt bad at the sadness on Edith's face as she turned to walk out the door with Charlotte. He didn't really want to hurt her, honest. *Edith's a good sort,* he mused, *but I can't let her know, 'cause then she'll try to smother me again, especially now that I've trained her to let me be. Besides, I can't let anyone be my friend. I just want to get big enough so I can get out of this dump.*

***

As soon as the door shut behind Edith, Marcus hurried into the kitchen. He opened the door of the fridge and searched the shelves to see what there was to eat. He reached into the back, behind the mayo and pulled out the can of Pepsi. There was only one. *Was she hiding it to save for herself, or did it get lost in the shuffle,* he wondered.

He wandered back to the living room, slurping the spill off the top of the can. Soon he got bored with watching TV. All of the stations just had a bunch of guys shouting or waving their hands. *That's why I don't want to go to church. Everyone's always hollering and telling people they're sinners.*

The room was too quiet. He found the comics and read them. They weren't very funny. He recognized a few faces in the sports section. Losing interest he let the paper slide off the couch and onto the floor.

"I wonder what Spiffer is doing? He probably misses me," Marcus sighed. "I wish I could still go over there to play with him. But I'm too big for a babysitter now." He flopped against the back of the couch and sighed again. "I wish I had my own dog."

His eyes whipped to the clock when he heard voices outside. It was just past noon. He went to peer through the gauzy curtains. He saw Edith holding Charlotte's hand to help her up the steps. Quickly he rushed back to the couch and pulled the comics onto his lap. He watched the door knob turn and lowered his head pretending that he'd been reading the paper the whole time.

The little kid came straight over to him and dropped a wilted dandelion right in the middle of the paper. He slapped it onto the floor and growled. "Get that stinkin' weed outta my face."

Now why did the kid have to start with the tears? Just to get him into trouble. Again! He watched in fascination as her lower lip quivered. *How did she do that? Aww what did she have to go and start crying for?*

One big teardrop formed on her lower eyelash. It hung there for a second before it rolled down her cheek as she stood and gazed at the rejected bloom.

And here comes the big scold from Edith. Marcus' lips protruded as he listened to her tirade.

"Marcus! How could you? Can't you see that she is only trying to be kind!"

"What does a stupid dandelion have to do with being kind? She can just leave me alone. That's what I call being kind." He stomped out of the room and down the hall. He slammed the door, but lost the sense of satisfaction when the door bounced back open. He shoved it again. This time it remained shut.

Chapter Nineteen

It seemed to have happened overnight, the 10 year old's growth spurt. One morning when Marcus looked into the mirror he saw a tall dark handsome boy with magnetic blue eyes. He had to bend his knees to see to comb the top of his wavy hair. It gave him a sense of self-confidence.

He smirked at the face staring back at him. *No one's going to dare boss me around anymore.* He patted his hair in place and strutted into the kitchen. When Edith wouldn't be intimidated by his new stature, he turned on Charlotte, "Get me a bowl of Cap'n Crunch!"

"The word is please," said Edith with a slightly raised chin, "And what's wrong with getting it yourself?"

Marcus tried to out-stare her. She didn't even blink. He shoved his chair back and muttered, "Who needs breakfast."

Edith and Charlotte didn't see him again that day.

After school Marcus practiced his new-found self-confidence on a couple of grade three boys who were headed to the monkey bars.

He stepped in front of them, narrowed his eyes and leaned his upper body real close. "Gimme your money!"

His height added to his intimidating stare. The boys quickly handed over the few coins they had in their pockets at Marcus' demand.

Success made him brave to take bigger risks. Not wanting to go home after school, nor excited about hanging out on the streets until after dark, he got an idea.

His next effort was to sneak into the theatre without paying. He watched for the right moment when the cashier was distracted. Then he swaggered past the line-up.

These peasants must think I'm on staff 'cause no one's questioning my right to cut in here. He grinned inwardly as he strode over to the snack counter.

It didn't take long for the staff to recognize him and realize what he was doing. Instead of calling him on it, they began to give 'the kid' odd jobs to make up for the price of a ticket.

It gave him a pleasant feeling when they said, "Good job" after he swept up all the spilt popcorn. One job he really didn't care to do was mopping up the sticky pop spills. It seemed that no matter how carefully he mopped up, his shoes still got dirty. Every step squeaked and the soles stuck to the floor. That was most embarrassing. But it got him out of the cold.

He delighted in the fact that now he could stroll in with head held high instead of having to watch for the right moment to sneak in.

Marcus tried to time his home coming to coincide with Edith leaving for work. *I have to get inside before she leaves with just enough time so she won't fret about my being out, but not long enough for her to nag at me. She still thinks a ten year old shouldn't be out after dark. Must be because she's so old...*

One Friday evening something went wrong with the projectors and everyone was sent home. Marcus got home too early. He didn't want to go inside until just before Edith left to drop Charlotte off at Collette's place. The night was cold and dark with a heavy mist. He shivered as he waited behind the hedge. His heart thumped loudly and he sucked in his breath when the leaves in the hedge shook and parted. What a relief! It was only the neighbor's cat. It came through the hedge and wrapped its tail around his leg. He reached down and picked it up. He pulled it close to his chest. The added warmth and the purring of the cat made it easier to wait.

At the sound of a door opening the cat strained against Marcus' arms and jumped down to the ground. The scrambling cat startled Edith. His half-smile at the providential distraction was hidden by the dark of night.

Edith breathed a sigh of relief as Marcus' appearance followed the cat. "Thank goodness you're home. I won't have to worry about you out in the cold."

In his room Marcus found his allowance on top of the dresser. He liked having the money. It was adequate to buy lunch at school and it saved the bother of having to make a sandwich. It didn't look cool to carry a paper bag. How could he intimidate others if he didn't look the part?

But, still, he hated it when Edith handed it to him. It made him feel angry and frustrated that he needed to accept help. It made him feel like he owed her something.

He tightened his fist around the bills as he was reminded of his last allowance. His features darkened as he could still hear his own voice. "I only take this because I have no other choice."

She'd made him feel even worse when she said, "What, no thank you?"

Like a dumb kid I mumbled a stupid thanks. His mutinous look glared back at him from the mirror. *One of these days I'll get a lucky break. Then I'll be rich and I won't have to grovel to anyone ever again.*

Chapter Twenty

When fourteen year old Marcus wasn't at the theatre, he was at the bowling alley. The seats at the back allowed him to learn who bowled consistently. Then he waited for an opportunity to make a wager. Sure, no one cared to bet large amounts, but he won often enough to make a bit of extra spending money.

But Marcus was getting desperate. *Will I ever have enough money to go away from here? As fast as I get a few dollars, they seem to disappear.*

Lips set in a firm line he headed out front, off of school property, to look for someone to bully. A devilish grin settled on his face when he found his quarry. "Gimme a smoke!" he demanded, towering over a kid that barely came to his shoulder. He loved the feeling of power his height gave him; of being in control. He didn't give a hoot about whether anyone liked him or not.

"Where's that lunch money?" He grabbed the second kid by the collar before he could back away. Marcus knew that when he spoke in an ominous voice and looked the kids straight in the eye they always gave in.

Marcus walked away without a backward glance. He shook the few paltry coins in his palm and sighed. *How long must I endure this? I want to make a pile of money. I can't rob a bank; that only happens on TV. There must be something…*

***

The angry boy worked hard to distance himself from everyone, at school and at home. "I don't want any ties when I leave this dorky town. Friends only complicate matters."

Marcus missed more and more time at home. As a teenager he had stopped getting indoors in time to alleviate Edith's fears. These days he always checked that no one was around before he entered the house. Hungry when he came home, he headed straight for the fridge. Most of the time he found clearly labeled containers of leftovers. "Edith must think that I'm hungry all the time – ha, no brownie points as far as I'm concerned," he growled as he scanned the shelves.

But it didn't stop him from taking a container of lasagna over to the microwave and heating it up.

"Good thing the old gal isn't at home. I'd hate to have to go to bed hungry."

He turned on the TV and slouched on the couch but shoveled the pasta into his mouth in haste. He'd rather starve than give Edith the satisfaction of seeing him enjoy her cooking. When he heard a car pull into the driveway, he plunked the dishes on the floor beside the couch and headed for his room.

Marcus quickly dropped his clothes and slid under the covers without bothering to turn on the light. *Let her think I've been in my room all evening.*

He strained to hear their conversation as Edith and Charlotte came in the front door. *Just listen to miss goody-two shoes.* He curled his lips in disgust at Charlotte's words.

"Mom, I know you're tired. Sit down and put your feet up while I start a fresh pot of coffee."

Marcus held his breath as he waited to hear what else they would talk about. He heard a creak. *That must be the old lady sitting down on the big chair. It always creaks.*

Marcus heard Charlotte say, "Thanks for picking me up. Sally and I got a lot done on our Science…" She stopped mid-sentence to exclaim, "Mom, you shouldn't have to pick up after him, especially after working all day. Let me clean up those dishes. I didn't see them there when I left for Sally's house."

Edith's murmured response didn't carry to his ears. He raised his head to hear better but there was only the clatter of dishes hitting the stainless steel sink. He pursed his lips. *The kid's probably earning some more brownie points as usual.*

But light footsteps indicated that Charlotte was headed to her room and the clatter in the kitchen continued. "Great, now it's my fault that the old lady has to clean up after a hard day's work."

Marcus rolled over and shrugged. He couldn't let himself care. It was bad enough that he was beholden to others. *I don't care. It's not my fault that I was left on her hands. She could've dropped me off at the Children's Aid.*

But that thought brought back dark memories, scary memories of what possible evil lurked there. His mother had never fully explained. She had said just enough to make him know that he'd never want to be under their control.

***

Skipping classes wasn't much fun. Edith was at work and Charlotte at school. The house was too quiet and there was nothing to distract him. Time dragged. He had to think of something to do until it was time to head over to the theatre – which wasn't until after school. What could he do?

His thoughts turned to Charlotte. No matter what he did, he couldn't wipe the smile off of her face. Oh sure, sometimes she'd go off and cry for a while, but then she'd show up again with that silly grin on her face.

"I'll have to spend less time away from the house, find more ways to bug her. Sooner or later she'll cave."

Marcus got an idea and headed outdoors. The neighbor, two doors over, had a chopping block in his backyard. He used it to made kindling to start a fire in his fire pit. "If I move the block just inside the hedge she won't see it until it's too late."

He smirked as he pulled the heavy chopping block across the lawn and stuck it on the edge of their sidewalk. After putting it in place, he went out of the yard and walked a few feet away to check if it was in the right spot. He retraced his steps. He had to step into the yard before he could see it. "Yes," he said as he rubbed his hands in anticipation. "Wish I could stick around and see her face when she flips over the stump. But that would never do. If she saw me, she'd suspect something was up. Nope, it's better if I'm not in sight."

Marcus jumped on his skateboard and kicked off. He headed towards downtown, the opposite direction from where she would come.

He had promised to vacuum the front entry at the bowling alley so he'd better hurry. He hated the need to kowtow to those guys for a few paltry dollars. What he really wanted was to earn big money! *If only... but never in this sleepy town. They don't even have a beer parlor. One of these days...*

Chapter Twenty-One

Marcus smirked as he let the door slam in Charlotte's face. He made sure to plunk his backpack in front of the door so she'd have a hard time opening the door. With arrogance he strode towards the living room and grabbed the remote before he hit the couch. He glanced sideways when the eight year old finally got the door open. Did nothing make that kid frown?

Her face was sweaty and her hair hung in tendrils, but there was only a smile of satisfaction when she stepped inside.

Marcus kept his eyes glued to the TV screen without seeing the busy cartoon until he heard Edith empty a pan of cookies onto the counter. Then he grabbed a handful and headed towards his room. Before he got there, Edith called after him.

"Hey, Marcus? Got any homework?"

"Not me. I never have homework. I leave that for the nerds," he flung the words over his shoulder. He stepped into his room and closed the door to avoid any further questioning. But he couldn't resist leaning his back against the door. As he listened he let the cookie melt on his tongue because chewing might make him miss something.

He heard Charlotte say something about going to the park for a music concert 'because Marcus might like it'. Her wistful tone bothered him but rather than admit that his behavior was shameful, he curled his upper lip and blamed her for being such a goody-goody.

Edith must have agreed to Charlotte's suggestion because she said, "Good choice, Sweetie. And it's tonight, isn't it? That means I won't have to cook supper. So we ALL get out of our homework."

The sound of their giggles filtered back to his room. Marcus finished the cookies and walked softly to his bed. On his back, he stared at the ceiling. How he yearned to be a part of the happy sounds – but he couldn't let himself give in to the yearning. They would just take advantage of him, or even worse, they might reject his attempt at joining them.

His thoughts were interrupted by a tap at his door and Charlotte's gentle voice.

"Hey, Marcus, want to go have supper at the park and listen to the music groups?"

Glad that he'd moved away from the door, he cleared his throat and said, "Sure, why not?" He heard her skip merrily back to the kitchen.

Marcus turned onto his belly and smiled in spite of himself. "I was going anyway but if I tag along with them I won't have to fork out any of my own cash for supper."

***

The half-smile stayed on Marcus' face as they walked to the park. He hated to admit that he was beginning to enjoy the banter with Edith and Charlotte.

But all too soon a couple of regulars from the bowling alley came along and kidded him about walking with the ladies.

Marcus hardened his heart. The mask fell back in place. How could he be so stupid and let himself trust anyone – because sooner or later they would disappoint him.

He forced himself to continue to walk beside them. Part of him wanted to drop the chairs and escape, but he remembered

Edith's pleased look when he not only walked with them, but had offered to carry the two lawn chairs...

Marcus decided to bear with the teasing. *I'll get even with them later.* Edith must have seen his hesitation because she immediately asked him, "Are you sure you'll be okay without a chair?"

He tossed his head to fling the hair off his face, "Chairs are for wimps. Us guys always find a tree branch to hang from."

A giggle escaped from Charlotte. "And do you guys hang by your feet?"

"Ya, right," Marcus grunted. He noticed the flush that accompanied Charlotte's smile. *Is she pleased that I'm with them, or did I say something wrong?*

There were a variety of local bands setting up for the evening's entertainment. The sound of testing mikes and tuning instruments filled the air as they found a place to leave their chairs.

Standing behind Charlotte in the line-up for hotdogs, Marcus said, "Good choice, Charlie." Her wistful smile filled him with a warm feeling, but it also made him feel guilty. *What's the big deal about calling her Charlie?*

Marcus disappeared into the crowd as soon as he had his hotdog and drink in hand. He was going to get ribbed enough as it was. No sense giving the guys more fuel.

Chapter Twenty-Two

M arcus charged in the front door, letting it slam behind him as usual. He noticed the phone in Edith's hand and her sorrowful expression as she listened to the caller.

Before she could say anything after hanging up he announced in a loud voice, "I need eight dollars for a field trip."

"A school field trip?"

He gave her a funny look, "Of course! What other kind is there?"

She gazed sadly into his eyes before she spoke. "That was your school, calling to say that you skipped classes again."

He colored guiltily as he muttered, "Stupid substitute Teacher...doesn't know the lesson yet expects us to. Why would I waste my time with such an imbecile?"

Quick before Edith could get back to where he'd been that day he asked belligerently, "So, do I get the dough or not?"

"Marcus, Marcus. Just remember that you, and only you, are responsible for what you do with your life, no matter what others do or say."

His body tense, he made no reply, just waited with raised eyebrows.

"Of course you can have the money, Marcus."

He tossed a crumpled permission form onto the counter and mumbled, "Needs to be signed."

Edith signed the note and held it out to him along with a ten dollar bill. He hated it when she looked at him with those tender, pleading eyes.

Marcus snatched the money out of Edith's hand and crammed it into his back pocket. She continued to hold out the note. He glared at her as he snatched it and shoved it into his backpack. He couldn't get out of the room fast enough.

Guilt made Marcus slam his door. It didn't latch. It bounced back and remained part way open. He didn't bother to close it. That way he'd be able to hear the conversation back in the kitchen.

"Mommy, why doesn't Marcus get a part time job for extra spending money? Lots of kids, younger than he is, work at McDonalds."

"Sweetie, Marcus feels that the world owes him." He heard the familiar sigh before Edith continued. "He'll need a change of attitude before anyone will want to hire him."

And the world does owe me, fumed Marcus. *I didn't ask to be born and then get dumped on a stranger.* He sucked in his breath as Charlotte's voice filtered back to his room.

"I'm sorry, mommy, that he doesn't see how much we have to be thankful for. In Sunday school we learnt how important it is to be thankful for what we have. I told Teacher that I'm most thankful that you are my mom."

Ha, buttering up again, fumed Marcus as he moved quietly over to his dresser.

***

Monday morning Marcus went to his home room and stayed just long enough to get signed in. He flashed the ten dollar bill in front of his classmates. "Guess where I got this?"

"You stole it!" shouted two of them.

"That's not a bad idea," he grinned, "But it's the wrong answer. The old lady forked it over."

"What sob story did you give her?" asked another classmate.

"Goin' on a field trip, and I am. Only not the kind she's thinking or the one planned by our sainted professor," laughed Marcus. "Nope, gonna hitch a ride to *tha big city!*"

Pride filled him at the looks of astonishment in front of him. "Yep! Gonna find me a job, maybe pushin' drugs."

One pair of eyes in front of him narrowed, "Why go to the city for that?" he asked. "You can make good money right here."

"No way, man," declared Marcus. "And risk getting caught by cops who know me?" He shook his head, "I'm not that stupid."

With head held high, Marcus left the school and made his way toward the center of town. *Trucks have to stop for traffic lights and I'm gonna grab the next one that has to stop for a red light.*

He was in luck. He didn't have to wait long. The driver for Abitibi was on his way to Winnipeg. Marcus had no trouble convincing the man. After the long lonely stretch from the USA border behind him, the driver was ready for conversation. Marcus was glad that the man did most of the talking.

Good thing he was so busy talking, I didn't have to make up an excuse about where I was going and why. Marcus chuckled as he swung out of the cab when the driver had to wait to turn at the Lagimodiere intersection. He called out his thanks and slammed the door shut before the surprised driver could ask any questions about where he was headed.

But Marcus' day in the city turned out to be a dud. Everyone was too busy to talk to him or to take him seriously. They sized him up, shook their head and turned away from him. No one was impressed with his cocky attitude.

He found a Video Slot machine in the lounge of a restaurant. He won a few and lost a few. At noon Marcus bought a sandwich and a drink. With a mirthless smile he headed out to the highway. In his pocket he fingered the same amount he had started out with, a mere ten dollars.

He had wasted his day.

Chapter Twenty-Three

1992 March 10th

Marcus stayed out late on his 15th birthday. He did not want a fuss made over him. It would only cause him embarrassment and maybe even shame. *I don't need that on top of everything else. Bad luck and more bad luck, that's all I ever get.*

He waited across the street until the lights turned off, all except the front hall light. Edith always left it on for him when he was out.

He turned the door knob quietly and paused a moment before he opened it all the way. All he heard was his own rapid heartbeat throbbing in his ears.

He stepped quietly into the house and made his way to the kitchen. On the counter was a piece of birthday cake covered in Saran wrap and two gift-wrapped packages. He shrugged and murmured, "Don't know why they insist. I'm almost surprised that they remembered."

The triple layer chocolate cake was separated by a darker chocolate custard filling. It was covered with a swirl of green icing. His nostrils quivered at the scent of mint. All it needed was a glass of milk.

Marcus opened the fridge door and found a supper plate ready for the microwave. *Seeing as she went to all this work, guess I'd better eat it.*

He poured the glass of milk while the microwave heated his supper. A T-bone steak! Marcus had never eaten one. It was delicious. So tender that he hardly needed a knife. The mashed potatoes and creamed corn were the perfect sides for the steak.

He opened the gifts before he ate the cake. He found a wallet with sixty dollars from Edith. *I sure didn't expect that, after all the grief I give her.*

He felt all around Charlotte's gift, trying to guess what it might be before he opened it. It was a twenty dollar bill stuck inside an empty toilet paper roll. He chuckled. *The disguise worked. I would never have guessed.*

His birthday had turned out good after all.

Chapter Twenty-Four

Time dragged for Marcus; all his dreams ended up fruitless; nothing to look forward to in his life. But it didn't stop Christmas from arriving.

Even without an alarm, he still woke up early. Marcus yawned. *I'm getting too old for all this kid stuff. Waking up early, then having to wait for Edith to tell 'the good news' before we get to open our gifts. It's not like we don't already know what she's going to tell us.*

"God loved you and me so much that He gave his only begotten Son to take our place." Marcus mimicked Edith's voice as he looked up at the ceiling. "Punished for *our* wrong-doings, He paved the way for us to come before God the Father." Marcus could hear her voice in his head, running alongside his. He rolled onto his side, "God adopted us as His very own children. He offers us a constant Companion so we don't ever have to walk alone."

Yeah, right. I've heard it a thousand times, if I've heard it once. It's just a fairy tale and doesn't mean anything in real life. Marcus shut out the voice in his head and rolled over onto his stomach. Maybe he could snatch a few more minutes of sleep. But his restlessness drove him out of bed. He reached for his housecoat and stifled another yawn. *May as well go and get it over with.*

Charlotte was already seated on the couch. She looked like a little kid with the twinkling lights from the tree reflected in her eyes.

He joined her on the couch and slouched low enough to let his eyes get mesmerized by the tree lights.

Edith bustled in a few minutes later and beamed, "My two favorite children. It is so good to be together like this." Almost immediately she began to tell the old story.

Marcus admired her tenacity. *Most folks, like school and everyone else gave up on me a long time ago, but not Edith. She keeps hoping I'll give in. And that'll take a miracle.*

Her words filtered into his mind despite his effort to shut them out, "All you have to do is accept this precious gift God offers you."

Marcus squirmed. She was looking right at him. He couldn't miss the yearning in her eyes. *I'm almost sorry to disappoint her. But it'll never happen. At least it's kind of her to keep most of her nagging to once a year.* He was relieved when she finally turned to Charlotte.

"Sweetie, do you want to be Santa this year?"

Charlotte eagerly agreed. She got down on the floor and began to sort through the gifts, selecting one for each of them. She sat back on her heals and waited for Marcus to open his first. It was a shaver.

Edith smiled at him and said, "I thought it would be the perfect gift. You're such a fine looking young man and with your dark colored hair, you're going to need to shave often."

Marcus managed a smile. He'd heard that once you start to shave it becomes a daily task. "Thanks, it'll come in handy." He rubbed a hand over his lower jaw. "I'll have to try it out later. Any day now it will become a daily chore."

This year Marcus managed to stay in the room until all the gifts were opened. In fact he was kind of looking forward to the moment when Colette, Edith's sister-in-law, would arrive. He knew that she hated his guts. His plan was to deliberately irk her. He chuckled as he visualized his idea while pretending that the back of a comic book was so funny. *Maybe if I bug her enough she'll leave early.* He flipped through the comic book without seeing the words or pictures. *I wonder why she keeps on coming now that her husband is gone. It's not like she enjoys time spent with us. Then again, maybe it pleasures her to pick on others.*

Marcus grinned as he anticipated her discomfiture. *It's time someone turned the tables on her for how mean she's always been to Edith.*

True to his plan, Marcus stood up the minute Collette came through the door; without knocking, as was her habit. His eyes followed her every move but he didn't say a word.

She passed a quick glance toward Marcus and Charlotte. Then greeted Edith with a kiss in the air but her eyes were on the pile of opened gifts scattered on the floor and the couch. "Still spoiling them, I see."

Collette gave Marcus a funny glance as his eyes never blinked while he continued to stare at her. She huffed and tossed her nose in the air. "When will they be old enough to get rid of?" she asked as she walked into the kitchen.

Marcus walked just a step behind her. When she turned, she had to look up at him. He didn't make eye contact, just stared at her forehead. He chuckled to himself as he watched her hand come up and brush away an imaginary hair.

"What's with you?" she finally demanded.

He only raised an eyebrow and shrugged.

All through the meal he kept watching her as he ate the delicious turkey dinner. He couldn't help but notice how uncomfortable she became, uncomfortable enough that she forgot to criticize the meal or to deliver her usual tirade about Edith fussing over good-for-nothing orphans.

They hadn't even reached dessert when Collette shoved her chair back and stood up declaring, "I've had enough of this insolence." She stormed off without a backward glance. She even forgot to check if there were any gifts for her under the tree.

Marcus finished his meal with a satisfied look on his face.

Edith said, "I wonder what got into her. She never leaves without her gifts, or complaining about them being the wrong color or scent or something else."

Marcus rubbed his hands together under the table but did not confess to his plot.

But he gave Edith a mental 'high five' when she said, without looking up, "It must have been you paying her so much attention."

Chapter Twenty-Five

1994 June

Afraid of public humiliation in case of possible failure, Marcus didn't show up until the last part of the graduation exercises. He walked in and leaned against the back wall in time to listen as they called out the individual names for the diplomas. He had positioned himself behind a tall man so he wasn't noticed from the stage when they called his name.

Standing at the back, he caught sight of Edith seated in the middle section. She kept looking around. *She's probably trying to spot me in the crowd.*

The ceremony over, Marcus pushed his way in against the exiting crowd. He approached the row where Edith still sat. He thought he saw a look of pride on her face. Could she be proud of his accomplishment? They hadn't read his name in the list that passed with honors, but they had named him in the group that graduated. He watched for any sign of hesitation when she caught sight of him. But her smile seemed genuine. He heard a sigh along with the smile. Was she as relieved as he was that he'd passed? Or was she just happy about his appearance?

"I know you didn't have to come, but thanks," he said as he half lifted a hand and then dropped it back to his side.

She stood up and pulled out a fat envelope with a red bow tied around it. She handed it to him and said, "It's not a car, but I hope it will tell you how proud I am of you. I know you've had your issues and struggled because of them, but you finished! And that's what counts."

Embarrassed, he took the envelope and mumbled, "Sorry about the bad days."

"We all have those," she admitted. Then she patted his arm and said, "I've got to get over to Charlotte's school. Her teacher wants to see me." Thankfully Edith left without making a fuss about him opening the gift in front of her.

Marcus stuffed the envelope into the inside pocket of his leather jacket. He couldn't imagine what it might be, but whatever it was he didn't need an audience when he opened it.

He waited until he was back at the house in his own room before he pulled it from his pocket. His eyes grew wide. It was a wad of money. When he counted them, there were twelve one-hundred dollar bills! "I can't believe the old lady had that much available." He chuckled as he read the note attached to the first bill. A hundred dollars for each year you had to suffer in the name of education.

He slapped the wad of bills against his hand. He hadn't expected anything, for sure not this. "My first bit of luck." He whistled. "What am I going to do with it?"

It never entered his mind that he could save some of it. No, it was too busy with plans on how he could double it.

***

Sadly, the large amount of cash quickly disappeared. Instead of doing odd jobs at the theatre, he paid for his tickets and played the hotshot by giving impressive tips.

He kept making bets and losing. And the winner already knew Marcus well enough to demand immediate payment. He groused about things not being fair as he watched the thick wad melt away.

One evening a fight broke out in front of the bowling alley. It had happened on numerous occasions and the owner was tired of the damage to his business. He called the police.

Marcus was dragged off to the remand center along with the four who were involved in the fight. This time he'd been an innocent by-stander. The other boys begrudgingly admitted as much.

The police called Edith. She hurried over with money in hand to pay for his bail.

But the desk clerk held up his hand. "No need for that Mrs. White. The boy was picked up because of his proximity to the fight. Apparently he wasn't involved." His eyes twinkled as he added, "I'm sure he'll be glad to see you."

Marcus heard the policeman's words. It angered him all over again; the injustices that kept happening to him. And to top it off, Edith didn't drive away. Instead, she began to preach at him as soon as they were in her car. He slouched down in the front seat. His dark eyes glared at the windshield and his arms were crossed tight against his chest. He resented every word she said.

"Marcus, God's love and His grace know no bounds; His forgiveness will never run out. It is unlimited. But be aware that your time may run out."

Edith's earnest manner made him squirm. He did not appreciate her next words either. He was sure they came straight out of her Bible.

"Seek the Lord while He may be found. Call upon Him while He is near. Marcus, I fear for you. If you don't mend your ways, big trouble is heading your way." She reached toward him without actually touching him. "I wish I could make everything better for you, Marcus. I really do, but I can't."

He muttered, "It's always the same, nothing works out for me." He watched her put the car in gear and ease out of the parking spot. Thankful for the silence in the vehicle and that he was headed for home instead of being back there with the cops, he started to relax. Then Edith had to go and spoil it.

"Marcus, first you will have to recognize the need to change your attitude and then you'll have to want to change." She shook her head, "Until then you can only expect things to keep on going from bad to worse."

Marcus fumed the rest of the way home. *There goes the bit of peace and quiet we had for a moment. Even when I'm not guilty I'm in trouble. I give up.*

Back home he stomped down the hall without consideration that Charlotte might be asleep already. He even forgot to thank Edith for coming to his rescue. All he could think was *why does everything bad happen to me?*

Chapter Twenty-Six

1995

Bored, eighteen year old Marcus headed to the sidewalk in front of the high school. He knew better than to go on the school property now that he was no longer a student. He leaned against a light standard and waited. He had timed it right, barely a five minute wait and the kids began to spill out of the front doors.

He straightened up and tugged at the hem of his black leather jacket. It was time to see what was going on, to see who was looking for a dare. Not a dollar left in his wallet, he had to con somebody. He could usually find someone in the mood to take a dare. He watched for the kid with the biggest swagger. Marcus peered through narrowed eyes at the trio coming toward him. The middle one had definitely set himself up as the leader.

He's so full of himself he wouldn't see a con job if it hit him in the face. Minutes later Marcus chuckled at how easy it had been to taunt the guy into confusion and then hit him with 'heads I win, tails you lose'. The bet was made. *Let the kid fume over his loss or maybe he'll smarten up and admit to his stupidity.*

It was only a five dollar bill but it was better than nothing. Marcus patted his pocket and self-satisfaction glimmered in his eyes. He wheeled out his bike and took a quick step before he threw the other long leg over the cross bar.

It was time to go place a few bets at the bowling alley. *Let's see if my luck holds out.* It was amazing how often he could double his money in one evening. The problem was he could lose it just as fast.

The tires on his bike sped along, but not as fast as his thoughts were spinning. *If only I could find a way to make big money. I'd leave this burg so fast no one would know what happened.*

Up ahead he noticed Charlotte walking with that good for nothing red-headed kid from her school. *Well it's time we put a stop to this. If she doesn't know what's best for her, I'll just have to help open her eyes.*

In one smooth move Marcus hopped off his bike, smacked the books out of the boy's hands and knocked him to the ground. Straddling over him, Marcus smashed his fist into the nose of the thirteen year old. Blood spurted everywhere.

"Please, Marcus," begged Charlotte. "Please let him go."

He chose not to respond to her plea. He landed a few more punches and listened with satisfaction at the sound of the kid's 'oof' with each blow.

"You tub of lard, if you ever come near her again you won't live to tell about it," he snarled as he stood up. He grabbed Paddy by the back of the neck and yanked him to his feet. Then he shoved the kid forward. "If you know what's good for you, you'll get lost and stay lost." Breathing heavily to catch his breath he added, "Remember, I'll be watching you."

Marcus exuded hate as he glared at Paddy. He watched the boy stumble, regain his balance and send a shy grin at Charlotte all at the same time.

That oaf has the nerve to smile at my sister! Marcus couldn't believe his eyes. They narrowed into daggers of warning as Paddy tucked his shirt into his pants.

The kid picked up his books and dared to wave at Charlotte before he started down the street.

Marcus turned to her with a sneer on his lips, but he held his words when he noticed her tear-filled eyes and heard her whisper, "I'm so sorry, Paddy."

Marcus forced himself to turn and watch until the boy turned the corner. He muttered, "Why would you pick such a loser? You won't get anywhere in life with that piece of garbage. Don't you know that he'll just drag you down?"

Before she could reply, he hopped on his bike and sped off toward the bowling alley.

Later that week Marcus heard Charlotte talking with Edith about Paddy. It sounded like he had disappeared from school.

Good riddance. But somehow Marcus didn't feel as good about it as he ought to. Charlotte sounded so sad.

Chapter Twenty-Seven

1996 February

Snow pellets pinged against the window as the wind whistled around the corners of the cozy bungalow. Marcus was glad for the indoor warmth as he stretched out his long legs. Content, he half listened to the happy chatter in the kitchen as he flipped through channels on the TV. He stopped at a new show called Everybody Loves Raymond. It looked like it might be a good one, so he settled back to enjoy it.

Edith and Charlotte finished the dishes and quietly joined him to watch the rest of the show. As the program ended and the credits rolled by, Edith started to talk.

"Children, we've been a family for almost twelve years. Can you believe that? What do you think about making it official?"

Marcus raised one eyebrow and asked, "What brought this on?"

Edith replied, "Actually it came up at the lawyer's office yesterday. Daniel Rand suggested that it might be a good idea to make it legal, seeing as I want to write both of you into my will."

"What about ole sister-in-law? Isn't she going to be pi…" Marcus blushed, embarrassed at what he'd been about to say. He changed it to, "Won't that get her all riled up?"

130

"Probably," laughed Edith, "But then everything I do bothers her. She'll just have to deal with it."

Marcus shrugged his shoulders and focused on the TV. "Well, I'm too old to be adopted so it doesn't make much sense in my case. But squirt here needs all the help she can get. Sounds like a good idea for her," volunteered Marcus as he glanced over at her. He noticed Charlotte's cheeks colored at his comment and her hands were busy, twisting the gold chain at her neck. *I wonder, does that mean she's pleased or upset?*

There was none of the usual tension as they chatted. It must have pleased Edith. She had a big smile instead of that pinched look that folks have when they worry.

"Yes, Marcus, you're almost grown-up and legal adoption wouldn't change everyday things, but I want things to be legal for after I'm gone."

Marcus nodded. *Sure hope I don't have to wait until she croaks before I come into some money. She looks too healthy.*

His thoughts halted abruptly when he heard Edith say something about his future.

"Now that you've been out of school for a while, have you thought about what career you'd like to pursue?"

His eyebrows lowered. Without answering her, he turned back to watch the last of the credits roll by. *Now what did she have to bring that up for? There's no future for me in this town or anywhere else, unless I can make some big money.* He glanced sideways at Edith. Her face looked like she felt bad about bringing up the subject that destroyed their amicable evening. And so she should. He was relieved when she turned her attention to Charlotte.

"What about you, Charlotte? Have you ever thought about adoption? Just remember that whether we make it legal or not, you will always be in my heart." She looked over to include both of them, "You too, Marcus. I hope you'll always remember that."

Marcus pouted and pretended not to hear but he heard Charlotte's response.

"I feel the same way, Mom. You and Marcus are the only family I've ever known so the idea of adoption has never crossed my mind. But if the papers make a difference, then let's do it."

For just a few minutes he felt a warm glow spread through his chest. The idea of belonging felt good. But he couldn't bring himself to say it out loud and soon his thoughts took a downward spiral. *What's the use? It won't change anything.*

Without a word of explanation he jumped up and got his jacket from his room. He closed the front door behind him and immediately wished he'd taken his toque as well. He pulled the gloves out of his pockets and put them on. But even the brisk walk over to the bowling alley did nothing to warm his shivering limbs or alleviate his frustration.

Chapter Twenty-Eight

On June 30th, Marcus headed for home much earlier than usual. He was in a snit. The guys at the bowling alley were upset with him. They refused to take any more bets and had the nerve to accuse him of cheating. *They can't get it that I don't need to cheat. They're just too stupid to follow my sharp thinking, or to catch on to my swift hands.* He fumed all the way home.

As soon as he walked through the front door, he remembered that it was Charlotte's 13th birthday. The trouble was that even if he had thought of it earlier, he had no money to buy her a gift.

Shame fought with self-pity. Marcus refused to let shame stay. He chose to be disagreeable.

Charlotte's secret smile as she hovered over the cake before blowing out the candles made him even more irritated.

He was glad to see her smile freeze when he laughed at her. It made him push harder. After a loud guffaw, he sniggered and mimicked a young girl's voice, "I wish for a Barbie doll."

Angry at everyone including himself, he slouched in his chair. Self-absorbed, he whined, "So are we done with the sentimental stuff yet?"

He glanced up. Edith's sad eyes and Charlotte's stiff back made him drop his eyes, but he didn't apologize. Instead he muttered, "Can we have cake now?"

***

Marcus had rubbed his hands in anticipation when he'd heard that Charlotte had gotten a job at Duffy's Café. *She'll probably get lots of tips. And I know how to make her hand it over. It'll be easy money.*

As usual, he entered Duffy's Café with a smirk on his face. But the first person his eyes connected with was that waitress, Irene. He hated her. She was altogether too wise. He'd already discovered that his charming smile and his even row of white teeth flashed at her did not fool her. Too bad she wasn't as gullible as so many other innocent folks. Instead, her eyes mocked him. It galled him.

He moved to a table and sat down. He would have to corner Charlotte behind Irene's back. But that was next to impossible. Irene seemed to notice everything, especially if it concerned Charlotte.

His mood darkened as he held up a menu without reading it. It was bad enough that Charlotte tried to avoid him. He had noticed that whenever he came into Duffy's, she would slip into the back. *She ought to know better. It's not like she can get away from me. And now that waitress seems to have crowned herself as Charlotte's protector.*

He gazed around the busy café. People were laughing and talking to each other. Their friendliness included both Irene and Charlotte. His lip curled in disgust.

Marcus ordered a Pepsi when Irene came to ask what he wanted. He glared at Charlotte through narrowed eyes as she cleaned the table next to him. It felt good to make her squirm. *What's wrong with making her hand over the few paltry coins, she doesn't need money like I do.*

He finished his Pepsi and set the can down with extra force, shoved his chair back and left. When he passed Charlotte he whispered, "I'll see you at home."

Outside, he ambled down the street with his hands in his pockets. Marcus couldn't think of anything to be happy about. He was too busy counting his woes.

***

Day followed night, night followed day as Marcus made his disappointing rounds. He hated the sighs at home and stayed away except to sleep. Angry when he found a plate of food, "I can look after myself." And angry when he didn't find it, "They don't care about me."

He grouched through another Christmas.

When his twentieth birthday rolled around, he decided to get drunk; on an empty stomach. He'd heard that it affected people quicker that way. Having steered clear of the stuff until now, it didn't take much to befuddle his brain.

Marcus ended another disappointing day hanging over the toilet bowl. The putrid smell of the green bile made him heave again and again. He wished he could die.

Chapter Twenty-Nine

Marcus did not notice that Edith's car was parked down the street. The empty garbage can at the curb meant the truck had already come. *Edith and Charlotte must still be at work or they'd have taken the garbage can to the back. Good* he thought. *I can find a bite to eat, get cleaned up and be outta here before they get home.*

The key turned easily in the door. "Someone must have forgotten to lock it," he surmised as he stepped into the house. He stumbled, taken by surprise. Both of the women were standing at the kitchen counter, their faces turned to look at him as he entered. By their serious expression, it was obvious that they'd been talking about heavy stuff. The silence as they watched him made him uncomfortable.

"What?" His belligerent tone of voice was louder than usual, as if he'd been caught doing something wrong.

Charlotte looked at Edith before she spoke, then back at Marcus. "You need to know that Mom got bad news from the doctor."

"It's not necessarily bad news, Charlotte." A cough stopped Edith from saying more.

Marcus looked from one to the other. He couldn't imagine what kind of bad news would make his miserable life any worse. "So?" He lifted one shoulder and waited with raised eyebrows.

Edith looked up and gave a bit of a smile. "It seems that I'm not long for this earth." She raised both hands, palms up and shrugged. The effort cost her. She struggled to suppress another bout of coughing.

He stared at her for a moment; opened his mouth but no sound came out. He clamped it shut and raised his chin, eyes narrowed to half slits.

For just a moment Edith thought she'd seen a look of fear in his eyes, then again, perhaps not.

Marcus turned around and walked back out the front door. He closed it gently behind him, deep in thought.

What was going to happen now? He hadn't realized how good he'd had it. *I should have seen it coming, all that coughing; looking so shriveled and skinny. But not long for this earth? Can it be that bad? What's to become of me? I'll have to get a real job, but there's no such thing in Steinbach; At least none that will pay enough for me to live comfortably. Oh, what am I going to do?*

Hands in his pockets, shoulders slumped; he watched his feet. He realized that Edith hadn't argued with him as much lately; not that he'd been around much of the time. But when he was, she'd been quieter, even gentle with both him and Charlotte. Yes, he should have seen it coming.

He roamed the streets. He couldn't bring himself to face them again. He didn't want to see anyone at the bowling alley either.

Marcus ended up on the arched bridge in the park. The water looked dark and cold. He shivered but knew it wasn't deep enough for him to drown if he was foolish enough to jump in. What was he going to do?

It was in the early morning hours when he finally made his way home. The stillness, when he closed the door behind him, made it feel like death was already in the home. Sleep evaded him. The morning sun brightened his room, but he stayed in bed until the Edith and Charlotte left the house. A hot shower and peanut butter toast made him feel better for a short while.

But soon the peanut butter toast reminded him of life with his real mother and how she had left him. The pain he thought he'd buried returned in full force. *This can't be happening to me again. It's not fair.*

Marcus half pondered the idea of faith. Edith and Charlotte depended on it to face their days. They were quick enough to share, whether he liked it or not.

He shook his head. *No. It seems to help them but it's not for me. Anger is the only way to get what I want.*

He left the house as soon as he finished his breakfast and did not return again until he felt sure they would both be asleep.

To his surprise they were both sitting in the darkened living room. The front hall light made them visible. With a curt nod in their direction, he headed past them down the hall.

"Marcus, do you want some supper?"

He paused at Charlotte's question, shook his head without looking back and muttered, "No thanks." How could he tell her that his stomach hadn't quit churning since he heard the news of Edith's illness; that he couldn't walk fast enough or far enough to distance himself from its reality? He just wanted it all to go away. If only things could go back to the way they'd been.

In his room he dropped onto the bed and pushed his shoes off his feet. They landed on the carpet with a dull thud. Both hands tucked behind his head, he stretched out. His long body reached from the headboard to the bottom edge of the bed.

He'd left his door open and couldn't help but overhear Charlotte as she talked to Edith. She said that Pastor Mac had reminded her that the heavenly Father was going to continue to be with them, even after Edith would be gone.

138

Ha. Like God's done a good job up till now. All three of us have lost someone. I don't call that taking care of us. It's more like abandoning us to the whims of nature.

Marcus turned onto his side and stared at the window. *If only it were that simple.*

A big sigh and he turned onto his back, his eyes on the ceiling. *I can't believe that anyone's up there. So it's up to me to look after me. I'm not going to waste my time talking to the air.*

Restlessly he tossed and turned. Footsteps in the hall told him that the women were headed to their rooms. He went and opened the window. The June air felt warm and fresh against his hot cheeks. He bent his upper body forward so he could rest his arms on the window sill. The muted sounds of the city came to his ears. The sound seemed to come from another world. Nothing was real anymore.

He heard a rustle in the hedge. His eyes narrowed to focus on the dark shadows in front of him. The street lights did not penetrate the bushes, but let him see a silhouette. He could make out the pointed ears of a cat. Marcus held his breath and waited, but the cat did not come closer. *Oh well, it's probably not the same one anyway. My friend must be long gone by now.*

The gurgle of his stomach suggested that it was time to find something to eat. He straightened up; closed the window and walked across the room. He stopped at the door and listened. No sound but the pounding in his ears disturbed the quiet house.

Marcus eased out of his room and went to the kitchen. Once again he found a plate of supper neatly wrapped, waiting for him. He frowned. Was it Edith, or maybe Charlotte...*don't they think I can look after myself?*

Chapter Thirty

Before long a couple of nurses took turns staying at the house. Marcus noticed that a cot had been set up in Charlotte's room. *More people in the house*, he grumbled. *You can't turn around without bumping into some stranger.* He was frustrated that it had to be, and angry that he couldn't fix it. *Now I've even lost the privacy of my own home.* He growled at the injustice.

Marcus began to wait until after the theatre and bowling alley closed for the night before he ambled towards home. It was easy to sneak into the house to get a pillow and a blanket. Everyone was in Edith's room.

He made a makeshift bed in the back seat of Edith's car. She wasn't going to work anymore, so the vehicle remained parked on the driveway. No one would bother him in there. "At least it's better than being stuck inside with all that's going on," he muttered as he shifted again to try and find a more comfortable position.

During the daytime Marcus ambled around town to pass the time. He glanced at the front window as he walked past the house but couldn't bring himself to go inside. Death was waiting in there and it scared him. He wasn't even hungry these days as he pondered what was to become of him.

Charlotte's 14th birthday came and went unnoticed by Marcus. He spent long hours sitting at the back of the bowling alley. He did not see the people in front of him. All he saw was a long dark tunnel with no light at the end.

One day his ears perked up at a conversation two lanes over. It gave him an idea. It was an evil idea, but if he didn't look after himself, who would? He grabbed a score pad and pencil off the nearest table and made an outline. Only he would know what each notation meant. *Gotta have it all figured out ahead of time. It'll have to be done in a jiffy with no one suspecting anything.*

It was time to go home.

He snuck inside the front door and stood for a few minutes. The only sound in the house besides his hammering heart came from the old lady's room. It was not a sound he had heard before. *It must be that machine she's hooked up to, to help her breathe.* He shuddered. It was too spooky. He edged over to the corner where the computer sat. It took only a few minutes to complete his well laid out plan.

Marcus couldn't believe how easy it was to get into the old lady's bank account. Over the internet, signed in with her password and on her computer, no one questioned his actions. *They can't hear my voice.* He gave a dry chuckle as he pretended that he was Edith, a caring mom, who wanted to open an account for her son's college education.

"Yea, like that could ever happen to me," he whispered.

He hit enter and waited for the transaction to be completed. He frowned at the monitor as his thoughts darkened. Condemnation argued with the need for self-preservation. Busily excusing his behavior, he sighed with relief when it said transaction complete. He turned off the computer and hurried to the bedroom. He felt ashamed, yet wasn't ready to admit that what he'd just done was wrong. Instead he let his thoughts feed his anger at how unfair life was and that he was only doing what anyone else in his shoes would do.

When Edith died he'd have to look after himself.
Charlotte was young enough and a nice kid. A good family
would take care of her. He hoped.

Marcus continued to make himself scarce, not even
coming home for the odd meal. He lost interest in his old
haunts. Instead he walked in the park or sat on one of its
benches, refusing to think about the trouble his actions would
add to Charlotte's life. He decided that it would be better to
wait a day or two before he accessed the new account.

The few times he ran into Charlotte he could see that she
was worried about him. He didn't know why. The way he
degraded her, she should be relieved that he kept out of her
way.

Chapter Thirty-One

Marcus didn't show up for the funeral service. But he rode his bike to the grave site, staying behind the long line of cars. He pulled in behind one of the larger head stones. One foot on the ground to steady the bike, he sat and watched. *It's a good thing so many folks showed up. I won't be noticed.*

He did notice that Charlotte glanced around a couple of times. *She's probably wondering where I am.* He scuffed the ground with the toe of his sneaker and looked down, half wishing that he could go and tell her he was sorry that she was an orphan again. When he glanced up, one of the nurses that had been staying at the house had put her arm around Charlotte. He let out the breath he'd been holding. *It's better this way. I'll get out of her way and they'll look after her.* As silently as he'd come, he wheeled around and left.

Back at the house he quickly crammed a few pieces of clothing and his shaver into a backpack. He tied his jacket to the shoulder strap. "I sure won't need it today, but the nights might get cold." He reached into the bottom drawer for his blankie. It lay there, folded into a neat square. He pulled his hand back, tightened his lips and slammed the drawer shut. That was a part of his past life which he was leaving behind.

All the cash he owned, which wasn't much, he tucked into his shirt pocket. But that was about to change.

Marcus didn't take time to stop and think about what would happen to Charlotte after he left; nor about what would happen when it came time to pay the bills. His only thought was to be as far away from here as possible before anyone knew what had happened.

At the Credit Union he withdrew $200 in small bills from his account and asked for a certified cheque for the rest. *The world owes me after all I've been through...* his thoughts were interrupted by the clerk.

"Take a seat," she said as she motioned to the row of chairs beside the receptionist's desk. "It'll take just a few minutes."

Marcus' feet tapped out a rapid beat. His fingers drummed on his knee. Every few seconds he shifted in his seat. He wiped at the sweat that trickled from his brow. *What is taking so long?* When his anxiety reached its peak he got up and walked over to the coffee pot. He poured himself a cup. Stirring in sugar and cream, he tasted it before he sat down again. His watchful eyes roved back and forth from the spot where the clerk had disappeared, to the open area in front of the service counter. *It'd be just my luck to have the cops walk in right about now.* He rubbed one damp palm on the side of his pant leg and shifted the cup of coffee so he could wipe the other hand. Marcus drained the cup and got up to toss it into the garbage bin.

He blew out his breath when he finally saw the clerk come toward him with the certified cheque in her hand. Her smile looked calculating but she handed over the cheque. *I wonder if she suspects anything. Ha, all the more reason to get out of town as quickly as possible.*

Marcus left by the back door of the Credit Union and hurried along Elm Street. At the corner before Elmdale school he stopped at the bench placed in honor of a previous mayor. The sight of his old school filled his brain with memories. He shook his head. No sense in getting maudlin. He pulled out the map of Canada he had picked up at the travel agent. He closed his eyes and picked a spot with his finger. He opened his eyes and read the name of the closest place. It had landed in the province of British Columbia near the city of Kelowna.

"Yes, that looks like a good place to go," declared Marcus. "From what I've heard, lots of rich folks live there. Maybe I can get lucky and make my fortune." He patted his pocket.

The certified cheque gave him a feeling of security. Two hundred dollars in small bills made a nice bulge in his wallet. *There's no sense in alerting folks to the fact that I'm leaving town.* He decided to head toward the northwest side of Steinbach. He picked up a long branch and used it for a hiking stick. *It will look good if someone sees me. They'll think I'm out for another walk.*

Marcus trudged along the edge of farm fields. The hot sun beat down on his head and made him wish that he'd taken a hat. *Oh well, with all that money in my pocket I can buy one when I get to a store.*

After only a few minutes of walking along the #311, Marcus heard the sound of a motor gearing down. He stepped sideways and held out his thumb. A few pieces of gravel flew past him into the ditch as the pickup truck slid to a stop beside him.

"Goin' far?" a friendly voice hollered from the interior.

Marcus ducked his head to look into the truck. The hearty voice matched the sturdy farmer who sat behind the steering wheel. One beefy hand hung onto the open window frame beside the driver, the other reached over to open the passenger door.

"Thanks." Marcus tried to keep his voice even, despite the rapid beating of his heart. Hot air from the motor filled the cab and pressed against his already overheated body.

"Where ya headed?" asked the driver in a friendly manner.

"Winnipeg," replied Marcus, "To the bus depot."

"Sure thing, it's just up the road from where I'm going," said the farmer as he put the truck in gear and the motor roared into action. As soon as the vehicle had quit fish-tailing and straightened out on the road he glanced over at Marcus with a big grin plastered across his sun-burned face. "Only thing better than startin' and stoppin' on a gravel road is that first-winter's drive; ya know? The streets are so slippery you can do a donut right in the middle of an intersection." His jovial laugh filled the truck and spilled out the open windows. He gazed ahead of the vehicle for a few moments and shook his head, the grin of a specific memory imprinted on his face.

He shot a look at Marcus. The eyebrow closest to Marcus was raised into a perfect arc. He asked, "Ya do any driving?"

Marcus shook his head, "Only a bicycle."

"Just wait, son," chuckled the farmer, "You'll see what I mean." Then he cautioned, "Of course you want to make sure there's no other vehicle around to tangle with."

For the next few minutes Marcus watched the road fly by as silence reigned in the cab. He turned his face to the open window and closed his eyes with a sigh of relief, grateful for the moments of quiet in the cab. The breeze created by the speeding truck cooled his flushed cheeks.

Now and then the farmer commented on the fields along the way but didn't seem to expect a response from Marcus.

In the city, the driver shifted gears with a flourish at each street light. It seemed to please him. A block before the bus depot he turned onto a side street and stopped.

"It's just down the street, that way," he said as he pointed Marcus in the right direction.

"Thanks," said Marcus as he jumped out of the hot interior of the cab, only to be met with stifling heat waves flowing upwards from the sun drenched sidewalk.

The truck driver nodded, "My pleasure, son; my pleasure." Grin still intact, with a wave of his hand he revved the motor and sped off in a cloud of dust.

Half a block away Marcus could see a number of buses parked on the pavement. A crowd of people got off one bus.

Some headed into the depot, others hurried to get onto another bus. Marcus quickened his step.

Upon inquiry he found out that the bus he wanted was leaving in twelve minutes. *Luck is finally on my side.* He patted his pocket. *I got money in my pocket and I don't have to wait around and risk getting picked up by the cops.*

"I'll have to leave off buying a hat until later." He shrugged a shoulder, "Not like I'll need it on the bus."

He found a window seat near the back. He tucked his backpack between his feet and settled against the seat. Not quite comfortable, he rolled up his jacket and shoved it behind his head. *There, that's better.*

Thankfully no one came to sit beside him. No one would bother him with questions he didn't want to answer.

The ride was boring. Mile after mile there was no change in the scenery. Marcus hadn't thought of getting a magazine or any kind of entertainment. *No time actually, I had to get out of there before anyone found out and tried to stop me.*

He twisted in his seat to stretch out his long legs. He tried to lean his head against the side of the bus. But it bumped and bounced too much, so he sat up straight and leaned forward for a change of position. Absentmindedly his fingers fiddled with the strap on the backpack tucked by one knee.

Thank goodness, the bus finally pulled to a stop. Marcus couldn't wait to get off. While the passengers crowded into the convenience store, Marcus walked up and down the sidewalk beside the bus. He waited for the majority of folks to make their purchases before he entered the store. Inside, he browsed through the magazine rack and picked out a couple of Archie Comics. He took them over to the cashier.

Outside he waited for the driver by strolling around the parking lot. A couple of young ladies were giggling and whispering to each other behind their hands. It didn't take a genius to know what, or rather who, their topic was. Their eyes kept darting his way, hoping he would notice them or start talking to them. He ignored their attempts to flirt with him. He wasn't interested in anything that would deter him from his goal. All he wanted was to strike it rich; to have so much money that he could lord it over others.

Their intrusion into his space angered him. Besides, he didn't want to attract any attention that could leave a trail for someone to find him. He headed back inside to the only place he'd be safe from those gawkers, the men's restroom.

Marcus felt boxed in, yet he forced himself to stay in the bathroom until it was time to get back on the bus.

He had only twenty more hours to try and avoid attracting attention. At each stop, quickly making his purchases, he disappeared into the restrooms or hid behind the bus with a cigarette.

The sun sank below the horizon and the countryside rushing past the window morphed into gloomy shapes, until all he could see was the dim light from inside the bus reflected in the window.

When he managed to doze off, the bus hit a bump or swerved to pass. Numerous times he refolded his jacket and tucked it behind his head.

That last stop couldn't come soon enough for Marcus.

Chapter Thirty-Two

After 24 hours Marcus stepped off the bus in Kelowna with a dare-devil attitude. He straightened up to his full height. *No one knows me in this city. I've got lots of money and no one's going to push me around.* He walked along the street with a swagger.

His first mission was to look for a posh hotel. He booked a room under the name of Mark North. Not having a credit card he knew he'd have to pay cash. He was prepared with a wad readily available. *All the better,* he thought. *No way for anyone to know where I am or what I'm doing.*

The elevator moved swiftly and silently up to the top floor. If he hadn't been looking at the door, Marcus wouldn't have realized that it had swished open. His footsteps made no sound on the plush carpet in the hallway.

In the room, he tossed his backpack on the neatly made bed and headed to the bathroom for a shower. He stood under the cascading spray of hot water until his travel weary bones started to relax. *Looks like I won't have to worry about using up all the hot water.* He laughed as he stepped out of the shower and secured a towel at his waist. His dark hair shone and waves rippled smoothly across the top of his head after he used the blow-dryer. Satisfied with what he saw, Marcus reached for the thick bathrobe that hung on a hook behind the door. It fit perfectly.

"Now this is what I call living," said Marcus as he glanced once more at his reflection in the mirror. A change of clothes from his knapsack and he was ready to go find something to eat. Before he left the room, Marcus stuffed his dirty clothes in the bag provided for laundry and tossed it on the dresser. He left a twenty dollar gratuity on top of the bag.

The glitter in the dining room dazzled his eyes. He tried not to look as inept as he felt. Shoulders back and eyes focused straight ahead, he strode after the maître d'. The chair was pulled out for him as if he was royalty. His eyebrow quivered slightly, *I sure could get used to this in a hurry.*

The menu was big enough to hide behind. Gold colored tassels hung from the edge. Prices were not included but Marcus didn't worry. He was practicing for when his ship came in.

He sat back after the delicious meal and enjoyed a steaming cup of hot coffee. His eyes roved over the crowd in the well filled dining room. *I'm surprised I didn't have to make a reservation. But perhaps that's because I arrived before the dinner crowd.*

Jewels sparkled on fingers, on almost bare shoulders and even in hair. Sparkling stars in the ceiling gave just the right amount of light so as not to intrude. Tinkling music wafted all around Marcus. The muted chatter was barely discernable, even from the next table.

A momentary look of shock crossed his face when he saw the total on his bill, which he quickly replaced with a bland expression. From his wallet he pulled out the two large bills needed and added an extra twenty dollars for the tip.

Back in his room he settled on the bed and stared at the ceiling. Even it sparkled down at him. "I'll just have to get used to all this opulence."

Marcus reached for the remote and switched on the TV. The first program was Everybody Loves Raymond. He quickly flicked away from it. *That reminds me of home. I can't go soft, not now.* The next station had 7th Heaven. *Does everything have to be about families?* The third channel showed The X-Files. That was better. He stuffed extra pillows behind his back and let himself get involved in the storyline.

The last thought before he drifted off to sleep was, *tomorrow I have to find a bank and open an account. Hope they won't give me a hard time about depositing that certified cheque.*

***

After an easy time at the bank with no uncomfortable questions asked, Marcus set off on foot to explore the city. Beautiful trees lined the streets, giving plenty of shade from the hot July sun. He paused in front of a Men's Clothier and admired the handsome suits. But he didn't waste much time window shopping. What he was looking for didn't require fancy clothes.

Marcus searched until he found it; an opportunity to double his money. He thought he'd found his niche when he entered a busy bowling alley.

He walked around and chatted with the bowlers. They were too tense. He had to kid around for a while before they relaxed enough to take note of what he was suggesting. No one seemed to have thought of playing for money before. Grins began to flash out as the idea began to take root. Soon the betting became intense. Those who had never taken a risk before were hesitant to put up anything larger than a dollar. Marcus played on their fears, taunted them and more times than not, ended up with most of the winnings in his pocket.

To show that there were no ill-feelings, he bought a round of snacks for everyone. He loved the feeling of being in control. He could choose to be generous. He made them feel indebted to him.

Each evening he strode proudly through the streets back to the hotel, rejecting the idea of taking a taxi. Now that he was

Mark North, a man with money, he wanted the world to see him.

When he entered the hotel, some of the staff tipped their heads in recognition. The maids giggled and blushed when he paused to speak to them. Finally he was in the place he wanted to be; primed for his big win.

***

But the glitz didn't last. It wasn't long before Marcus realized that his big bank account was dwindling much faster than he had anticipated. The chance to strike it rich had not shown up around the corner. It wasn't even a dream any more. The heat of summer had disappeared, followed by chilly autumn days. *Just like my life* he thought as he shivered, more from his lack of prospects than from the cooler weather.

All too soon he had run out of risk-takers. It saddened him and made him angry at the same time. This wasn't working out the way it was supposed to. How could it have happened so quickly? According to his plans he should have amassed a big bank account by now.

Instead he was nearly broke. Nothing left in the bank; the weekly payment of his hotel room had been kindly extended by the clerk, much to Marcus' chagrin. He'd been embarrassed further when they wouldn't let him charge his meals to the room anymore. That had put a big dent in the final withdrawal from the bank. It was time to move on.

He sat in sullen contemplation at the tables in the bowling alley. Just enough coins to buy a fast-food meal or two clinked in his pocket. He sipped the dark, syrupy liquid and watched the pins fall on the lanes in front of him as he lamented his situation.

It's just not fair. Why do I have to have such bad luck all the time? He sighed heavily. *What am I going to do? I can't go back to the hotel until I pay up. With the way things are that's never going to happen.*

Disheartened he traced a path with his index finger through the condensation that his drink bottle had left on the table top. Mesmerized, he watched how quickly the path disappeared as soon as he lifted his finger. He leaned back and stared across the room without seeing anyone. *Too bad it all had to come to an end.* He took a sip of pop and stretched out his long legs under the table. His toe bumped against his bag. *Good thing I remembered to bring my backpack when I left.*

Marcus sensed someone sit down on the stool next to him. A pop bottle, grasped by a huge hairy hand, appeared on the table.

Chapter Thirty-Three

1997 October

The hair stood up on the back of his neck. Marcus sensed that he was under scrutiny but wouldn't give that person the satisfaction of looking up. He heard a man chuckle and couldn't resist giving him a quick sideways glance.

"So, no more takers, eh?"

Startled, Marcus straightened up, "What do you mean?"

"I've been watching you. You're smooth, I'll give you that. And your face, it don't give none of your thoughts away. I like that in a man. Comes in *real* handy when needed."

Marcus shrugged and turned his attention back to the drink in front of him. Knowing someone had been watching him made for a few moments of uncomfortable silence. When he finally lifted his eyes, he found the man still watching him with a smirk. The rough looking, thick necked man did not look like anyone Marcus wanted to associate with.

"The name's Abe Ziofuldiogh," said the man. A bland look replaced the smirk. Huge hands were clasped loosely around the bottle in front of him, but looked like they could crack the glass with ease.

Marcus was glad the man didn't expect him to shake those hands. Just the thought of it made him feel queasy. And he especially hated to be laughed at. Without a word, Marcus stood up to his full six foot height. The short man beside him wasn't intimidated.

"Sit down, kid. I got a bizness proposition for ya."

Marcus didn't even glance at him as he turned and walked away. He stood for a moment outside the building. Where could he go? "No money, no friends." He straightened up, "But I don't like the looks of that guy," he muttered as he headed downtown. "Maybe I can find a warm place inside the bus depot.

***

For days Marcus walked the streets until his feet were sore and his legs ached. No matter how many shops he stopped at, there were no job openings. He couldn't find one place to agree to hire him, not even the fast food joints.

Miserable, hungry and cold, Marcus found the men's restroom at the Mall. He gazed sadly at his reflection in the mirror. Six feet tall, charming and handsome had turned into a haggard face that needed a shave. He frowned in disgust at the sight of his disheveled hair. His rumpled clothes had food stains and smelled strongly of perspiration. *No wonder I can't get a job. I wouldn't hire me either. This sink is too small to wash my hair but hopefully no one will give me a hard time if I give myself a shave.*

The stench of dirty clothing assailed his nose when he opened the backpack to get out his shaver. *If I didn't need the bulk for a pillow, I'd throw the whole thing out.* The shave only made him feel worse, more keenly conscious of the rest of his unkempt appearance.

At the end of another luckless day he humbled himself to digging for food in the big garbage bin behind the McDonalds restaurant.

Cold burgers and dried up fries aren't half bad when you're hungry. Good thing people throw out so many ketchup packets thought Marcus as he squished the last bit over a cold French fry. *It adds good flavor and kills the after taste.*

Marcus fashioned a paper drinking cup out of a discarded tray liner and went to the bathroom at the all-night gas station for a drink of water. Only a couple of drops of water escaped from the makeshift cup. *Guess they taught us a useful skill at school after all. But I never dreamt I'd ever need to do this.*

Back out on the sidewalk Marcus shivered and wished he had a warmer jacket. October, even in Kelowna, felt a lot colder than he was prepared for.

Leaning against the cold stone wall he let his mind wander back to Steinbach. The good meals that Edith had provided were gone forever. The fun times at the theatre and the bowling alley were but a memory. He let out a heavy sigh. Remembering was a futile project. Edith wasn't there anymore and with the money he'd stolen Charlotte would hate him… Marcus shook his head. No, he could never go back.

His head bowed in despair. He noticed a good sized cigarette butt. A tiny swirl of smoke still rose from it. A few puffs and the end began to glow. Heat from the smoldering tobacco warmed his fingers, but not his heart.

After the cigarette was finished he made his way over to the garbage area. The sign attached to one of them stated that it was for Cardboard Only. Marcus peered over the edge. In the dark it was hard to see what was inside. The cold wind blowing past his ears and up the back of his jacket encouraged him to take the risk. He pulled himself up over the edge and dropped down onto a pile of broken up boxes. Marcus shivered as he curled into as tight a ball as he could. The cardboard was too stiff to make a good blanket. When he tried to pull a piece over top of himself, it just slid off again.

The knapsack under his head smelled familiar and even nice compared to the reek in the garbage bin. *I guess there's more in here than just cardboard.* His teeth chattered and he

156

hugged his arms tightly to his chest. *Sleeping in here is warmer than the ground behind a park bench.*
But he had to be alert. Every truck that went by woke him up. He had to listen for the truck coming to empty the bins. It made for a long night and not a very restful one.
The next morning he had to do it all over again. More often than not, his request for a job was turned down before he could complete his question. He looked down at himself. *Can't say as I'm surprised what with my smelly clothes and rumpled look. It would scare me away from giving me a chance.* His mirthless chuckle accompanied him out of the building.
Marcus kept his job hunting area close to the bowling alley. It gave him a place to warm up during the day and to rest when he got too discouraged from all the rejections. And it wasn't too far from the recycle depot, *my bedroom.* He gave a dry chuckle.
It was amazing how often he found some loose change on the ground beside the dumpsters. It wasn't much, but it did buy him a nice cup of hot coffee, a small bit of comfort in the midst of all his bad luck.

***

Days went by before the rough looking man showed up again. He sat down one chair over from Marcus and ordered a coffee. Without looking at Marcus he asked, "What's your name, kid?"
"Mar..k Nor…th" he stammered. His mind, dull from lack of proper food and the restless nights, wasn't thinking as fast as usual.
The man smiled knowingly.
Marcus hated that knowing smile. He gritted his teeth till his jaw hurt. His anger grew at the fact that the man could make him feel so uncomfortable with just a look. He wanted to

run as fast and as far as he could. It felt like the man knew his shame; that he was at his wit's end. *Maybe he even knows about the stolen money, I don't know how he could. But what if he knows? He sure looks smug.* When the man began to speak, Marcus felt his skin crawl. All his senses told him to run. But a certain fascination with the man's demeanor made him waver. That and his desperate state kept him glued to his seat.

"How would you like to come and work for me?" asked Mr. Ziofuldiogh.

"Doing what?" Marcus asked tersely.

"Why don't we go over to my place, Mark, and I'll show you around. Then you can decide for yourself. You'll see. It's a nice place." He looked Marcus up and down. "With some nice clean clothes, you'll be a handsome addition to the staff."

On the street outside the bowling alley sat the same black limo Marcus had seen before. He followed reluctantly, but felt that he had no other choice. The ride was short, but nice and warm with the heater blasting hot air out of the vents.

Not many words passed between them on the short drive, but when they stopped in front of an elegant building, Marcus exclaimed in surprise, "Wow!"

Mr. Ziofuldiogh's smile was filled with satisfaction at the reaction.

Before Marcus could say anything to destroy that sickening smile, the man touched Marcus on the shoulder and motioned with his head, "Let's go inside."

Chapter Thirty-Four

Lights sparkled everywhere. People were kissing their money before they placed their bets. Some were getting change from the cashier's cage, while others sat bedazzled by the lights and bells of numerous slot machines. It seemed that everyone was very happy or very tense.

Marcus followed the man, eyes wide open and mouth agape. It was like he was in a whole new world. At a nod from Abe, someone offered Marcus a free drink and gave him a couple of tokens.

"Go try your luck, kid, while I look after some urgent bizness," said Abe before he turned to a man waiting a few feet away from them.

At last Marcus found himself at a roulette table. His few tokens earned him some very good returns. Excitement rose in his veins. *This is more like it! Maybe my luck's turned.*

Then just as quickly he lost everything. *Stupid game!* Before he could leave the table, Abe appeared at his elbow and placed a few bills in his hand.

"Don't worry. You'll earn it back in no time."

I shouldn't take this, but what if I can earn it back and more? Marcus' better sense put up a weak struggle, but very quickly the temptation to try one more time won out.

The lights dimmed. A voice came over the intercom to announce closing time. Marcus sighed; he hadn't won another round. He felt like the weight of the world was on his shoulders. Before he could stand up Mr. Z's big hand added to the burden. A paper with numbers was placed on the table in front of him.

"Tough luck, kid, but you'll do better next time." He quirked a thick eyebrow and winked at Marcus.

Marcus gave a mirthless chuckle, "Not likely."

He wanted to kick the guy, or even himself. *How could I have gotten into hawk for so much in one evening?* He glared at the IOU. *Can this be possible? Do I really owe Mr. Z over a thousand dollars? Surely it couldn't have added up that quickly.* He grimaced as he got up, shoved the note into his back pocket and picked up his backpack. Now what?

Thinking the man had gone, his heart jumped when he heard Abe clear his throat right beside him. He looked down. The man just stood there and watched him with dark, deep set eyes. It made Marcus' skin crawl. He felt like a fool. *What's the guy waiting for? He knows I lost every dime and that I can't pay him back.* Marcus raised his chin. *I'm not going to beg, whatever he thinks.*

Those eyes narrowed as they looked Marcus up and down, from his face down to his toes. It added to his feeling of angst.

After what seemed like forever the man reached into his shirt pocket and pulled out a key. "Number 214 is available. Go have a good sleep and we'll talk in the morning."

Feeling like he had no other choice, Marcus reached out and took the offered key. He headed for the stairs. There was no way he wanted to lengthen his humiliation by waiting in the spacious hallway. Nor did he want to be a captive in an elevator. No, the stairs gave him a bit of control over his life.

Briefly, very briefly, he paused at the revolving doors with the thought of escaping. But he had nowhere to go and no money to find a place. Plus the big debt had to be atoned for. He had no options. He looked back, *and there's Mr. Z standing by reception, watching to make sure I don't leave.* He waved sheepishly and continued down the hallway. His long stride quickly took him past the elevator to the stairs. He took them two at a time. *Why can't I resist the flattery over my good looks and my smart brain? I'm such a wuss...* Marcus hated that about himself but not enough to deal with it.

He had no problem finding the right number on the second floor. The room was clean and the bed looked very inviting. He opted for sleep first. He would shower in the morning. Marcus opened the window. He hung his pants and shirt on separate hangers and slipped them onto the drapery rod.

"Maybe they'll smell better in the morning," he murmured as he crawled into bed and pulled the soft blanket up to his chin.

Chapter Thirty-Five

It was mid-morning before Marcus woke up. The shower felt great but his lip curled with disgust when he shook out his dirty clothes. He had no clean things to change into, so he got dressed and headed down the stairs. It was time to go see what Mr. Z had up his sleeve.

Out in the hallway, Marcus averted his eyes as the door next to his room opened. He sensed rather than saw that there were two people in the doorway. One of them walked away.

Marcus was on his way to find Mr. Z. *That man is probably livid by now. I'm surprised he didn't send someone to get me.*

Marcus hadn't planned to sleep in, but it had been a long time since he'd slept in a clean bed with warm blankets. He took the stairs in a hurry. *No sense in extending Mr. Z's aggravation.*

The main room he marched through looked very different from the previous evening. Empty of people and noise, it smelled of stale smoke. Housekeeping was busy with the vacuum cleaner.

Ugh. I sure hope that won't be one of my jobs. The smell of bacon drew him in the direction of the kitchen.

He had no trouble finding Mr. Z. Just as he reached to push on the door, someone pulled it open from the inside. It was Mr. Z.

The grin didn't quite make it to his eyes as the man looked up at Marcus. It looked more like a smirk. "So glad to see that you enjoyed your room, m'boy," he said as he stepped aside and made an elaborate motion with his hand, bidding Marcus to enter. "Come, let our staff feed you. After you're done, come to my office," he said as he motioned down the hall.

Marcus stood and stared as the door swung shut behind the man. He'd forgotten how much Mr. Z resembled a goon. That five o'clock shadow no matter what time of day it was; thick upper body with arms almost reaching to the knees; chin jutting forward... and yet, he seemed to own what looked like a very profitable business.

When he turned to face the room, three people were watching him. The question on their faces made him shrug and say, "I'm not sure why I'm here but the man said to have breakfast. What've you got to eat?"

A sudden clatter ensued as skillets and dishes were set and filled by the kitchen staff.

The rosy-cheeked chef declared, "One Cheesy Omelet coming up." He grinned over his shoulder, "You want rye toast with that?"

Marcus nodded and pulled out a chair at the side table. Immediately a cup of coffee was placed in front of him.

"Sugar or cream?" asked a pretty blonde haired woman.

"Both please," said Marcus.

The girl waited but when he didn't look up to flirt with her or say anything else, she nudged his shoulder with an elbow and said, "Another quiet one, eh?"

Marcus raised an eyebrow, "Another one?"

"Yeah, Abe seems to prefer that kind." She tossed her head in the direction of the third person in the kitchen who was obviously the dishwasher but she kept her eyes on Marcus. "So, where'd he find you?"

"Under a cabbage leaf," replied Marcus with a gleam in his eye. Literally, he thought but didn't voice it out loud.

"And a weird sense of humor. Who would've thought," she grinned and Marcus didn't take offense.

"The name's Gila." Arms akimbo, she stood and waited.

He looked at her and said, "Mark." Then he turned his attention to the arrival of his hot breakfast.

The chef set the plate in front of him and wiped his hand on his apron before he reached out to shake Marcus' hand. "Bill, here. Sam's our dishwasher." He motioned to the waitress with his head and said, "She's a hard worker and she won't put up with no nonsense from anyone. But she's easy on the eyes."

Marcus glanced over at Gila. He nodded at Bill and turned his attention back to the breakfast plate in front of him. "Thanks, this looks great."

It was delicious. The waitress didn't let his coffee cup get empty. When Marcus couldn't eat another bite, he sent a smile of thanks toward Gila, sat back and patted his stomach. After a final sip of coffee he wiped his mouth with the table napkin. Although he wasn't looking forward to it, it was time to find out what the man wanted him to do.

Marcus stood up and pushed the chair back under the table. Gila took it upon herself to point him in the right direction even though she knew it wouldn't be hard to find.

Marcus nodded and headed down the hall. He knocked and waited for the bid to enter. He stepped inside and let his eyes sweep over the luxurious furnishings without moving his head. He almost laughed when he saw Mr. Z dwarfed by the huge desk in front of him. When he stood up to greet Marcus, he looked no taller than a kid.

"First we must get some suitable clothes and a cell phone for you," suggested Abe. It actually sounded more like a command than a suggestion, thought Marcus.

Abe opened his cell phone and ordered his limo. The next thing Marcus knew, they were off to the stores.

When he says first, he means first, thought Marcus as he found himself seated in the limo. It was a smooth ride, in total comfort. *What a difference from yesterday. I can hardly believe this isn't just a dream.* Their business didn't take long. Abe's chauffeur knew where the stores were and once inside, the clerk seemed to know what was wanted.

The new clothes felt very comfortable. Marcus enjoyed the feel of the material as he ran his hands down the smooth front of the jacket. He was thankful that Mr. Z had let him choose the style and color when he looked into the long mirror. It revealed how handsome he looked, even with his rather gaunt face. But with a regular job it shouldn't take long to get his weight back to normal.

Happy to have clean clothes, Marcus stepped out of the store and paused on the sidewalk to take a deep breath. Immediately he felt Mr. Z's hand on his back, urging him toward the limo waiting at the curb.

"We'll just put that on your tab for now."

Marcus hadn't even looked at the price tag. *How could I have been so stupid?* He could have kicked himself because with no idea what his new outfit cost, Mr. Z could mark his debt with whatever he wanted. He did not trust the man. A worried Marcus remained in grim silence on the return to the Casino.

When Abe offered him a cigarette, Marcus just shook his head and kept his eyes forward in an effort to remain calm. *If I took one, he'd probably charge me for a whole pack.*

Back at the office seated across from Mr. Z, Marcus noticed that he wasn't the boss. The name plate said Associate, so he didn't own the Casino. That made the man accountable to others. *That should make me feel better, but what if the others are just as bad?* Abe's voice made Marcus sit up and pay attention.

"The boys will have a cell phone for you by the end of the day," said Abe.

He seems to be waiting for me to fall all over him with gratitude. Well, I'm not thankful, so I won't say it. Wonder what he'll bill me for that?

Frustrating the man with his lack of response, the questioning soon ended and Marcus was given his first assignment.

"Be in the games room by three this afternoon. You can help with crowd control."

Marcus thought, *in other words I'm one of the bouncers.* "You expect me to throw people out the door," he stated pragmatically.

"Oh no," said Abe with a wave of his hand, "All you're there for is to keep folks honest."

"You mean intimidate them?" asked Marcus.

"What's with all the questions?" The man asked, glaring at Marcus. He changed the subject abruptly. "There are times when we'll need for you ta make some deliveries for us. Do you have a driver's license?"

Marcus shook his head and said, "No."

Mr. Z's raised eyebrows indicated his unbelief.

"Never needed one," clarified Marcus.

The man sat back and sighed in exasperation, "Well, we'll have to look after that problem because it will definitely be required around here. We'll need you for picking up at the airport, deliveries to the bus depot and stuff like that. Let's see about getting that fixed right away."

He glanced through some papers on the desk in front of him. "You don't actually need ta be in the games room until supper. It's usually pretty quiet around here until then. Hang on a minute."

Mr. Z pulled out his cell. "Hardy? I got a client for ya. Can he start taday? Sure. Yeah. I'll send 'im right over."

He closed the cell phone and looked up at Marcus. "Hardy's driving school is just around the corner. He can fit ya in right now. Make arrangement for mornings ta do your driving practice. That way you'll be available for work the rest of the day."

Marcus nodded and asked, "What do I look for?"

"What?" asked Abe as he frowned at being interrupted, probably had his mind on another item of business already.

"What school?" clarified Marcus.

Abe grimaced, impatient with the kid. "You can't miss it. Just go out the door and walk to the left. At the corner look left again and you'll see the sign."

Marcus shrugged and waited.

"Whatcha waitin' for?" asked the funny looking little man behind the desk as he picked up a bundle of papers. "The guy's fittin' ya in between other clients so git a move-on."

Marcus unfolded his long body from the chair and left the room.

Mr. Z hollered after him, "Don't take all day! And when you're done, get back ta me."

***

Marcus proved to be a natural. After a few words of verbal instructions, the instructor eased him out into the traffic. Good thing it wasn't busy.

Before the hour was up, Hardy said, "Okay, take a right up ahead and let's get back to home base."

Marcus sent a questioning look his way.

Hardy lifted an eyebrow, "You're doing great. We'll take a drive every morning and by the end of the week, I bet you'll pass with flying colors."

Marcus shook his head, doubting he'd heard right. "You're sure?"

"Hey, this is how I make my living. You can trust me. I know a natural when I see one." He shrugged a shoulder and laughed sheepishly. "You could pass the driver's test today. The only reason I'm giving you a week is 'cause Abe's paying."

Marcus glanced over at Hardy and joined him with a flicker of a smile. "Okay then, sounds good to me."

Chapter Thirty-Six

Back at the Casino, Marcus found Abe pacing in the front lobby. It was almost humorous to see the relief on his face when he caught sight of Marcus coming through the revolving doors.

He motioned abruptly for Marcus to follow him. Instead of going back to the offices, they headed for the elevators.

"I'm going to introduce you to a pretty lady." The man's smile of self-satisfaction changed into a frown sent Marcus' way. "But she's not for you." He stretched to his full height, which brought him up to Marcus' shoulder. He kept his eyes focused on the numbers indicating the elevator's progress. "I want you ta look her over real good. Memorize every little detail 'bout her 'cause one of your jobs'll be ta look after her. We need ta keep her safe." Grim determination emanated from him.

Marcus sent a questioning look at Mr. Z. There was no explanation forthcoming.

"Why?" asked Marcus after they stepped into the elevator.

"She's too valuable. And she owes me." The last sentence was said through a clenched jaw.

Marcus pulled into himself and narrowed his eyes. He didn't know if he wanted to know more. He also owed this man a lot of money. Was he going to find a guard set on his heels as well?

The elevator dinged to announce their arrival at the second floor. Marcus thought they were headed for his room. He tried not to show his surprise when Mr. Z stopped one door short of room #214. And he was even more surprised when that man pulled out a room key.

Abe gave a quick one-two tap and opened the door. It opened to reveal a neatly made bed. Behind it he could see the back of a slender female figure, her arms hugging her mid-section. The most beautiful woman Marcus had ever laid eyes on turned to stand in profile beside the window.

She pivoted slowly, and gracefully lowered her arms. But her hands remained tightly clasped in front of her. She raised her eyes to look at him from across the room.

Marcus sucked in his breath as he caught sight of the utter sadness in those eyes. He noticed the rapid pulse at the base of her throat. There was something very vulnerable about her. She made him think of a wild bird trapped inside a house, desperately trying to fly through a closed window.

How could someone so beautiful be so sad? Abe's words were lost to him. "This is Myrna," was all he heard. He stood entranced, his gaze focused on the woman in front of him. There was no change in her glance; nothing to make him think that she might be even a little impressed. Then he reminded himself of his own situation. They were both prisoners. Frustration and bitterness settled over him. He wondered no more at her great sadness. He empathized totally.

"Ready to go?" Abe's harsh words brought Marcus' thoughts back to the moment. He watched as the woman nodded and stepped away from the window. She reached for her jacket lying across the foot of the bed. *Everything about her is beautiful and graceful.*

"This here's Mark North. He's accountable to me." Abe motioned with his head toward Marcus and a thumb to his chest. He watched Marcus through narrowed eyes, as if to emphasize the veiled threat before he added, "He'll see you safely home."

Marcus glanced quickly at Mr. Z. *Was that said to intimidate her or a warning for me?*

Silence reigned as the trio stepped out into the hall.

Abe placed a hand on Marcus' arm, "Remember where she lives 'cause you've gotta go back and get her this evening.

"Don't forget to check in with me when you get back. I wanna make sure you don't get lost." His raucous laugh followed them down the hall. Neither of them smiled. This time the threat was clear.

Out on the street the two walked the city sidewalk in silence, Myrna gesturing when it was time to turn at a corner.

Marcus wanted to lash out at the injustice. They should both be free, not enslaved to that boorish coot. A gentle sigh drew his attention. Myrna was looking at him with a questioning glance. He said, "Are you afraid to ask why I'd be working for him?"

"Actually, I believe I know why. You owe him money."

"How did you know?" asked Marcus in a defensive voice.

"Abe is a heartless man who preys on the innocent and those in need. He knows how to manipulate you till he has you in his debt, all the time making it look like he's this great benefactor."

Marcus nodded. His face turned grim, "You've got that right." His pace quickened with his anger, until he realized that she wasn't keeping up. "I'm sorry," he said as he slowed down. He offered the crook of his arm and she readily accepted. When she placed her slender hand on his arm, Marcus felt a strange desire to protect her sweep over him. He frowned as he asked, "Does he always lock you in that room?"

She shrugged, "When I don't have a client. That way Abe gets to decide when I'm free to go home. He knows that I have two children at home; two children that I was supposed to have aborted. He hates them even though he's rarely seen them. They conflict with my 'availability'. He likes to keep me busy earning money - for him."

Marcus frowned and shook his head in disbelief. "That man is evil, through and through. He doesn't deserve to live."

The walk lasted a number of blocks. His clenched fists relaxed little by little as they walked and talked. "How did you get involved with Mr. Z?"

She shook her head and the sadness returned to her eyes. "I came for a summer job. I had applied at the City Recreation Center and they asked me to come for an interview. It was only for two months, but the hours would allow me to look for a permanent position. You can imagine my disappointment when I found out that the position was filled before I arrived for the interview. They apologized for not getting back to me in time.

"I was in big trouble. The little bit of my earnings that I had managed to save at my previous job covered my bus fare and a bit of food along the way. I'd quit that job because of being harassed."

Myrna gave a hollow laugh. "How often I've wished that I'd been born ugly." Her shoulders sagged. "So there I was; no job, no money and hungry. Abe found me sitting at the counter of a burger joint. He presented himself as a kind fatherly gentleman and bought me a meal. He must have recognized how naïve I was because he got the whole story out of me before the food was gone.

"Next thing I knew I apparently owed him a huge sum of money. He demanded immediate payment, knowing full well that I didn't have a job or any cash. He'd set me up." Myrna shuddered at the memory. "To pay him back I was ushered into a hotel room where a man waited for me. I was ordered to 'please the gentleman or else'. That day, I died inside."

She caught her breath before she continued. "I had left my last job because I couldn't stand the come-ons, trying to stay out of corners, making sure never to be in the copy room by myself. But eventually it just got to be too much and I quit."

She gave a mirthless chuckle, "Now my situation is so much worse than being cornered in an empty room. I'm thrown into a hotel room and someone else holds the key."

Her sad face touched Marcus' heart in spite of himself. "I'm so sorry. I wish there was something I could do to help you but as you can see, I'm in big trouble myself."

She touched his hand and looked up at him, "Thank you, Marcus. It's very kind of you to even want to help."

He gave a harsh laugh, "I'm not kind. It's just that we have a common enemy."

She shook her head, "No, you are kind. It's too late to help me but if anything should ever happen to me, maybe you can help keep my daughter out of Abe's clutches."

Fear, almost panic, filled her eyes. "My very dear friend, Sherry knows what Abe is like. She is doing her best to help me keep Dora and Davy out of his sight, but there is only so much she can do."

Marcus heard the urgency in Myrna's voice. It rekindled his own anger at the man. "I will make it a priority. I don't know how it will look, but I'll kill him before I let him rob another young girl of her innocence."

Myrna's shoulders relaxed a bit. "It's good to know that you understand. I haven't said much to my sweet Dora because I don't want her to live in constant fear, but it's getting harder and harder to hide her. Abe keeps showing up at the apartment without warning."

Marcus' face darkened, "I know what it feels like to be helpless; to have no control over what happens to you or the situation around you."

The street was deserted as they approached her apartment. He turned to her. Even though she must be a number of years older than him, Marcus saw a beautiful face that looked far too young to be enslaved to such a brute. Impulsively he said, "Let's run away together."

She gave him a sad smile as she shook her head, "You don't know Abe if you think there is anywhere that you could hide from him."

Scowling, his voice heavy with bitterness, Marcus said, "Guess I don't really know him. I just know that he has the art of making peopled indebted to him and then he owns them."

Myrna stopped and looked Marcus full in the face. "I'm so sorry that he got his hooks into you too. I want out of this business for my children's sake, but I don't hold out much hope that he will ever let me go." She turned to keep on walking. Sadness replaced the look of concern, "I bring in too much money." She spoke without pride, merely in resignation.

They continued to the next corner. Marcus broke the silence and said, "You mentioned Sherry. I don't remember meeting her."

For the first time, a smile appeared on Myrna's face, "That's because she got free from Abe's chains. I don't know how she managed it, but she doesn't turn tricks anymore. She says Jesus did a miracle. I have to believe her because nothing else makes sense."

Their footsteps echoed in unison on the sidewalk. Marcus liked the sound of it. He could almost forget his own problems while he walked alongside this kind person.

"I'm so happy for Sherry that she doesn't have to work for Abe anymore." continued Myrna, "She has sworn to run away with my kids if anything happens to me, even if it's just to the cops. I know that isn't a possibility, but I love her for thinking of it."

Marcus nodded grimly, "Well, I'm here to help keep your children out of Mr. Z's clutches, in whatever way I can."

"Mr. Z?"

"Yes, his last name is too long to remember and I'll never be on a first name basis with that fiend."

174

Myrna's hand touched his arm, "Thank you, Marcus, for wanting to help. It warms my heart to know that Sherry won't be alone if anything happens to me."

He replied bitterly, "You're welcome, for whatever it's worth."

They continued in silence for a few moments, then Myrna said, "But I also have a hope now."

At his raised eyebrows she answered his unasked question. "I went to the Mission with Sherry last week. Somehow she heard that my client had failed to show up and she snuck up the room. Don't ask me how she got the key, but she dragged me out of that room and rushed me down the back stairs so fast I hardly knew what happened. On the street she hauled me along, whether I wanted to or not, babbling about how this was all in God's plan."

Myrna glanced up and saw that Marcus' curiosity had him waiting for her next words. "After seeing the change in Sherry and with all her talk about Jesus having freed her, I had to admit that I was curious to see what it was all about. So I risked Abe's anger and went along with her."

She walked a few steps in silence as if deep in thought.

Marcus watched the changing expressions on her face and was angered anew that such an angel should be chained to that devil of a man. It wasn't fair.

Myrna shook her head and continued, "The beautiful music and the words spoken by the man at the front made me cry. I wanted to be freed from my situation just like Sherry. An older woman came and talked to me, asking if I wanted to give my life to Jesus. I said yes."

She shrugged as if she still couldn't quite believe it. "Marcus, I can't explain the incredible peace that flooded my heart and my mind as soon as I said yes. And it hasn't left me since. I know it will take a miracle, but I'm praying that God will show me the way out of this mess."

Marcus listened attentively as Myrna talked. He admired her spirit but he hoped she wouldn't be too disappointed in the end. He couldn't fathom how anything would ever free her from Mr. Z's clutches.

"Myrna, you sound just like my foster mom. I remember how her sister-in-law hated the idea of Edith taking in abandoned kids like me and..."

Marcus stopped. He couldn't continue because it made him think of what he'd done and how he'd left Steinbach. He burned with shame. He did not like that feeling.

At Myrna's questioning glance, Marcus cleared his throat. "I…I'm glad for you about this Jesus thing…but it's not for the likes of me."

Marcus noticed the sad look that settled on her face after his comment. He waited until a noisy bus took off from the bus stop just up ahead. "Even though I can't go for all that God stuff – there are too many evil things happening for me to believe that he exists – but you have my word, I'll stick by you."

Myrna raised her beautiful eyes and said, "My greatest joy, Marcus, would be to see you learn to know my Jesus."

The almost gentle look on his face changed back to a scowl. He turned away and looked up the street, "Ha, as if your God would want anything to do with the likes of me." His frown deepened and he threw back his shoulders. "Besides, he wasn't there for me when I was a kid. Why would it be any different now?"

They stopped in front of Myrna's apartment, "Marcus, thank you for being a good listener."

He changed the subject. "It sounds like I'll have my driver's license by the end of next week. Maybe I'll get a limo to drive you around."

"Thanks, but I actually prefer to walk. It gives me more time in the outdoors." She paused at her door, took a deep breath, closed her eyes and raised her face to the skies.

Marcus said, "Same time, same place tomorrow," as he turned to head back to the Casino. Anger increased with each step, at the man who had made such bad luck for both himself and Myrna. He shook his head. *We're both stuck in this evil web with no one who can help us get out of it.*

Chapter Thirty-Seven

By late summer of 2002, Marcus owed 5 grand to Mr. Z. *I'm never going to be rid of this debt. The harder I try, the worse it gets.*

All the staff members were charged for daily meals whether they ate at the Casino or not, with no employee discount. Marcus grew more agitated every time he was reminded that his debt was larger at the end of the day.

In frustration he flared up when Mr. Z handed him his latest statement. "How come you add interest to these already inflated prices?"

"Hey, it's just part of the real world." Abe's derisive laugh made Marcus want to punch the man's lights out. Instead, he turned on his heel and walked swiftly toward the door.

Mr. Z's voice stopped him. "I hear you're getting real chummy with that woman. You'd better not get any ideas into your head. You just make sure she don't miss her next appointment or else I'll hafta add a hundred bucks to your account fer lack of performing your duties…with interest of course. And don't forget to pick up that 'parcel' at the airport. It's been waiting for over an hour."

Frustrated at his helplessness in the situation, without looking back, Marcus paused only long enough to hear the man out. Then he stomped out of the door to do Mr. Z's bidding.

His footsteps ended up a mere thud on the lush carpet in the hallway. His steps slowed but his heart rate didn't.

What's the sense in hurrying? He'll just find other, more obnoxious stuff for me to do. I guess Myrna's right. This guy is just plain evil. I'm surprised no one's tried to stop him.

***

There was something real fishy about the 'parcel' Marcus had been sent to pick up. He never even had time to get out of the car. As he pulled up to the curb someone opened the passenger door, tossed a package onto the seat and slapped the roof of the car. Then he took off on a skateboard before Marcus had a chance to see the kid's face.

When he arrived back at the Casino, Mr. Z was waiting in the alley. He snatched the parcel from Marcus and without so much as a thank you, disappeared into the night.

Marcus entered the building and was filled anew with anger at his situation. *How will I ever get out of this hell-hole?* He gritted his teeth until his jaws hurt. Then he had to massage his temples. It was all so hopeless. Swiftly and silently the elevator arrived at his floor but it didn't change his situation.

He frowned at the two ugly looking men who lounged against the opposite wall as the elevator doors parted.

They straightened up as soon as he stepped out. When he reached his door to unlock it, they were on either side of him. They 'helped' him into the room and the next thing Marcus knew, he couldn't breathe. The punches to his gut left him doubled over in pain. They slapped his back so hard that he crumpled to the floor. A guttural laugh rang out in the room as they gave each other a high five before they turned to go. One of them decided a good kick in Marcus' side was still needed. At the door they looked back and said, "Don't think of doin' nothin' funny. We're watchin' ya."

Marcus stayed where he'd fallen. Hot tears filled his eyes and dripped onto the carpet. The room that he had thought so nice after his cardboard boxes was now his prison cell. *Oh how could I have been so stupid? What was it Edith used to say, If it looks too good to be true, it probably is. She was right and I should've known better.*

Marcus got up and made his way to the bathroom. In the mirror, his eyes revealed that he was in pain but no bruises were visible. *I guess those goons know how to keep up appearances.* A dry chuckle was cut off by the pain it produced in his chest.

The next few days he noticed that the same two ugly thugs were in evidence every time he turned around. He also realized that they'd been around for some time. The car they drove was the same one that had been in his rear view mirror a number of times on trips to the airport. But he'd been too taken up with the pleasure of driving a classy limo to take notice of his surroundings. *How could I have been so blind?*

Chapter Thirty-Eight

Gila came over to Marcus and handed him a note. She gave his shoulder a quick pat before heading back into the main dining room.

He finished his meal before he read the note. It demanded Marcus' immediate presence in Mr. Z's office. Marcus finished his coffee and wiped his mouth with the serviette.

No one was there when he arrived but the door was open. He went in and closed the door behind him. Soon he began to pace in the small area as he waited for the man to show up. "Wonder what else he wants to add to my long list of things to do? This is wasting my time." growled Marcus. He glanced at his wristwatch, "It's almost time to get Myrna, the only relief I get from this place."

The door to the office opened soundlessly on oiled hinges. Marcus sensed someone enter behind him. He twisted around like a panther, ready to pounce. He relaxed only slightly when he saw it was Mr. Z.

The man walked with silent tread around the desk. He rubbed his hands together, but his mouth was a straight line; his eyes mere slits in a flushed face. Marcus watched closely but couldn't decide if the man was pleased or anxious.

"I've got a delicate job for you, Mark. I don't trust anyone else to take care of it." He paused to let the words sink in.

Marcus stood quietly and waited; unimpressed that he was the chosen one.

"I need you to waste one of my girls," said Abe.

Marcus sucked in his breath and took a step back. Before he could argue, Abe continued. "Word is out that she's planning to go to the cops. I can't let that happen."

Marcus stiffened. With fists clenched, he glared at Mr. Z, "You know I won't carry a gun."

"But my man, you're going to have to." Abe reached across the desk and poked Marcus in the chest with a stubby finger to emphasize his point, "Myrna is a threat to all of us, including you."

"What! Did you say Myrna?" gasped Marcus, "There's no way I could lay a finger on her." He was ready to not only poke the man in the chest, but to punch his nose so hard it would come out the back of his head, whatever the consequences. "Myrna's a good woman and you know it!" He shifted his weight backwards, onto his heels and crossed his arms, "I refuse to be any part of hurting her."

Abe pounded the desk top with his fists and snarled, "You get this job done or else you go ta jail. I'll fire you and demand full payment of your debt. You'll find yourself in jail so fast you won't know what happened."

Marcus turned and strode out the door. He took the first set of stairs and ended up in the kitchen. Without a word to any of the staff, he exited via the side door. A delivery truck had just backed up to the door. While the goods were being unloaded, Marcus sprang into the passenger side. Pressed back against the seat to lessen visibility, he waited until his heart slowed down. Then he reached over and did up the seat belt. *I'd love to run to Myrna and get her to safety but that's the first place his goons will look for me. What can I do to help her? If only I had some money.* His frown deepened. *But I don't! It's all in Mr. Z's pockets.*

The driver hopped in and glanced at Marcus. The thunderous look on that face warned him not to ask any questions. He shifted gears and merged onto the busy traffic.

Across town the driver stopped at a traffic light. Marcus undid his seat belt and turned to him, "Thanks." A quick nod of his head and he disappeared from view into the mass of shoppers that crowded the street.

Marcus ducked down a back alley and leaned against the cold brick wall of a Home Hardware Store. He dialed Myrna's number. Sherry answered his terse request for Myrna.

"She's not available at the moment."

Marcus didn't wait for explanations. He whispered into the phone, trembling with fear and anger. "Sherry, you have to warn Myrna. Mr. Z has decided to kill her before she can go to the cops." He heard a sharp intake of breath and then a gentle 'thanks for letting us know' came across the air waves.

He closed his cell phone and pushed it in his shirt pocket before he continued down the back alley. He waited for a crowd of people and then mingled with them to cross the street. Then he ducked into another alley. He knew where the truck depot was and the quicker he got there the better his chances for getting away. *Here's hoping one of them is headed east. Mr. Z's goons are probably out looking for me already. I sure don't want them to get a hold of me.*

Luck was with him. There was a load headed for Toronto. It was just what he needed. As the truck rolled along, Marcus' mind was busy.

He calculated that it was about five years since Edith had passed away. She had promised to leave everything to him and Charlotte. Although he already had his share of the inheritance by taking the cash, there should be more money from the sale of the house...because of course the kid wouldn't stay in such a big place all by herself.

He didn't remember her as being a big spender. Surely by now she would have some money saved up that he could borrow. *No, not borrow.* His face darkened at the thought; *money to give me because I'll never be able to pay it back. I've got to get money, and lots of it.*

Marcus shrugged deeper into his jacket and watched the sign posts along the TransCanada Highway slip by one after the other. The more he thought about what he needed to do, the darker loomed his possibilities. *I guess I'd better sneak into town. They probably have a warrant out for my arrest for emptying Edith's bank account. It seems like everywhere I turn I have to be on guard. It's not fair. How can I keep my eyes and ears open all the time?*

The cab was filled with hurtin' country music, turned up loud so the driver could sing along. It just matched Marcus' heart and mind, hurting and hopeless. The words did nothing to cheer him up but at least it kept the driver from trying to make conversation.

***

About mid-morning on Friday, October 4th, the truck pulled off the highway and coasted onto the shoulder just past the #12 intersection.

"This here's as far as I can take you. I'm headin' for Kenora and then on to Toronto." He laughed, "Unless you've changed your mind and want to head further east."

Marcus shook his head. "Thanks. Much as I'd like to, there's business that needs to be looked after."

"Maybe next time, buddy."

Marcus got out and stepped away from the truck. He stood and listened to the motor roar into action and gears shifting as his ride pulled back onto the highway.

By the time he made it to Ste Anne his feet hurt and his teeth chattered from the cold. Even though the cigarette drew in warm air, it did nothing to warm his insides. His shoulders hunched forward against the brisk breeze as he forced himself to keep moving.

The business suit was fine back in Kelowna but here in Manitoba...he desperately wished that he was wearing a warmer jacket. He was thankful that the truck driver had given him a cap for a souvenir. It was only a baseball cap but it helped to keep in some of his body heat.

As Marcus walked on the shoulder of the highway, every few minutes he looked back. He didn't think Mr. Z's goons would realize that he'd left town already, but he knew it wouldn't take them long to figure it out. He had to remain alert in case they followed his trail.

I wonder if Charlotte's still working for Duffy. She'll be done school by now; probably married. But to whom? surely not that red-headed loser. A bitter laugh escaped from him that ended in a harsh fit of coughing. *Who knows? A lot of things can happen in five years.*

The second cigarette was done. He flicked the butt towards the ditch and buried his hands in his pockets. Still shivering he spotted McDonalds up ahead. His need encouraged him to hurry. It was as good a place as any to use the bathroom and warm up with a cup of hot chocolate.

He jingled the few coins in his pocket. *I sure hope I find that girl before night. I need a warm place to sleep. And a good home-cooked meal wouldn't hurt.*

Chapter Thirty-Nine

Marcus made his way to Reimer Avenue. From up the street he could see a bunch of kids close to the old place. When he got closer he looked for the hedge but it was gone. A couple of the teenagers moved out of his way as he neared the driveway. They stepped into the yard that had belonged to Edith.

Too embarrassed to ask what they were doing there, he just kept on walking toward the next intersection. A few steps past, Marcus took a quick look over his shoulder and saw that they were going into the house.

They look too young to be Charlotte's friends. Could it be that she doesn't live there anymore? I guess it makes sense. It's like I thought, the place would be too big for one person.

Marcus rubbed a cold hand over his eyes. Slowly he retraced his steps to Main Street. It was almost lunch time. He sure wasn't going to go into Duffy's Cafe and risk meeting up with Irene. For whatever reason, that waitress had appointed herself as Charlotte's bodyguard. *She'd recognize me before I could set foot inside and probably have the cops come pick me up.*

At the intersection he looked down the street toward the Café. What did he see but Charlotte getting out of a vehicle! It had to be her. The young woman was taller than he remembered Charlotte, but that long brown pony tail still swung the same way. And she got out of the driver's door!

Would wonders never cease? Before he could make up his mind whether he should risk approaching her in front of Duffy's or not, he noticed that she was meeting some people, an older couple.

It was an interesting development. Not surprised that they went into Duffy's Café, he slunk around to the back of the Credit Union and tried to make some plans. He leaned back against a car. It was still warm. That felt good. He bent at the waist and looked into the driver's window. The keys were still in the ignition.

"These hicks haven't changed a bit. They're so naïve!" he muttered, "Leave the keys in the car just waiting for someone to help themselves. I must remember that, in case I need it. "

After his cigarette was finished, Marcus sauntered around back to the front where Charlotte had parked her car. *That mahogany mist paint job is pretty cool. I wonder what she had to pay for that.* He stayed well back from the Honda CR-V but wrote down the number on the license plate before he crossed the street and went down to M.J.'s Kafe for a bowl of soup. In the restaurant he kept his eyes lowered to avoid conversation with anyone who might be able to identify him. Probably no one remembered him but why take the risk. He didn't dawdle too long in case Charlotte had a short lunch. He sauntered back up the street and found a corner sheltered from the wind, to keep an eye out for her. Her car was still parked in the same place. He began his vigil.

Teeth chattering, he hugged himself and rubbed his upper arms. Whoever she worked for must be pretty lenient if her long lunch was any indication. Finally they came out of the restaurant. *Good grief, she's hugging those people. Who are they anyway?*

Marcus peered across the way. No one he knew. He wrote them off as not important. Charlotte got into her vehicle and drove right past him. A big smile adorned her face. "Still happy as ever," he muttered. His long stride ate up the sidewalk as he kept his eyes trained on her car. She took the yield heading north. *Most of those businesses along the highway are close to the street. It shouldn't be too hard to spot her car.*

He looked left and then he looked right, checking each parking lot as he walked along the highway. His legs were trembling by the time he reached the Day's Inn. He decided that he'd go in and sit in the lobby, just to warm up for a few minutes.

Just then he spotted a car that looked like Charlotte's. He quickened his steps to see the license plate. It was hers. He looked up at the building. A sign out front said it was Rand and Associates. It was a law office.

"What could she be doing for a lawyer? But if it's her workplace, she'll probably stay put until after four. Now is a good time to look for another car with keys in the ignition." Marcus glanced across the parking lot. "Not enough vehicles," he whispered, "too easy to be noticed."

Part way down the street, sitting in the driveway was just what he needed, a nondescript clunker. *If only the keys are in there, it'll be a piece of cake. Take a few corners and no one will remember it.*

"Yes!" he uttered with glee as he spotted the keys in the ignition. He got in the driver's side and gently closed the door. No need to alert anyone unnecessarily. The gas gauge showed that the tank was full.

He waited till a car came up the street before he started the Ford. The motor purred to a start. It took only a minute to roll out of the driveway and turn up the street. Going to Park Rd, he made a U-turn and headed back down Highway #12. Signaling a left turn, he drove to the back of the Inn. It gave him a nice view of Charlotte's vehicle in the next parking lot. And a nice warm place to wait.

He hated the fact that he had to take the risk of staying so close to the place where he'd stolen the vehicle but what else could he do.

His stomach growled. He paid it no heed. There would be enough time to eat later.

Shortly after five o'clock Charlotte came out and got into her vehicle. Marcus watched to make sure that she headed toward the highway before he left his parking spot. Keeping his distance he wondered *would she feel afraid if she knew someone was following her.*

He followed Charlotte all the way out to the small community of Zhoda. When she turned onto the service road he slowed down to see where she was going. She pulled into the third driveway from the end. Marcus signaled left and pulled onto the other end of the service road. He parked in front of the building next door to the one she had stopped at. Choosing not to rush in after her, he sat back and checked out the place. It was a nice little cabin set among some huge pine trees. The windows sparkled in the late afternoon sun. *It looks like she's still a neat-freak. I wonder if she lives alone.* He watched until dark to see if anyone else might come and go from her place.

Satisfied that there was no one else and that she was settled for the night, he drove back to town. It was too late to go to the bank so it would be better to wait until the morning to confront her about money. It was time to go see if any of his old buddies still gathered at the bowling alley.

Marcus parked the clunker on the side street so as not to advertise his whereabouts. He hurried along the sidewalk, shivering in the cold night air after exiting the warmth of the car. The parking lot hadn't changed over the past five years but he didn't recognize any of the vehicles in it.

A few dollars right now for food would come in mighty handy he thought as he entered the building.

He found a new crowd. There was no one to remember how slick Marcus could be. A few small bets were made; a little chagrined humor at the 'heads I win, tails you lose' ploy, and he had enough money for a meal at A&W. He was content for the moment.

The Teen Burger hit the spot. He tipped the glass to sip the last drop of Root beer. These days he didn't waste any food. Eating from garbage bins was a too-recent memory.

Marcus walked through the empty restaurant with tray in hand. He tossed the paper garbage into the receptacle and left his mug on top of a very clean stand. He almost felt guilty messing it up. He kept his face turned away from the staff behind the counter and headed out the door.

On the sidewalk he paused and glanced back. "Guess they were waiting for me to leave," he murmured as he saw the lights flick off in the interior.

His steps echoed in the empty street. Suddenly he paused. He moved swiftly off the sidewalk and stepped into the shadows beside the fence.   Something was wrong. He could feel it. The stolen car - it was gone!

Not that I should be surprised but I did have plans to sleep in that car tonight. What am I to do now?

"Rats!   I'll just have to keep my eyes open for another car to steal." Marcus made his way to the nearest back alley. *I'd better disappear from here. Being the only one out on the sidewalk makes me the most likely suspect.*

Main Street was just as deserted. There were no cars on the street. A few neon lights blinked off and on, displaying the fact that everything was shut down for night.

Where will I find a place to hide out until morning? I can't remember…Do they have recycle bins in the downtown area?

Marcus walked along the sidewalk until he reached the corner of Barkman and Main. "Ah, the Thrift Store. I remember the big bins in the back."

He was in luck. A couple of bags filled with clothing and a quilt had been deposited beside the back door.

"That big garbage container is just what the doctor ordered," he chuckled grimly as he threw the bag and quilt over the side. His tired muscles couldn't haul him up the side. He looked around and found an old TV set. "That's just about the right height."

Marcus tugged and pulled the old cabinet TV closer to the bin and managed to pull himself up over the edge. It reeked in there, but the newly donated quilt had a fresh smell and it was definitely warmer than being out on the street.

Saturday morning traffic along the street woke Marcus. He shivered when he threw back the quilt. It was no easy trick to climb back out of the bin. Feet skidding on the side finally caught a protruding bolt and gave him the needed foothold to hoist himself up the rest of the way. He brushed at the dirt and dust on his pants, but it was of no use. The stubborn stains and wrinkles weren't going to disappear without a good wash. He had no other choice but to move along.

Marcus made his way back to Charlotte's workplace. His feet hurt and he was hungry. There were a few cars in the lot, but her CR-V wasn't among them. By the time he'd decided that she wasn't coming to work it was too late to head out to her place in Zhoda and still make it back in time to hit the banks. He needed to find another car to steal since his first set of stolen wheels had been found by the owner or retrieved by the cops.

He plodded back to the bowling alley to try for a few more dollars. He found no takers. They must have wised up overnight.

Besides, the majority of folks bowling looked like they were there with a personal caregiver. Marcus didn't have the energy or patience needed to explain his game to them.

Hands tucked into his pockets for warmth, he scuffed along the street thinking of his miserable, lonely life. He ignored the few happy events and chose to dwell on the injustices, real or imagined that he'd suffered.

Head bent in dejection, Marcus spotted some loose change beside the curb. He picked it up and jiggled it in his hand to shake off the dirt. A hollow laugh at the clinking sound of the few coins ended with a sigh. There was enough change for another burger or maybe a toasted bagel. He purchased a burger to-go and made his way to the park. After his meal for the day, Marcus wandered through the park and along some of the side streets. Somehow it felt safe. He relaxed his watch for Mr. Z's goons.

He was glad when dusk descended. It was time to head back to the bins. Thank goodness there had been no garbage pick-up that day. The quilt and the bag of clothes were still where he'd left them. Before Marcus climbed in, he threw a block of wood into the bin. It would help him to get out in the morning. He curled up into a fetal position and pulled the quilt up over his head. It was a lot warmer than out on the street.

Chapter Forty

2002 October 6th

"Hmm, it's Sunday morning. Most of these good people will be at church. Good time to go find another sucker who's left keys in the car."

Marcus strode along one street after another. It was not as easy as he'd hoped. He got tired and hungry.

"Wonder why they don't have a fast food at this end of town," complained Marcus. "It's a long way to walk back to McD's."

Late in the afternoon he was ready to give up and just hitch-hike out to Zhoda. But his luck changed and he found what he was looking for. The driver's side had a big dent. *That silvery gray paint job will blend in nicely with the traffic; a few corners and it'll be just one of many. But why would anyone leave their keys on the seat, in plain view? Unless the driver is coming right back...*

Marcus leaned against a light standard and waited. Quiet continued to reign. *The owner is probably having a Sunday afternoon nap* he thought.

His luck held. Not only were the keys in the vehicle but the gas gauge showed a full tank. Careful not to slam the door, he got away without anyone trying to stop him.

The road out to Zhoda was lonely. No one passed him. There was only one other vehicle and it stayed way back of him; too far away for someone to recognize him. "Good thing. If no one sees me, no one will tell."

He pulled onto the service road and backed into the shrubs beside what looked like a machine shed of some kind.

Good place to be inconspicuous. This vehicle has enough dents that it'll just look like it's waiting to be repaired.

Marcus was in no hurry to leave the warmth of the vehicle. He could sit in comfort and still keep watch on Charlotte's yard.

"No need to bother her tonight," he mumbled as he leaned his back against the door and stretched out his legs along the bench seat. The warm interior made him drowsy but his mind continued in a whirl of what-ifs. He sat up straight to force himself back into alertness. *So many things to go wrong and all I can do is sit here and wait.* He thumped his fist against the steering wheel and complained, "It's just not fair."

The minutes turned into an hour and he grew bleary-eyed as he strained to see through the darkness. Trying to rationalize his plan took a lot of energy. He fought desperately against the drowsiness that was determined to take over. "With a nice spread like this, she must have found some rich friends." He yawned and let his body settle back against the seat. "I'd better wait until tomorrow so she can ask them for assistance."

His eyes traveled around the area. *All the neighbors must be away. It's so quiet and the pine trees do a good job of hiding the light from that one yard light. No extra lights to brighten the dark night or give my hiding place away.*

It was time to recline the padded seat and call it a night. It was a lot more comfortable than the garbage bin the last two nights. Even with all the rags and the quilt, it had still been lumpy and cold. He shivered at the memory. "I sure could use a few nights of undisturbed rest in a real bed."

As the night wore on, the cold seeped through the interior of the car. *Sure wish I could leave the motor running but it would draw someone's attention* thought Marcus as he tried to curl up into a ball. "It still beats sleeping in a bin." He pulled his collar up around his ears. "I wish I had that quilt."

The wind blew through the pine trees and sounded like a mournful voice trying to give a warning. Was it for him or for Charlotte? His mouth tightened. As if he had a choice. This was the only way to get Mr. Z and his henchmen off his back.

Marcus raised his head and let his eyes do another sweep of the area before he settled back and let them close in sleep. He mumbled, "And by the look of things, Charlotte's doing okay for herself. She shouldn't mind sharing."

Chapter Forty-One

2002 October 7th

Monday morning Marcus sat tight until after Charlotte left for work. He watched for any movement in the neighborhood. When he sensed that the coast was clear, Marcus eased out of the car and cautiously approached the cabin.

He had no problem breaking into the house – a screwdriver pressed in just the right spot and voila! The door swung open.

The first thing he looked for was food. On the clean but cluttered counter sat a loaf of bread that looked homemade. *Charlotte didn't even put it back into the bag, and a dirty knife? She must have been in a hurry.*

Marcus cut a thick slab of bread and slathered it with the peanut butter and honey left beside the loaf. He leaned a hip against the counter as he chewed slowly, savoring each bite. While he was eating he let his eyes rove around the room.

The computer brought a sly smile to his face. Passwords and numbers for her different accounts were written on sticky notes and pasted all around the front edges of the monitor. There was no need to hurry.

"Some milk would go nice with this," he said as he turned to look for a cup.

The cupboard above the sink didn't have doors. Dishes were in plain view set out neatly on two shelves. The bottom shelf was edged with a strip of eyelet lace. *Makes me think of Charlotte, it's so girly.*

Marcus grabbed a glass off the top shelf and went to the fridge. He stood in front of the open door to fill the glass. Back at the counter, he finished a second piece of bread and guzzled the rest of the milk.

He wiped his mouth on the tea towel and pulled a pack of cigarettes from his shirt pocket. He squinted through the smoke as he breathed out after his first drag. "Now this is more like it." He took another puff and made his way over to the computer desk in the corner.

"This'll be as easy as taking candy from a baby. I don't even have to memorize these passwords and account numbers to gain access and empty them," said Marcus as he turned the machine on. He inhaled some more smoke and reached to turn on the computer. "It's so easy that I almost feel guilty; almost, but not quite," said the thief as he clicked the internet icon.

He was startled when he heard the sound of a telephone dialing. "What gives?" he gasped in surprise. "Oh, now I get it," he eased back in the chair. "This place is out in the boonies. Dial-up must be the only thing available. I'm lucky that they even have internet."

He stretched out his arms and cracked his knuckles. He leaned back in the chair and waited. "What is taking so long? There's almost enough time to take a nap!" he complained. Marcus blew out a sigh of relief when the machine was finally connected to the internet.

It was time to get to work. He crushed the cigarette butt with the heel of his shoe. Not a sound disturbed the room as the desperate man began his heinous task. He hardly dared to breathe, refusing to think of anything but to get the job done.

First step was easy – open a new account for Mark North and transfer Charlotte's money into it. All the needed information was readily available on the posted notes in front of him.

Marcus looked at the final balance and clenched his teeth. He jabbed his fingers into his hair and held his head in frustration.

"I need more!" he cried out. "This isn't enough." He slammed his open hand down on the desk. "Ouch!" He sat and rubbed his hand. It hurt. But what Mr. Z was going to have his goons do to him would hurt a lot worse.

"What am I going to do?" Marcus scrunched his forehead; his hands propped under his chin. Eyes, mere slits, gazed across the room but didn't see what was in front of him. He tried to visualize the future.

"What if Mr. Z carries out his threat and has me thrown in jail? But that's hogwash! He wouldn't because it would implicate him too. Still…"

Marcus jumped up and paced around the room, "I wonder if she has any money stashed someplace else." He had already checked for sugar bowls and found none. He began a thorough search of the cabin. Gingerly lifting the mattress, he let it fall back in place when there wasn't even a stray feather. He opened each drawer and pawed through its contents. He came up empty each time.

A dog barked outside. Marcus, naturally cautious because of past experiences, moved to the window and peered through the sheer curtains. He gasped. A sleek black car had parked across the road from where he'd left the stolen car. He could see two people in it and they were watching the car.

"Oh no, it can't be!" whispered Marcus. "Why would Mr. Z send his goons after me all the way to Manitoba and how did they find me? I'm sure I left no tracks. I guess Myrna was right. There's no place to hide from him."

Marcus eased back from the window and realized it was time to quit the useless search. "I've got to get out of here. Too bad, I was going to make myself some lunch. Maybe I can come back later. Yes, that's what I'll do. I'll wait until Charlotte gets home from work. She's *got* to have more money. She just has to. Or maybe she'll know where she can get some."

The black car was far enough down the road that they wouldn't be able to see the side door. Marcus slipped out and crept through the bushes at the back of Charlotte's property. After he'd made his way past two neighboring yards he spied a bicycle leaning against a garden shed. Keeping low, he sidled over to the fence. His breath came in shallow gasps. His heart raced as he waited. When there is no sign of activity, he crawled through the fence, grabbed the bike and hoisted it over to the other side. He walked the bike until he came to a dirt road. It was little more than a footpath but wide enough to ride. He jumped on the bike and pedaled like crazy. Branches slapped in his face and caught at his hair. Panic lent him the needed strength to keep going.

Marcus arrived in town just after lunch. He straightened his clothes and brushed the leaves and twigs from his hair before he entered the bank. The line-up at the service counter was short. Only two people ahead of him, it didn't take long until he heard, "Next." It was his turn. Marcus hoped his smile would distract the clerk from his rumpled attire. He didn't waste any time with small talk.

"I need a certified cheque, please," was his simple request. He didn't give the clerk any unnecessary explanation, just what he needed and how much.

He was prepared for the request that he take a seat. He knew from the last time that he would have to wait for it.

Chapter Forty-Two

Marcus left the bank with a frown settled on his face. His whole body sagged in frustration as he pedaled back to Zhoda. He still needed more money and he didn't know of anyone else besides Charlotte whom he could press for more. *Charlotte has got to have some stashed away...but where? If she's living out there on that country property, what happened to the old lady's house? Was it sold? Is she renting? I really doubt that. And if she's buying the cabin, she'd have needed a sizeable down payment. Selling the house in town would have given her that, but surely there would have been money left over.*

A gopher darted onto the road just ahead of Marcus. It scampered back into the ditch just before he reached it. His interrupted train of thought clicked back into gear. *She's going to have to hand it over. I've got no choice. Hopefully this sum of money will get Mr. Z off my back. But I want more. I want to be free from his claws! Totally free! I don't want to do any more dirty jobs for him.*

By the time Marcus reached the Sarto turn-off, his lungs felt like they were going to collapse. Since working for Mr. Z he'd gone soft. He had lost his zeal to exercise, to pump iron. There had been no need for muscle to carry out his tasks. And it was never the right time to get out and exercise.

His naturally lean body had become almost emaciated. At the Casino he felt like every bite put him farther into debt. Away from the Casino, he had no cash.

He eased back on the pedals when his leg muscles felt like they were on fire. He hadn't ridden a bike since he'd left Steinbach five years ago. Determination and necessity forced him to keep on moving.

When he neared the community of Zhoda he looked up ahead and noticed that the stolen car still sat on the service road, exactly where he'd left it. But, the black car had disappeared. Not taking any chances he jumped off the bike and snuck to the back of the row of properties. As silently as possible he walked the bike up to the last house before Charlotte's cabin.

Marcus leaned the bike against a white picket fence instead of returning it to where he'd found it – just in case he would need it again. And if not, the owner and the neighbor could wonder about how the bike had gotten there.

Marcus eased forward to check out the possibility of making it to the side door. Just when he'd made up his mind that it was still clear, the black vehicle rolled to a stop across the road. This time the cabin's side door was visible from where they parked.

"Just my luck," he whispered as he ducked back behind the fence. "I wonder if they saw me on the road. Now they're waiting for me to give myself up." He curled his lips and gave a mirthless laugh, "Ha, like that's going to happen. They'll have to shoot me first."

Marcus slowly lowered himself down to the ground and rested his back against the fence. He'd wait until dark. Time dragged on. He didn't dare light a cigarette lest it should give him away. But he was determined to outwait them.

Charlotte must have some friends, he thought as he sat and shivered, trying not to think of the dampness seeping through his trousers – *maybe some rich friends, like that couple she*

had lunch with on Friday. How else can she afford to live in the country?
That possibility kept Marcus waiting for Charlotte to return. It put him at risk of being caught by those goons. But he wouldn't get caught. No way! They were soft from their cushy job. City dudes, they'd get tired of waiting in the silence long before he would. No, he couldn't get caught. They'd leave him more dead than alive, and with empty pockets. Mr. Z might get the money but it would never be credited to his account. Marcus yawned and shook his head. *I have to stay alert if I want to remain alive.*

He got to his knees at the sound of an approaching car. His limited view made him impatient. When the CR-V pulled into the driveway he sighed with relief.

"But what's Charlotte doing home this early?" Marcus' whispered question hung unanswered in the air. His eyes darted over to the black car. It was still there, but they were watching the stolen car, not Charlotte's house. Relieved, he sat back to wait until they left or until the darkness would cover him. "No need to involve her with those rotters."

Marcus must have dozed off in spite of the cold and his discomfort. Startled wide awake by the sound of a car door slamming, he moved his head to peek through the fence. It was the neighbor behind whose yard he was hiding. *A Porsche! Wonder what year it is?*

Marcus eased back against the fence, careful not to alert the woman of his presence.

Too bad I can't hang around here for a while. She might be worth getting to know now that I have my license. I wouldn't mind the privilege of getting into that beautiful machine. His humorless smile left as quickly as it had appeared. *Lotta good my license has been so far; just driving from one place of bondage to another.*

He looked up when he heard some birds twitter in the tree tops. They flitted from one branch to the other, coming closer to the ground. It looked like a game of Follow the Leader. The setting sun made it hard to spot them when they settled among the leaves. *It should be dark enough pretty soon. Then I can finish up here and be off – off to secure my freedom.*

Marcus pulled his knees up to his chest and rested his forehead against them. He could feel his warm breath seep down to his chest.

He tensed up when he heard a rustle in the shrub beside him. He peered at the place where the noise had come from. A sassy squirrel resting on its haunches, with an acorn between the front paws, sat perfectly still watching him. Unblinking eyes seemed to demand an explanation of this stranger's presence in his territory. Marcus almost burst out laughing at the squirrel's arrogant stance.

Slowly the dusk deepened. His impatience couldn't speed it up. At last one streetlight blinked on, then another one. Still he waited. He pulled at his collar but it couldn't cover any more of him than it already did. Soon, yes soon, the dark would hide his movements and he could get to the side door.

While he waited, Marcus let himself dream of his freedom. And maybe he could work something out with Mr. Z for Myrna's release. Make her swear to him that she wouldn't talk. So she could change her identity and make a new life for herself – someplace else – free from the clutches of that evil man. His face darkened at the thought of him. Fat chance that Mr. Z would let her go, she brought in too much money and now that rumor that she was going to talk to the cops...Not likely.

Suddenly he sat up and clenched his fists. *What if he got someone else to waste her already? I sure hope she's still safe.*

A quick look over his shoulder showed that the car was still parked across the road and still occupied. He settled back against the fence, shifting back and forth a couple of times to find a more comfortable spot.

If only I could light up a smoke, he fumed. *I could almost enjoy the quiet back here. Almost.*

When his eyes refused to see past his feet, Marcus uncurled his tall thin body. It was time.

Chapter Forty-Three

2002 still Oct 7th,

He snuck to the side door. To his right, the light from the front room sent a beam across the driveway. *Good, she hasn't gone to bed yet.* Marcus gave an abrupt knock with his knuckles and stepped back into the murky darkness. With his back pressed against the side of the house, he listened for her footsteps.

Heat flared momentarily into his cheeks at the thought of his appearance. He brushed at the dirt on his pants, but to no avail. He ran his fingers through his tangled waves and flicked away the twigs and leaves that stuck to his hands. He fidgeted. He stuck his hands in his pockets and frowned. *She's sure taking her time.*

When the door finally opened he entered swiftly and pushed it shut behind him. A scent of sweat and stale cigarette smoke swirled in with him. Marcus leaned against the door to support his shaky legs. His tense frame and furtive manner seemed to increase the uneasiness in the room. He watched her through narrowed eyes. *Why doesn't she say something?*

His eyes darted around the room, toward the window and then back to her face. They never stopped moving.

"So, little sister..." His words were halted as he wheezed and pressed a hand against his chest to suppress a cough. "Nice place you've got here."

Marcus pulled out a cigarette and lit it. He leaned his head back and closed his eyes as he took a deep drag. Finally! But his enjoyment of it ended in a fit of harsh coughing.

He opened his eyes and somehow moved the cigarette to the side of his mouth without touching it. "And…" The single word accompanied with raised eyebrows implied that he was looking for an explanation.

"When I found out about this place, I came to see it and knew immediately that I had to move out here. Our house in town sold for a fair price." Charlotte stood with hands clasped tightly in front of her as she talked. "I divided the money and put your share in the bank, just like Mom wanted. With interest, it should be just over $30,000."

His look questioned her statement even before he blurted out, "And you expect me to believe that?" His words burst out like bullets. "Nobody does that for anyone."

A brief moment of shame flickered through him at the pain he saw in her eyes. And his brain tried to tell him that one of the accounts he'd emptied had indeed been just over the thirty thousand. But before thoughts of doing what was right could take root, he pushed them aside and focused on his present need. That justified his actions.

"I need money, lots of money. And I need it now."

"Be reasonable, Marcus. The bank is closed. It will have to wait until the morning."

"What about those hoity-toity friends of yours I saw you with?"

"They'll be asleep by now. I'm sorry Marcus, but I can't give you any money tonight."

He threw his cigarette butt to the floor and ground it out with the heel of his shoe. Fear of what might happen if he didn't get the money raced through him. Frustration at the reality that she couldn't help him tonight filled him with rage. *Why did those goons wait around? Just to make sure that the*

206

banks would be closed? Why do I have to have such rotten luck?

His upper body leaned forward until he was almost nose to nose with Charlotte. "Oh yes you can help me," he spat out, "And you will or el…"

His words were halted by the ringing of her phone. Marcus' eyes turned wildly towards it. Mr. Z's goons were onto him. They knew he was here!

Like a wraith of mist, he slipped out into the dark. His heart pounded as he ran across lots, retracing his earlier steps. For just a moment he hoped that they would go easier on Charlotte if he wasn't in the picture. He ran, jumping over dark objects, staying close to the fences. He ran until his lungs ached and he gasped for breath. "Should have… remembered...to grab…the bike."

He reached a side road and jogged along it towards Hwy #12. He noticed a small truck stopped up ahead with its brake lights on. It seemed to be waiting for him to catch up.

As Marcus came up beside the vehicle, the driver had the window rolled down. He called out, "Going to town?"

"Yes," gasped Marcus. "Buddy of mine lives on Springfield Road."

"Hop in," said the man without seeming to notice how out of breath Marcus was.

"Thanks, man," breathed Marcus. He had no energy left to say more.

"No problem, I'm headed to the Club's flying field. I left my radio transmitter there. It was stupid of me to forget. Guess I got too busy talking with Adam. That guy sure can make you think – anyway, got my trusty flashlight." The man patted it on the seat beside him. "Now if only some do-gooder didn't move it, I know just where it is." His hearty laughter filled the cab.

Marcus didn't let his thoughts show, although his bottom lip curled. *Are all these folks around here daft? Leaving an*

expensive piece of equipment like that lying around and keys in
their cars; and then expect stuff to be there whenever they
decide to return...

Marcus sat and tried to regain his breath. He was glad the
man talked nonstop, not expecting Marcus to say anything.
Thankfully they were soon at the corner where the man
signaled to make a right turn.

As the vehicle came to a brief stop, Marcus took advantage
of the opportunity and jumped out. He grimaced at the man's
protest that the car hadn't fully stopped yet. With a "Thanks,
buddy" over his shoulder, Marcus hurried across the
intersection and down the service road.

"Hey, fella, you're headed the wrong way!" called the
man.

Marcus waved a hand over his head without turning back.
He yelled, "Thanks again," and kept on trudging. Head down,
his long stride ate up the road. After the respite of the ride, he
was eager to get out of the area; away from Mr. Z's goons. He
had no wish to let them get their hands on him ever again.

At the Blumenort intersection, a semi from Steve's
Trucking pulled onto the highway. The truck did not pick up
speed. Instead the driver edged it over onto the shoulder and
waited for Marcus to catch up.

It was rather noisy in the cab as the driver kept shifting
gears. There was no talking until highway speed was reached.
Once again Marcus mostly listened.

The driver laughed good-naturedly, "Anyone walking past
that corner is bound to need a ride. There's nothing for miles."

Marcus nodded in agreement.

"I'm heading north of Portage La Prairie."

"That's good. I'm going to Brandon," said Marcus.

Close to midnight they approached Deacon's Corner. The
driver turned on his signal and glanced over at Marcus, "I'm
ready for a bite."

Marcus shrugged and thought *and my preferences would make a difference?*

"I've got enough to get you a burger too," the driver grinned as he pulled onto the parking lot.

"Sounds good," Marcus said with a nod of acceptance. *I wonder if he'd be so willing to pay for a burger if he knew how much money I'm carrying.*

Before eating the driver bowed his head and uttered a simple prayer of thanks to God for the food and a blessing on 'this young man'.

Marcus was tired and hungry. He sat hunched over his food and nodded as the man talked about God.

"So, are you ready to meet your Maker?" the man asked with a questioning look.

"No plans to do so any time soon."

Marcus' indifferent attitude did not deter the driver. He cheerfully continued to talk about how God cared about each person; had prepared the way to an eternity in heaven, but wouldn't force it on anyone.

Between bites of his meal he emphasized that each person had to choose to believe that they needed a Savior; and that only Jesus could save them. By not making a choice, a person was in fact refusing the gift of eternal life.

Sounds just like Edith's gibberish. Marcus took another bite of his burger. *At least if he keeps talking, he won't bother me with personal questions.*

By now they were back in the cab. Marcus muttered, "Thanks for the burger," and leaned his head against the side of the truck. The driver took the hint and stopped talking and began to whistle a tune. It sounded just like one of those songs Edith and Charlotte used to sing after they'd been to church.

At least I'm safe from those goons for a few hours, thought Marcus. *I can put up with a bit of religion in trade for not having to keep watch over my shoulder.*

He must have fallen asleep because the noisy sound of gears shifting startled him. Marcus gasped and sat up abruptly. Then he remembered that he was safe for the moment. He sat back and rubbed his eyes. It felt good to roll his shoulders to get the kinks out of his neck.

He looked over and noticed that the driver was signaling to turn right. *This must be the city route through the town of Portage la Prairie.* Marcus glanced over at the dashboard. The clock showed that it was almost three in the morning.

"I'm heading north from here," said the driver as he pulled over. Before Marcus could open the door, the driver placed a hand on his shoulder and said, "Think about what I said, son. And who knows, if we don't meet again here on earth, maybe I'll see you on the glory side."

Marcus ducked his head and mumbled a soft, "Thanks for the lift," as he jumped down. He trudged back to the highway and set off at a brisk pace. He felt somewhat refreshed after the food and his nap. But the tension of keeping a lookout for Mr. Z's goons was back. Plus the guilt for taking Charlotte's money and the problem that it still wasn't enough, soon robbed him of the newfound energy.

Chapter Forty-Four

Shivering against the cold of the early October morning, Marcus hunched forward against the stiff breeze as he hurried along the highway. There were no trees to hide him whenever car lights appeared. He had to lay flat on his face in the ditch, hoping that he'd blend in with the dried grass. Thank goodness there were more trucks than cars at this time of the day.

Dawn lightened the sky, making it harder to hide but at least he didn't have to hide from every vehicle; only the sleek black ones.

Marcus had reached the town of Virden before another semi slowed down to pick him up. He breathed a sigh of relief as he let his tense body sag against the seat. A few miles down the road, he pushed his shoes off his feet and wriggled his toes. *Ahh, that feels good.* He closed his eyes. *I'm safe from Mr. Z's thugs for a little while.* The steady drone of the engine, along with his extreme fatigue, soon lulled him to sleep.

The driver geared down as they approached Swift Current. The air-brakes gave a sharp hiss and then all was quiet. They had come to a stop beside the gas pumps. Marcus nodded when the driver said, "We've got time to grab a bite to eat while the truck is being refueled."

Marcus headed for the Dairy Queen. He was startled to see a girl that looked just like Charlotte getting on a bus. *But it can't be. She's back in Zhoda.*

On the road again, the sight of that girl made Marcus's thoughts turn to Charlotte. He hoped that Mr. Z's goons hadn't shown up at her door. He hoped she'd know enough not to open the door to strangers. *But she probably would, she's such a goody goody, just like she opened it for me without knowing who had knocked at the door. But she deserves better than getting hurt by those goons. I mean, she didn't even yell at me for asking for money. She was just being reasonable when she said she couldn't get it tonight.*

His mind kept accusing and excusing himself. *But there's nothing I could have done about it. They'd just hurt us both. Without me, they might just ask her a lot of questions. God, why do all these problems keep coming? What am I going to do?*

His heavy sigh drew the driver's attention. He looked over at Marcus and asked, "Are you okay, buddy?"

Marcus nodded and opened his mouth to say that he was fine. He gulped back his words because just then a sleek black car pulled in front of the truck and braked. To avoid hitting it, the truck driver swerved into the left lane.

As they picked up speed again, Marcus pushed back against the seat to be less visible. He eyed the driver of the black car as they passed it. "Oh no," he muttered, "It's Mr. Z's goons alright. How do they know so quickly where I am?" His quiet words were covered by the noise in the cab.

They passed the auto and pulled back into the right lane. The driver shook his head in wonderment, "What's the matter with that driver? Why in the world would he pass, only to slow down in front of a big rig like this? Does he think I can stop on a dime?" He shifted gears a couple of times before he said, "It makes you wonder what some folks are thinking, or if they're thinking at all."

Marcus nodded in agreement and allowed a smile to appear for a moment. He could taste his relief at being safe in the truck instead of out on the road. *There's no way they can see me in here.* His shoulders began to relax. He hadn't even realized how tense he'd become. But he kept a careful watch on the car. In the side view mirror he saw when the limo turned off the road. Marcus felt great relief that the truck driver kept on going. But he mustn't take any chances. He needed to be extra cautious now that he knew they were headed back to Kelowna.

In Lethbridge Marcus said thank you to the truck driver and headed over to McD's. Fifteen minutes later he was back on the road. Fear of being spotted by the goons, Marcus kept a sharp ear out for any approaching vehicles from behind him. This tension took extra energy and created a great weariness in him.

A pick-up truck slowed down as it passed him and pulled over onto the shoulder a few yards in front of him. It backfired and Marcus froze to the spot. Color returned to his face when he realized that it had not been a gunshot.

Hillbilly music poured through the open windows. Marcus kept his eyes wide open and approached the vehicle with caution. The driver reached over to open the passenger door for Marcus to get in.

"Howdy." The greeting was abrupt, but kindly. The older man was chewing on a piece of hay or wheat or straw.

Marcus didn't know which it was. He nodded a return greeting and huddled sideways against the corner.

The man reached for the radio and turned down the music, "Keeps me company since the wife passed away."

Marcus nodded again but still didn't say anything because he knew his teeth would chatter. He shivered and crossed his arms for a bit of protection against the cold wind blowing through the open window.

The old man must have noticed. Without a word he rolled up both windows and turned on the heat. Marcus was thankful that the man didn't need to carry on a conversation. As the warmth seeped into his body, drowsiness crept over Marcus.

His head drooped lower and lower. Twice he jerked it back upright. Each time he sent a quick glance at the old man, who seemed to be content to listen to the music.

Finally Marcus allowed himself to relax and sleep took over.

Chapter Forty-Five

2002 October 9th

When they reached the outskirts of Kelowna, Marcus said, "Thanks, this will do." He jumped out of the truck and hurried to a city bus stop. Passengers were still getting off the bus as he approached. Marcus was glad that he didn't have to wait out in the open. He felt very vulnerable knowing Mr. Z's goons were headed west again. All he wanted was to get to the Casino and hand over the money. Even though it wasn't the full amount, he was desperately hoping that Mr. Z would make a once and for all deal.

Marcus paid the fare and made his way to an open seat near the back. He ignored the covert glances sent his way. He knew that his clothes were beyond dirty and crumpled looking. His dirty fingernails bothered him too, but not enough to stop him from heading straight to Mr. Z's office.

At the Casino he caught sight of his disheveled hair in one of the many mirrors as he strode down the long hallway. He tried to finger comb it before facing Mr. Z but the tangles were too thick.

Marcus found the office door partially open. He pushed at it with one finger. Its hinges creaked. Mr. Z jumped up from crouching behind the desk. His face blanched and then turned crimson.

He's acting mighty suspicious thought Marcus as he stepped into the room. *What's he hiding, a safe in the floor?*

With raised eyebrows but not a word, Marcus stepped forward and handed the money over to Mr. Z. He took a step back and waited.

Abe glanced from the certified cheque to Marcus. He cleared his throat before he crumpled it and straightened it again, to make sure it was genuine. "What'd ya do ta come up with this much dough?"

"Does it matter?" retorted Marcus.

Abe chuckled mirthlessly and raised a hand, "Hey, don't get your shirt in a knot." He stuffed the cheque into his pocket and said, "I got a new job for ya."

"What? Who's looking after Myrna?" demanded Marcus. Angry eyes and a deep frown showed his disapproval that he wouldn't be the one walking and talking with her. He'd been planning to share about his harrowing trip back to the old home town. Myrna was the only one who would understand.

"She's gone." The finality in Mr. Z's voice made Marcus pause, even as it raised troubling questions in his mind. He hid his frustration and waited for further instructions.

Abe's shrewd eyes narrowed as they tried to pierce through Marcus' wall of defense. Finally he gave up, shrugged and laughed.

Marcus kept his clenched fists at his side. He hated the sound of Mr. Z's mocking laugh and wanted nothing more than to punch the guy's lights out.

"Go get cleaned up. Ya look like you've been through a mighty rough bout. Then come and sit for a round of your favorite game. You need to relax." It wasn't a request. It was an order.

But Marcus shook his head, "Don't want to. I just need more work so I can pay off the rest of that IOU"

"What's the matter with you? Are ya sick?"

Marcus straightened up to his full height and pulled his shoulders back. Dirty and rumpled as he was, he must have still made an imposing figure because Abe quickly took a step back.

Marcus realized that through it all, Mr. Z was extra tense. His suspicion deepened. *Something isn't right. I wonder what happened while I was gone.*

***

Abe was seldom around in the days that followed, but all his assignments kept Marcus tied to the Casino. It seemed a conspiracy that he was not allowed out on the street. His time was spent walking the floor, taking care of problematic guests or escorting folks to the requested table.

The crisp fresh air that came in with people increased his longing for his old job, when he walked and talked with Myrna as he escorted her to her home. When he dialed Myrna's number all he got was a recording that said the number was no longer in service. How frustrating!

These days his duties were never given in person. He found notes that demanded immediate attention. The only time he got outdoors was when he had to drive the limo on an errand. When he had packages to deliver, the drop-off was never in Myrna's part of town. And Marcus was always given a narrow time slot, which did not allow for him to make a side trip. He fretted and worried about all the possibilities.

Marcus noticed that whenever Mr. Z showed up it was early in the morning or late at night. He was always in a hurry, casting furtive glances over his shoulder.

What happened while I was gone? I know Mr. Z was usually uptight but this is unreal. Something is definitely not right. I wonder; did Myrna get to the cops? Is that why Mr. Z is hiding out?

Marcus' thoughts sped along. Tension hung in the air as the President of the Casino, who had been mostly invisible up till now, seemed to be everywhere barking orders at everyone.

None of it made sense. Marcus' wondering about what must have happened during his short absence increased, especially as no one talked. And there were new guys walking around silently. They seemed to be spying on everyone, eavesdropping on conversations and always in someone's way.

Even the kitchen staff that usually cheered him up was tight-lipped and non-communicative. No one made eye contact as they worked feverishly at their given tasks.

One thing Marcus was glad about, the goons seemed to have disappeared. *Perhaps they were in hiding with Mr. Z.*

Chapter Forty-Six

The week before Christmas Marcus heard angry voices
coming from the big boss' office. He thought that one of
the voices sounded almost like Mr. Z. *I wonder what trouble
he's in. Not that that would make me sad. He's such an evil
man.*

The office door swung open just as Marcus passed it. He
glanced over his shoulder. A short man with a crooked body
was scuttling toward the back elevator. It wasn't Mr. Z.

The President came to the door. His face had a grim look
about it. When he saw Marcus he nodded at him. "Please step
in here for a minute."

He obeyed without a question. After all, this man owned
the Casino. The first thing Marcus noticed when he stepped
into the room was the huge desk. Every inch of it was covered
with folders and unopened mail. Definitely not the clean desk
he would have expected. The few times Marcus had seen this
man at the Casino, he'd been dressed to the nines, strutting
through the Casino with hands behind his back and a satisfied
smile on his rugged face.

Now it seemed that he had become involved with every
detail of the business. Marcus turned his gaze to the man and
waited patiently to be enlightened.

The President cleared his throat before he gave Marcus a
forced smile. "I just want you to know that I've noticed your
diligence and capable handling of our clients. I'd like you to

take over as host in the games room. The players' confidence in our establishment needs to be reestablished."

The fact that he was being offered a cushy job with more pay didn't lessen the angst that filled Marcus.

Steely grey eyes focused on Marcus. The hand that reached across the desk to shake his was cold and hard. The grip almost crushed his fingers. He shivered. It brought back vivid memories of the goons' attack.

The man tapped his hand on the folders spread out in front of him. He stopped on a red one. "I'm curious. Can you explain why there is such a big debt noted beside your name?"

Marcus' face flushed. He swore under his breath. He leaned forward with his eyes fixed on the red folder even though it was closed. "It's less than a thousand, Sir. I gave Mr. Z a cheque for the rest. And I swear that I haven't taken another cent from him since."

The president narrowed his eyes and stared at Marcus for a full minute before he said, "Well, there's no record of any credit besides the weekly sum being deducted from your wages."

With a quick intake of breath, Marcus declared, "I gave him a certified cheque!"

The man opened and closed the file a couple of times before he spoke. "Seeing as it appears to be a personal debt to Abe and he seems to be making himself scarce these days, we'll put it aside and let him deal with it."

The President changed topic so fast Marcus could only stare at him. The questions being fired at him were all about Mr. Z's possible whereabouts. Marcus could only stammer that he did not know.

Just as quickly, the man backed off and said, "Go and enjoy your day. But if anything comes to light about where Abe is at, you'll be sure to let me know." It was an order.

Over the next week, the President slipped some very generous tips into Marcus' hands. He winked as he explained that these tips were from the women that Marcus had escorted to the tables. Marcus wasn't going to look a gift horse in the mouth. It just meant more money to pay off his debt. Most of which should already have been paid.

He gritted his teeth, "That crook! I should've known that Mr. Z would pocket the cheque! And after all I went through to get it."

He'd hoped to be free of this place by now. His shoulders sagged and he slumped against the wall. "Now I'll be old and grey before I get out of here."

Day and night undercover police were crawling all over the establishment. The staff had quit talking to each other lest something they said would be overheard and used to incriminate them.

The President appeared at any given moment with questions, trying to force a confession out of someone. He wanted information about Abe's extra activity, especially as it had brought big trouble to his business, and he had no one to blame.

Marcus did not have any answers either, not even for his own questions. *I wasn't gone that long. I wonder what happened for Mr. Z to make himself scarce. I didn't think anything could frighten that man. Myrna must have got word to the cops.*

Marcus stood in the middle of his room and heaved a big sigh. *If only I could find out about Myrna? How are her disappearance and Mr. Z's odd behavior connected?* He shook his head as if to erase the horrible possibility.

***

December 25^{th,} 2002 was a just another day of work, except busier than usual. By the end of his shift Marcus barely made it to his room. He fell across the bed, face down and didn't wake up until mid-morning. Stiff and sore from not having moved all night, he groaned as he got out of bed. "Here's hoping that a shower will wake up my bones."

His thoughts returned to all his unanswered questions as the hot water eased his aches and pains. If only it could calm his tortured mind as well.

Marcus had tried Myrna's number numerous times. Each time the line was busy or he heard the recording that stated the number was no longer in service. His angst quickly turned into anger at the thought of harm coming to Myrna. His promise to help the daughter was out the window. He couldn't even help himself. Hot water streamed from his clenched fists as he grappled with his rage. Anger mixed with the feeling of helplessness and frustration almost overwhelmed him

***

The New Year had come and gone. The police had disappeared and the President had left off with the questions. Tensions lessened for everyone except Marcus. He missed Myrna. It felt worse than when he'd been abandoned by his mother.

The kitchen staff couldn't understand the great sadness that enveloped him. Things were back to normal, weren't they? So what was the problem? Trying to think of how they could cheer him up they checked the records for his birthdate.

On March 10th Marcus walked into the kitchen to shouts of "Surprise!" A birthday cake with 26 unlit candles sat in the middle of the table. The same number of balloons hung in his usual corner.

"What!" he asked in surprise. "Who?" he sank into the chair, "How did you know?"

They laughed and shouted at him all at the same time. Gila edged over with a cigarette lighter and did the honors of lighting the candles. She chucked him under the chin and said, "Enjoy."

Marcus forced himself to be charming. He smiled and ate and thanked them for such a caring act. He told them how much he appreciated it because he had no one left to celebrate with and no one to care about what happened to him.

Chapter Forty-Seven

M arcus felt like the restraints woven around him were prison walls. He seemed to be hedged in at every turn. He was kept too busy and he was too tired and discouraged to take a walk by himself. For whatever reason, he no longer got to drive the limo. How could he find out what happened to Myrna when he was stuck indoors and Mr. Z wasn't available for questioning.

Today as his eyes roved over the crowd looking for troublemakers, Marcus mused on the fact that it was June 30th, 2003. Charlotte would be twenty years old. He wondered what she was doing and who would celebrate the day with her.

Regret filled him whenever he thought of how he had had to rob her. But that was something he couldn't change. He had needed the money to get out of Mr. Z's clutches. He was sure Charlotte would have wanted to help him if she'd known about his situation. His chest tightened when he remembered that now it was all for nothing.

That evening Marcus looked up her phone number. But as soon he heard it ring he chickened out and hung up. "What will I say? Hope you're having a good birthday, even though I stole all your money?" His sardonic laugh echoed off the walls in his room.

An hour later he sat up in bed. He couldn't get Charlotte out of his mind. He dialed her number again. Marcus almost panicked at the sound of a voice. Before he could hang up again, he realized that it was a recording saying that the number was no longer in service.

He hung up and frowned at the phone. Only two phone numbers that could matter to him and both were no longer in service. *Of all the rotten luck! Why me?*

He walked to the window and gazed down at the few vehicles still on the street. *I wonder what happened to her. Did she move? Perhaps she can't afford to live there anymore.* He slumped down on the edge of the bed and dropped his head in his hands.

***

A narrow window of free time opened for Marcus in the middle of July. The President sent him on a personal errand. He slid behind the wheel of a beautiful shiny, dark grey Mercedes-Benz. The sun was shining as he merged with the busy traffic. His destination was two blocks from Myrna's building. A bit of a smile appeared on his face at the thought of being near her place.

With a few minutes to spare after the job was completed, Marcus decided to risk being late and drove to Myrna's apartment. He saw Sherry come out the front door and pulled over to the sidewalk. He pushed the button to roll down the passenger window and called out, "Hey, Sherry, I've only got a minute."

She came closer to the car and leaned down to look inside, "Oh, it's you Marcus. I didn't recognize the car."

"It belongs to the President. Where is Myrna?"

A strange look crossed her face and her hand came up to her mouth. "Where have you been, Marcus?"

Something was wrong. His heart beat painfully in his chest as he waited, dreading to hear her words, even though he'd been expecting them.

"Marcus, she was shot."

He gasped. His mouth snapped shut. Then he ground out between clenched teeth, "So it's true. I didn't want to let myself believe it. How did it happen?"

"Back in…" Sherry knelt beside the car, "Are you okay? You look like you're going to be sick."

Marcus glanced at the clock on the dashboard. "I have to get back but I need to hear more." Eyes narrowed to mere slits, he growled, "When do you have free time?"

She stood up. "Ha, it's more like when don't I have free time these days. You just come by when you can. Don't even bother to call, just come."

"Thanks, I'll try to come tomorrow before work. That is - if I can escape. It feels like I'm in jail and I'm beginning to understand why," said Marcus with a grim voice. He waved at Sherry, turned on the signal and pulled out into the street.

***

Next morning, shortly before five o'clock Marcus got off the bus. He was just in time to see a young woman come out of the apartment. She looked exactly like a young Myrna. His heart skipped a beat even as he realized that it had to be her daughter, the one he was supposed to protect from Mr. Z.

He saw Sherry standing at the top of the stairs. She waved at the girl who hurried down the street. Marcus strode quickly to where Sherry stood.

"That's Myrna's daughter? How old is she, about fifteen?"

"She'll be eighteen on her next birthday. Her brother Davy is fifteen," said Sherry.

"Pretty girl," he murmured. "No wonder she didn't want Mr. Z to get his hands on her."

Sherry watched the girl until she crossed at the corner. Then she turned to go indoors. Marcus followed her into the apartment. She held up the coffee pot and motioned to see if he wanted some.

"Sure." He pulled out a chair and sat down at the end of the table. Silence filled the room as each took a swallow of the hot brew. Then he raised pain-filled eyes and asked, "What happened?"

"Abe shot her. I didn't see him do it. I was out looking for work, but I just know it was him. Dora won't say a word. She just walks around with a haunted look. She jumps at the slightest sound and hovers over Davy, trying to protect him like a mother hen. Whatever happened, that girl is scared stiff. She was always a quiet kid but now she is a quiet, terrified kid!" Sherry spat out the words.

Her angry look changed to concern. She looked up at Marcus and said, "I'm so glad you weren't around. I think Abe wanted to put the blame on you. He got raving mad when he couldn't find you. He kept coming around, asking about you, wanting to know if we'd seen you."

Marcus reached out a trembling hand and covered hers where it rested on the table. He wasn't used to hearing such caring words.

"By the way, where were you?" she asked. Her face turned red. She pulled her hand free and dropped it into her lap. "I…I'm sorry, Marcus. It's none of my business but I was so worried for you."

"I ran away." His eyes were mesmerized by the dark liquid in his cup as he explained. "Remember when I called to warn you? Mr. Z wanted me to waste Myrna. I told him that I could never shoot anyone and especially not her."

He felt his cheeks warm with embarrassment as he caught her keen scrutiny of him. "I'm sorry I took off after I called." He added in a bitter voice, "I wouldn't have been much help anyway. I had to get away because of Mr. Z's goons. They beat me up before and I didn't want to fall into their hands again."

He saw Sherry grab at her throat and catch her breath. He quickly added, "I really am sorry. I should have stayed, especially knowing what they are capable of. I don't deserve it, but thanks for caring. No one else does."

The wall clock ticked away the minutes in its relentless beat. Both of them sat quietly, each caught up in their own thoughts. Sherry got up and refilled their cups.

Marcus asked, "So why did Mr. Z have to kill Myrna? I've never met a nicer person. How could he do such an awful thing?" Marcus slapped his hand on the table and Sherry jumped. "Sorry, didn't mean to scare you."

"It's okay," she shook her head and wiped a drop of spilled coffee from her hand. "Please continue. What reason would Abe have?"

"I should have known as soon as he told me that she was gone. But I didn't want to believe it. The reason he wanted her done in was because he heard a rumor that she was going to rat on him. Yep, that's what made him do it."

Marcus realized that he had been musing out loud. "Sorry for blabbering."

"No problem," she smiled in sympathy. "I have to pray a lot not to hate that guy."

"Well, I have no problem hating him," Marcus retorted. "Why wouldn't you hate him?"

She shrugged a shoulder and replied in a softened voice, "Because it wouldn't change a thing. It would only drain me of energy and imprison me."

"*He* ought to be in prison!" exclaimed Marcus.

"I totally agree," said Sherry, "But I still must choose to forgive him, otherwise the hatred will destroy me."

"Now you sound just like Myrna and like my foster mom."

"Thank you, Marcus. I believe you could pay me no finer compliment."

"Sorry, Sherry, but I can't see it your way. If the law won't punish him, then I will."

Sherry cried out against his dark threat, "Oh no, Marcus! Please promise me that you won't take things into your own hands."

"Just give me the chance." His clenched hands, low voice and narrowed eyes showed that he was not kidding.

He opened his fists and stretched his fingers to ease Sherry's distress. "You don't have to worry yet. I haven't seen him since shortly after I returned. It looks like he's on the outs with the President of the company. At least that's who I've been getting my orders from these days."

Marcus noticed the time on the stove clock and stood up. "Thank you for the coffee and for filling me in about Myrna. But since this trip is on my own time, I have to catch a bus. Hopefully I'll make it back on time."

Sherry followed him to the door. "Sorry that you have to hurry away but I'm glad you stopped by. Any time you want to talk more about this whole situation…just come over."

"Thanks. I will. Right now I've got to run. I don't want to give them any excuse to dock my pay. I want that debt paid off so I can get out of there." He paused at the door and turned to face Sherry, "Then I'm going to hunt down Mr. Z. He needs someone to teach him a lesson."

"Please promise me that you won't do anything foolish, Marcus. And be very careful, I don't trust Abe."

Chapter Forty-Eight

His phone rang. Marcus' breath quickened at the sound of
Mr. Z's voice. "Sure I can meet you." His eyes narrowed
to mere slits. "No, I won't be late."

The call ended and he went in search of a co-worker.
Marcus knew that the man always carried a piece. It was part
of his job as security. It was just what he needed for this
meeting with Mr. Z.

"Sure you can borrow it. But, do you even know how to
use it?"

"Just show me how to aim and shoot," said Marcus. He
didn't grin like the oaf in front of him. He was deadly serious.

As luck would have it, Marcus did not have to report for
duty until after his appointment with Mr. Z.

When he got off the bus Marcus saw the man's car parked
in front of Zack's Diner. He knew the place well, having
dropped off many 'parcels' at the side door. Now he
approached with caution. He needed to be in control of the
situation and that meant taking Mr. Z by surprise. He snuck
past the side door and paused to listen at the window. He heard
Mr. Z's loud voice arguing on the phone even though the
window was closed. The timing was perfect.

Marcus pulled out the gun and didn't even think of the
instructions he'd been given about its use. He smashed the
window with his left fist. Right hand extended, he stepped
through the broken glass with the gun aimed at Mr. Z's head as

he shouted, "You double crossin' imbecile! Why did you have to kill Myrna?"

Abe dropped the phone, whipped out his pistol and fired in one smooth move. He missed because Marcus tripped over an extension cord and fell to one knee at just that moment. The bullet whistled past Marcus' right ear. A scream ripped through the air, followed almost immediately by a police siren.

Marcus' gun flew across the floor as Abe shoved him out of the way and escaped through the broken window. Marcus staggered, already off balance; he fell heavily to the floor. The gun on the floor was pointing straight at him. It seemed to mock him. He got up onto his knees in bewilderment. Things were definitely not progressing as planned.

Then he remembered the scream. In haste he crawled on hands and knees over the broken pieces of glass. He peered out the window and saw the still form of a young lad. Quickly he clambered out and reached for the boy. He cradled the bloody head in his hands and cried, "Oh no, please, if there really is a God, please don't let him be hurt bad."

Before Marcus knew what happened, handcuffs were snapped on his wrists and he was jerked away from the boy. His sudden removal made the boy's head crack against the sidewalk. Enraged, Marcus lunged away from his captor and reached towards the boy, but the shackles stopped him.

"Leave the kid. You've done enough damage."

Marcus heard the harsh words; uncaring words; lies. He hadn't hurt the kid. It was Mr. Z's gun that had been fired. His gun had not even been discharged. But no one listened, or seemed to care to check out his statement.

"We're up to our ears with you guys." The words were snarled close to his ear. "You bunch of drug pushers and greedy cold-hearted pimps. Well we've got one of you now. Your gang's going down."

The words chilled Marcus to the core. He saw an ambulance pull up as he was shoved into the back seat of a patrol car.

At least the boy has a chance of being taken care of. Marcus' mind couldn't erase the sound of the poor kid's head hitting the pavement. And his anger at Mr. Z grew to include the hard-hearted officers. *Did they actually think I would hang around if I was guilty? They're probably too busy to see past their agenda to use some common sense. But I hope the kid doesn't die. I'll get blamed as usual; just my rotten luck.*

Marcus couldn't help but overhear the conversation in the front seat as they headed back to the station.

"The big guy has disappeared."

"Of course."

"What about the package we were told about?"

A guffaw came from the front. "Ya, like he'd leave that behind. Probably worth like a thousand bucks! Maybe even ten grand."

"Yea, I'd run too. But we'll get him."

"Who called in the tip-off?"

"I don't know. I heard it was some dame."

***

Marcus languished in the cell, a small room with only a narrow cot. Anger raged through him, mixed with frustration at his helpless situation. There was no one to care what happened to him; no one to bail him out. Sherry couldn't and the President wouldn't. *He only cares about keeping his hands clean.*

Marcus sat, hunched over on the side of the cot. His head hung low and his hands were clenched in his lap. A cigarette hung from his mouth. He did not notice the ray of sunshine shining through the bars, trying to warm up his cell.

When he was ordered outside for exercise, he must have been too slow to obey. One guard stepped over and jerked him off the cot and across the room. The second guard shoved him along the short hallway. Marcus remained mute, which only seemed to irritate his 'helpers'. *I guess they want to make me talk, hoping to get some secret information...if they only knew. I don't even know where Mr. Z hangs out away from work, never mind when he's in hiding.*

Out in the yard Marcus circled the fence, never far from the guards. The July sun beat down on him. The warmth felt good after being cooped up the cold cell. He tuned in to the guards conversation.

"The bullet doesn't match this guy's gun," he flicked his head toward Marcus, "But they're gonna keep him locked up anyway. They're hoppin' mad at all the crimes being committed right under their noses."

The guard went face to face with Marcus when his steps took him close to the two. "Someone's gotta take the fall and it looks like you're it." "And He gave a short derisive laugh.

The second guard glared at Marcus. "Yeah, it may as well be you, seein' as we got you nice and safe in here."

"And I heard the sergeant's keeping a real close eye on the big guy's lady-friend, hoping to nab him when he tries to sneak home."

"Lotsa luck there. I hear she don't seem to care much that he's in trouble."

"Yea, probably was her that called the cops on him. Who else would've known?"

Marcus tuned out all their surmising, and turned back to his own situation. *What's going to happen to me? I'm stuck in here and no one knows or cares.*

"Hey, move along, Bub."

Marcus was startled out of his reverie as one of the guards prodded him with a baton. He stepped away from the fence where he'd propped himself up and stretched to his full height.

It gave him a grim sense of satisfaction when the guard took a quick step back. *If they only knew how little they need to fear me. I can't even shoot a guy that deserves it.*

Back in the cell Marcus paused in his self-pity party. *I wonder what Myrna's daughter is doing. Who's looking out for her?* His eyes roved around the cell. *Now I can't even keep my promise to help protect Dora.* He dropped his head into his hands as his mind continued to whirl about wildly. *Does Sherry have the means? I know her heart is in the right place, but she can't even get a steady job. She probably has a hard time looking after herself. And what could she do against that big brute?* "Oh, how I wish that I could have won big. I'd have taken them all far away from here."

The black cloud of worry over his head grew heavier as he fretted and fumed, "And now I'll never get the chance to win big. I'm going down for a murder that I didn't commit."

"Oh God, why do I keep having all this bad luck?" He stretched out full length on the cot and sank into a stupor. He let his mind go to a blank place. That way there was less pain and stress.

Late in the afternoon a loud banging against his cell door woke Marcus and brought back the weight of all his problems.

"Someone to see ya," barked the guard and stepped to the side, holding the cell door open.

Marcus rose slowly and inhaled deeply. His muscles ached from lying motionless for so long. He wondered who on earth would come to see him. Determined to not let the guard see his anxiety, he moved forward with slow, deliberate steps.

"Hurry it up. Ya ain't got all day," growled the guard. Then he had the nerve to grab Marcus by the upper arm and pull him out of the cell. He prodded him along the hallway and into the room at the end. The room held a couple of inmates, each with a phone pressed to their ear.

Marcus was shoved into an empty seat and a phone was thrust into his hand. Begrudgingly, he shifted his eyes to the glass window, curious to see who the visitor could be.

"Charlotte?" He brushed a hand over his eyes. *This can't be real. What's she doing here, in this town?* In shock, he didn't hear half of what she was saying. *First I get arrested for a crime I didn't commit and now I have to deal with a ghost from my past. She has to be a ghost. Because what would she be doing here?*

His breathing became labored when he heard her say something about working at Zach's Diner. He glowered in frustration, trying to get in control of his thoughts. *She can't be serious. Why would she be...* He realized that Charlotte had closed her mouth and stepped back. *She must think that I'm mad at her. Actually I am. What a time to find me! As if I don't have enough to deal with already. Is she here to charge me with theft?*

"Marcus..."

He heard the apprehension in her voice. But he couldn't respond in a civil manner. "What are you doing here?" he growled.

"I left Steinbach about a year ago. I've been working at Zach's Diner here in Kelowna. Yesterday a kid was shot outside the building. Rumor said that you were in jail because you shot him. I couldn't believe that. But I had to come down here and check for myself, to see if it was really you." Her words rushed along too fast for him to comprehend.

He frowned at her, his lips a thin hard line. "What do you mean you work at Zach's? Do you owe Mr. Z as well?"

"Pardon me? I don't have much money but I'm not in debt."

A short moment of relief swept over him at the fact that she wasn't owned by Mr. Z. But it was hard to believe that she would willingly work for the guy.

Charlotte looked at him, blinked a couple of times and then stared at the wall behind him when he didn't say anything else. Finally she said, "I brought you some of Ted's cinnamon buns. They're declared to be the best in the world."

The hopefulness in her voice irritated Marcus as shame nudged his conscience. "Whatever," he grunted. "I imagine they'll feed me in here." Dark eyebrows lowered as he hid his angry eyes. *She can't be for real. It's got to be a bad dream. But if it's really her, it could only be to laugh at me, to get her revenge.*

Marcus looked up again and saw that her face was filled with worry. He had to believe her when she said, "I came as soon as I heard that you were here." But he hated her questions, mostly because he didn't have any answers; answers he desperately wanted as well.

But most disturbing was her claim to be working at Zack's Diner. That meant they were both working for the same evil shyster. Her voice pulled him back to the present.

"When you get out of here you should stop in for a meal. Ted is an excellent cook." She hesitated before she added, "And maybe...and maybe we could catch up on each other's life," she finished in a rush.

"Yeah, sure." He slouched back, "As if I'll ever get outta here."

"But Marcus, surely they'll prove your innocence and let you go."

"If only I'd shot him," muttered Marcus. Charlotte's gasp made him explain, "Not the boy. I mean Mr. Z. He's a liar and a cheat. A thief! And he killed my only friend." Marcus' face darkened at the remembrance. His body slumped down even further. "So I guess I deserve to be here, either way."

When Charlotte quickly offered to get Mr. Rand, her lawyer friend involved, Marcus laughed. "Ha!" It sounded like a sharp bark. "As if any lawyer would care to waste his time on the likes of me. Besides I don't have any money. Lawyers don't work for free in case you didn't know. Don't waste his time or yours."

Oh how Marcus hated to be incarcerated; to have Charlotte see him this way. He didn't know how else to deal with it but to let anger take the lead. Through gritted teeth he declared, "I don't need help from anyone and especially not from you!"

He turned away so he wouldn't have to see the tears in her eyes. As he pulled the phone from his ear he heard the words, 'I give up, Marcus. Have it your way, I won't bother you anymore.'

Despair filled him as he turned to the waiting guard. He was pulled and pushed with extra vehemence, but he didn't resent it. He deserved every bit of meanness that they could give him. The guard couldn't have helped but overhear his uncaring words to his sister. Add that to being a suspect of murder, it was no wonder they had it in for him.

At first he felt glad that Charlotte's voice had sounded mad at the end. That was better than having her pity him. But shame soon crept in and wouldn't be tamped down. His behavior toward her, after she'd made the effort to seek him out, was abominable. He was no better than Mr. Z.

He flung himself down on the cot and let the tears of grief flow freely. *She only means good. She doesn't deserve to suffer from my anger. If only I could tell her that it's not her fault. It's that boss of mine.*

Marcus grabbed the corner of his shirt and swiped at his eyes. But the tears, now that they'd been released, kept streaming down his cheeks. He cried until he was exhausted. Sleep finally overcame his anguish.

Next thing he knew, it was the wakeup call. The guards banged on all the doors. Marcus hoped that it meant breakfast. He was hungry.

Day followed monotonous day. No news of what went on in the outside world filtered down to Marcus. Listless from inactivity and no one to talk to, the days and weeks crept by.

One day a big ruckus happened down the hallway, but it stopped as quickly as it started. Marcus didn't hear what it had been about.

I wonder why nothing is happening in my case. Why haven't I been summoned to face a judge yet? At least then I'd know what was what. His deep sigh echoed loudly off the bare walls. *I'll probably rot in here.* He rolled over onto his side. *Charlotte kept her word. She hasn't come back again. Too bad I can't tell Sherry to warn her to be careful around Mr. Z.*

Chapter Forty-Nine

Marcus was freed as suddenly as he'd been jailed with no explanation. One moment he was sitting on his cot trying to keep sane in the quiet monotony. The next moment he was standing on the sidewalk in bewilderment with the cacophony of noises all around him.

He sauntered over to the side of the building to think. He had been apprehended with only the clothes on his back and that's all he had now. His wallet was empty and he hadn't even been given his breakfast.

Marcus was determined not to return to the Casino. That left him without a home. He'd made no friends beside Myrna and she was gone. He was too ashamed to go find Charlotte.

Alone and hungry, he pushed away from the wall and headed downtown. *I've survived on dumpster fare before and I can do it again. At least this time I know where the good restaurants are. Maybe one of them is looking to hire.*

Marcus went into the first restaurant he came to. When he asked to see the manager he was told to come back at ten. Marcus turned to leave and decided to zigzag to the left. One of the empty tables had a lot of food left on it. A fat biscuit and half an egg rested on one plate. Another plate had two slices of buttered toast and a rasher of bacon. *It's a good thing for me that folks are so wasteful.* He glanced over his shoulder. The maître d' was speaking to another couple. Marcus quickly snatched a table napkin and wrapped the food in it. As he exited he realized that it was a cloth one. "Oh well," he shrugged a shoulder, "Right now, survival is of utmost importance."

No matter how many places he stopped to inquire about a job, no one would hire him. Apparently his face had been plastered on the front page of all the newspapers. The curse of having such a handsome face was that everyone recognized him.

Weak from lack of proper nourishment and sleeping on the cold ground, Marcus grew more and more discouraged. He developed a cough which only got worse from his life of deprivation.

The day came when he decided to give up. He couldn't go on like this. His footsteps dragged. The few street lamps along the path left a lot of dark spots in the park.

He heard a flapping sound to his left. On stepping closer to investigate he saw that the wind had blown a large cardboard box into the park. It had become wedged between a maple tree and the park bench.

It's just what I need for my final resting place. They can bury me in it. He gave a dry laugh which ended up in a bout of coughing that left him exhausted.

When the coughing stopped he pulled the box free, opened the top flaps and crawled in. Try as he might, he couldn't pull or twist enough to get all of himself into it.

He shivered. Each breath intake rattled in his lungs. He felt goose bumps on the top of his head. No matter how tight he pulled his arms against his chest, it didn't feel any warmer. He tried to slow down his breathing. *I wonder how long it will take to die.*

***

"Hey there big fella."

Marcus stirred. The voice came again. It sounded far away.

"Come on out of there."

Marcus tried to sit up and then remembered he was inside a box. He groaned as he straightened his legs. At least he tried to but they wouldn't cooperate. He pushed against the sides with his hands and managed to slide out far enough that he could sit up. Through bleary eyes he saw a young man on his knees close by; a smile on his face and a hand held out for assistance. Marcus stared at the hand. The young man was persistent.

"Hi, my name's Davy. I know of a place, just a couple of blocks from here where you can get warm and a bite to eat."

Together they got Marcus up on his feet. Trembling legs and bouts of coughing made the few blocks seem to stretch out forever, but they finally made it.

Marcus held back when he recognized Zach's Diner, but the young man placed an arm around Marcus' shoulders and urged him forward.

"Just a few more steps and you'll see. No one asks questions here. These folks want to provide a safe place out of the cold. Apparently the Boss doesn't mind so long as it doesn't cost him anything. They have a group of singers, volunteers from a church. They're easy to listen to." Davy smiled in encouragement. "You're going to be okay, big guy."

One step through the open door and Marcus was face to face with Charlotte. He shook his head and tried to stammer a response to her greeting but the effort brought forth a racking cough instead.

The evening passed in a blur. There was food and hot coffee. Someone kept pressing more food on him. At times Charlotte sat across from him, but he had a hard time focusing on what she was saying.

Marcus was thankful that Davy had come to his rescue and had brought him to the Diner but he wasn't able to understand how he was connected to the others.

The days that followed were a blur. All he knew was that he was in a warm room, on a comfortable bed. A doctor kept hanging over him and talking to him but Marcus couldn't focus on what he was saying.

Then the nightmares began. He found himself in a cold dark tunnel filled with pain; always running, trying to keep one step ahead of Mr. Z's goons. Was he ever going to be safe? Charlotte's gentle voice was the only thing that could pull him back, away from the terror. Sometimes he heard her singing. The songs made him think of home and being safe.

In his more lucid moments, he heard them talk about a lung infection and wondered who they were talking about.

Too weak to argue, Marcus let Charlotte take care of him. He appreciated her constant presence and tried to tell her. But the words never seemed to leave his mouth. She didn't pester him with a lot of questions, just tended to his needs. And she never left him without a cool hand to his forehead. It felt like the touch of an angel.

He began to stay awake for longer times. Charlotte was always there, sitting beside his bed. It made him feel secure to have someone he knew nearby.

One day he murmured, "How can you be here all the time?"

She smiled and patted his shoulder, "Dear Marcus, I couldn't be anywhere else."

"Shouldn't you be at work?"

She smiled, though there were tears in her eyes, "A lot of folks are helping out. We all want you to get better."

He pondered that for a while. "How can you forgive me?"

She placed her warm hand on his, "Because we all need to be forgiven. You just rest and get your strength back. Then we'll talk."

Chapter Fifty

After a couple of weeks Marcus was definitely on the mend. He found out that his room was part of the suite at the back of Zach's Diner. He had only ever been in the sitting area when he came and went on errands for Mr. Z. He found out that there were two bedrooms and a bathroom besides the living room.

Charlotte had returned to work in the diner at the front of the building. This made it easy for her to stop and check on him every so often.

But with all that time alone, he was getting bored. Hanging on to the wall for support, he made his way into the living room. He made it across the room and dropped down onto the couch. He closed his eyes and rested his head against its back. *It feels good just to have a change of position.*

Eventually Marcus raised his head and looked around. There was no evidence left of his last time in this room, but his face saddened at the memory. Before his thoughts could become morbid the door opened.

"Sherry! What are you doing here?" He brushed a hand over his eyes. He couldn't believe that Myrna's friend had just walked into the room.

"I'm on staff here," she replied, "have been for a few weeks now." She beamed at Marcus. "I've been trying to be helpful so that my boss could spend more time looking after you."

"Charlotte's your Boss?"

"U-huh," Sherry sent him a conspiratorial grin, "I think she was beginning to miss the folks in the diner, so she agreed to let the rest of us help with your care. At first she insisted that you were her brother and it was her privilege, and her privilege alone, to look after you. She wouldn't leave your side."

Without realizing it, Sherry sent admiring glances across the room. It gave Marcus cause to wonder, but right now he needed to listen to what she was saying.

"Your sister is doing an excellent job as manager. And I for one am so thankful that she was willing to hire me. She's a real Christian!"

Sherry shifted her eyes to the far wall and her mouth tightened. "It was no fun going hungry, knowing that my chances of finding honest work were very slim. This job is a God-send and I'm so thankful." She used the corner of her apron to wipe a tear from her eye. "When Dora called to say that I should come in for an interview, I cried. I really did. I couldn't help it."

"Dora, as in Myrna's daughter works here too?"

She nodded and turned back to look at Marcus. "Yes. So when she called, part of me was filled with hope but the other part of me had been rejected too often to think that this time would be any different."

Still weak and prone to break out in a hacking cough, Marcus just relaxed and listened and wondered at Sherry's words. Would his sister's God give him a second chance as well? Was it fair to expect mercy when he had rejected God for so long?

He pulled himself up but the effort set off a bout of coughing. Hand over his mouth he smiled sadly at Sherry but didn't dare try to speak.

Without a comment, she stood up and reached behind his back to pull up the pillow that had slipped down. Her hand gave a gentle squeeze to his shoulder before she sat back down.

244

Marcus reached up and covered her hand, "Marry me."

Sherry's face turned bright red but she laughed and said, "I shouldn't be in here too long. Charlotte just asked me to check on you, to see if you need to get back to your bed."

He grinned at how neatly she sidestepped his question. He let go of her hand and said, "Needed a change." He kept his words to as few as possible. It looked like she understood. He gave her a smile and a little wave as she started to leave. Her reluctance to go left a warm feeling in the region of his heart.

But he was snoring gently before he had figured it all out.

***

It was late November of 2003. Marcus tried hard to listen to the doctor's advice to 'just rest.' The activity on the other side of the door was getting harder and harder to resist.

"Hey Davy," he called loudly, "Can you come in here?" He had heard the younger fella's voice in the kitchen.

When fifteen year old Davy entered the living room Marcus blurted out, "Any chance of a guy getting a glass of juice?"

"Sure," said Davy. "Be right back!" At the door he paused and looked back at Marcus, "Apple or Orange?"

"Make it Orange juice, please."

Davy returned with two glasses of juice. "I thought you might need some company by now," he grinned as he sat down in the big chair, one long leg dangling across the arm. He grinned, "Getting tired of talking to yourself yet?"

Marcus nodded. "I've been wanting to thank you for insisting that I come here. You probably saved my life, miserable as it was."

"Hey buddy, your life is precious. I'm glad God sent me that way."

"What do you mean, God sent you?" asked Marcus hesitantly, yet curious to hear the kid's answer.

"Well, I had planned to go in the other direction. Then I got a strong feeling that God wanted me to go into the park. Not knowing why because the path was empty, but I kept on walking. When I spotted you I knew exactly why God needed me in the park. Sorry, but I had to chuckle when I saw your long legs sticking out of that box. There was no way you were going to fit in there."

They both smiled and gazed across the room as they remembered the occasion.

"God or not, I'm glad you followed the urge. I would never have dared to try to find my sister." He rested his head against the back of the couch and closed his eyes. "She's all the family I've got."

Davy nodded, "And a very special sister indeed. I'm really glad that she is *my* sister's friend. She's helping Dora get over her timidity and she makes her laugh." Davy shook his head as he gazed at his clasped hands. When he raised his head, there was a serious look in his eyes, "Growing up, I can't remember ever hearing an actual laugh from her. Smile a bit perhaps, but laugh, never. She might have when we were young, but never like she does with your sister."

Deep in thought, they were startled when Charlotte showed up with a clatter of dishes.

"You guys are being too quiet. I decided it was time someone made a noise," she declared looking from one to the other. Marcus' lopsided smile made her giggle. "I see it. You can't fool me. You want to laugh. Come on, let it out!" She placed the tray on the coffee table in front of them.

Davy raised his eyebrows at Marcus, "See what I mean? She can't help herself."

Charlotte asked, "What can't I help? Spoiling you guys? Well, someone has to do it and I'll take full responsibility."

Soon both of the men had a smile on their face as they reached unabashedly for a muffin. Davy juggled the muffin from one hand to the other and blew on his fingers. "These must be right out of the oven," he yelped.

Marcus chose to put his muffin on a plate. He grinned at Davy, "No sense both of us getting burnt."

"Now you tell me," muttered Davy.

"You can make as much noise as you want to, Charlotte," declared Marcus looking over at her, "but only if the noise yields such good stuff."

Charlotte went over to Marcus and touched his arm. "Ted, who's been cooking up all that delicious food you've been eating, and I want to fatten you up so we can put you to work."

"Oh Ho!" he cried, "You don't want to spoil us, you just want cheap labor."

She shook his arm gently, "You know better than that."

Marcus glanced up at her and saw the sisterly love in her eyes. He lowered his own but nodded and said, "Soon. Soon I'll be putting you all to shame. You should see how much work I can accomplish in a very short time. Just ask her," he pointed at Sherry who had followed Charlotte with a tray of coffee, cream and sugar.

Sherry smiled and said, "Sorry, but I've never actually seen you do any physical work, Marcus. You were always walking, usually with your hands in your back pockets."

"I beg your pardon!" Marcus couldn't believe his ears. "I've *never* walked with my hands in my back pockets," he declared emphatically.

He saw Sherry's shoulders shake and there was a definite twinkle in her eyes. "But according to Myrna," her face sobered, "I do know that you were a good friend and did your job, even when you didn't like it."

"Tryin' to soothe my ruffled feathers, eh?" he teased.

"That is high praise indeed," declared Charlotte. She noticed the heightened color in Sherry's cheeks and pondered the reason.

For a brief moment Marcus was lost in thought. Then he raised his eyes to Sherry and said, "Thank you. You have no idea how good those words make me feel. I always hated how Mr. Z treated his ladies, and that I had to be a part of it. I'm glad you got out of his clutches. According to your friend, Myrna, that was a miracle. But guarding their lives made me feel like I was doing something good; protecting them from that evil man and his arrogant behavior." Marcus lifted his hand toward his chest but stopped midair when he noticed the questioning look from Charlotte. He laughed, "Your face is so telling."

The laughing and all that talking made him short of breath. He didn't have the strength left to explain. He waved at them and shook his head. He'd have to explain later.

"Sorry, Marcus, you came out of the bedroom for a change of scenery. Now we've overtaxed you." Charlotte pushed him back against the couch and spread a lap quilt over him.

Sherry lowered the blind and admonished, "Close your eyes and not another sound out of you."

Davy grunted, "You're outnumbered Marcus. Listen to your women and don't make a fuss or you'll never hear the end of it."

In the quiet that followed after the rest went back to work, Marcus' thoughts drifted to the past. He remembered the truck driver's words about being ready to meet his Maker. *What if I'd died? I'm not ready.* He could almost hear Edith's voice sharing the stories about Jesus and God's love each Christmas.

He sighed and wondered and sighed again. He murmured, "It sounds like a fairy tale. How could God's mercy be new every morning? Isn't he sick to death of all the times folks say they love Him and then they go and do mean and hateful things that must break his heart?"

It was more than his brain could grasp. He pulled his feet up on the couch and curled into a ball and fell asleep with the problem still unsolved.

Chapter Fifty-One

"One of the truck drivers that gave me a ride must have believed like you and Edith," volunteered Marcus as he and Charlotte relaxed later that evening. He felt toasty warm in the quilt that Charlotte had wrapped around his shoulders. "The man asked me if I was ready to meet my maker. He even bought me lunch. I wonder if he would have if he'd known how much money I had with me."

"How kind of him," murmured Charlotte.

"Yeah, he was a nice guy. But all my conniving and stress ended up to no avail," shrugged Marcus. "Mr. Z stuffed that cheque into his pocket and never bothered to credit it to my debt. I owed him 5G."

Marcus buried his head in his hands, "And I owe you even more than that." He shook his head and looked up at her, "I'm so sorry, Charlotte, so sorry."

"Don't worry, Marcus. We're doing just fine, excellent in fact. Consider the debt cancelled and try to put the past behind you. That evil man is gone now. Whether he took his own life or someone murdered him in his cell we might never know. But we do know that he will have to account to God for all he's done," encouraged Charlotte. Quiet reigned as they sipped at the hot chocolate in front of them.

"Have you heard anything about who's taking over his accounts at the Casino?"

Marcus gave a mirthless laugh. "Probably no one; I think the President wants to stay as far as possible from anything and anyone connected to Mr. Z. That side-business became an embarrassment to them when all this trouble started. The management probably turned a blind eye to those extra activities so long as they didn't become a public nuisance."

Charlotte nodded, "And his girl-friend, Tonya, has disappeared with Abe's money and their chauffeur. I doubt we'll ever see her face at the Diner again; or in town for that matter."

"It's a relief not to have to worry about that debt. But I'm still a vagrant. The only things I own are the clothes on my back."

Charlotte's giggle interrupted him. He looked down at the pajamas that he was wearing and said, 'Well, maybe not these."

She shook her head, "Sorry, Marcus. I tossed all your clothes. They were stained and torn beyond hope. I gave Ted, our chef, the sizes and he shopped to replace them. I hope you don't mind."

A slow grin peeked out as Marcus shook his head, "What's that thing Edith used to say to her sister-in-law about stuff, 'naked I came into this world and naked I'll leave it'."

"I don't remember that one,' laughed Charlotte, "But I can just imagine her saying it. Collette sure bugged Mom Edith about wasting her time and money on us, didn't she?"

"Did she give you a hard time after Edith died?" asked Marcus.

"She started to but Mom's nurse, Kay, stood up to her. I never heard from her again."

"Good for Kay," chuckled Marcus. "I'm glad somebody did."

"Kay was also a big help when our house in town sold so quickly. We had to pack it up in a hurry. I could never have managed it without her."

Marcus did not interrupt Charlotte's train of thought, as she sat and gazed into space. *I ought to have been the one to help her with all of that.*

Charlotte looked up and smiled at Marcus, "I made sure that all your things were packed up separately. I labeled the boxes with your name so they'd be easy to find when you returned."

He shook his head, "I don't know how you could even have thought that I'd ever return, after what I'd done."

Charlotte reached over to squeeze his arm. "Marcus, I worried about how you were doing. I knew that your anger would not allow you to get close to people, so I cried because I knew you'd be alone. How I wished that you'd come home. I kept praying that you would."

Marcus dabbed at the tears in her eyes with a Kleenex. "How could you want me back in your life? I was such a fool."

"Marcus!" she scolded. "We're family. Family always long for each other."

"Well, I'm here now," he smiled sheepishly.

"Yes. And I'm so glad. But I just wanted you to know that I had not given your things away."

Her shoulders sagged, "But then everything burned in the house fire back in Zhoda. Mr. Rand found out that it was the faulty wiring that started it."

"Thanks for telling me. I don't think there was much of value, except perhaps that photo of my mom at her grandparents place." Marcus reached over and patted Charlotte's knee, "I know you care. That's why you looked after my things, even though I didn't deserve it."

She raised an eyebrow at him, "Just like none of us deserve to be loved by God. It's a good thing love doesn't look for reasons to love, it just does. Jesus, the perfect, sinless, Son of God died on the cross to take everyone's punishment."

Silence filled the room, broken only by a few slurps of cocoa and a crunch as they nibbled at the Crispy Oatmeal Cookies.

Marcus looked up to see Charlotte watching him with an intense longing in her eyes. He grinned sheepishly, "I know, I know. Edith told it often enough. Jesus didn't stay in the grave. He's alive today."

Charlotte's face lit up as she grinned, "Then you must also remember how she taught us that Jesus is offering to live His life through each one of us. And that the offer is for anyone who chooses to believe."

Marcus was getting uncomfortable, just like in the old days. He was relieved when Charlotte changed the subject.

"So, tell me about how you met Sherry and why she blushes when you look at her. Do you have feelings for her?"

"Yes, Charlotte, I care deeply for Sherry. Myrna kept singing her praises long before I met her. When I did meet her, I noticed how fiercely protective she was over Dora. Like a mother bear, she'd hustle her out of sight the moment I got close. In fact, I never caught sight of Dora up close. Once I saw her leave the house and I was close enough to see the resemblance to her beautiful mother."

Marcus mused for a few moments.

Charlotte waited quietly.

"Actually, I didn't even know about Davy," said Marcus. Myrna and Sherry kept their personal lives hidden. Not that I can blame them. I think Sherry saw me as part of Mr. Z's gang, at least at first. Because of Dora's beauty, they were worried that the girl would get caught by and enslaved into Mr. Z's web of evil."

Charlotte sat up, "I'm so glad Sherry was there for them. It makes me love her even more."

Marcus grinned, "Yes, well, Myrna couldn't say enough nice things about Sherry either. How could I help but notice?"

Charlotte laughed and clasped her hands, "I'm so glad. I think Sherry is a wonderful person. If you can bring some happiness into her life, I'm all for it." Then she added quietly, "Just as long as there's room for me too."

"Charlotte," admonished Marcus, "You are my sister. I know I haven't been a good brother but things will be different from now on. You're all I've got. I promise never to abandon you again." His face shadowed, "Because I know how much pain comes with rejection and abandonment."

Once again quiet reigned in the room. Both sat and stared into space.

"I'm so sorry that I rejected all your efforts to show love."

"Hush, that's all part of the past. It's forgiven, just as God has forgiven me."

Marcus yearned to have the peace and joy that flowed from her. But he couldn't believe that it was meant to be for him. The heavy heart and sadness were his lot in life, just consequences of poor choices.

Chapter Fifty-Two

As Marcus regained his strength, he started to help out in the Diner. Sitting at the table with the staff, he was impressed with the gourmet meals that Ted, their talented cook, created with such ease. He was pleased to see Dora's shy smiles become more confident as she worked in the dining room. Cheery words of appreciation could be heard for her, coming from Charlotte and even the patrons.

Davy's whistle added a cheerful note when he popped in after school; and on weekends he rolled up his sleeves to help with the mounds of dishes.

Charlotte amazed him with her managerial skills. The timid little girl that he remembered was gone. This young lady handled the whole business efficiently and confidently. She brought a happy attitude wherever she went and was loved not only by the staff, but the patrons as well.

Marcus began to time his Coffee breaks to coincide with Sherry's. He loved to tease her just to see her blush, which she did whenever she came near him.

This easy-going camaraderie was a delightful change for Marcus. So much easier on a body than the constant pressure of the world that he had left behind; or rather it had abandoned him when he most needed support.

He joined the gang for Sunday evening service because he knew it would please Charlotte. There was no sense of personal need because he knew that God would never accept him.

Charlotte seemed to be okay with that. Marcus was glad because he wanted to be included in every part of her life – they were family now.

The mid-December air was crisp. It nipped at their noses as the gang made their way home. Charlotte, Sherry and Dora walked arm in arm at the front of the group. Ted, Davy and Marcus followed a step or two behind them. They kept a slow pace on account of Marcus still not feeling his best.

"I'm so glad that Marcus feels strong enough to come with us," said Dora.

"His strength is sure taking it's time to return." Concern laced Charlotte's voice.

"It probably stems back to all the stress of having to work for Abe. I know how his evil plotting seemed to enmesh a person. Before I knew what had happened, I was hopelessly indebted to him." Sherry was speaking from her own bitter experience. "But thankfully God gave me the courage to stand up for myself. I don't know why, but although Abe threatened to hurt me, it never happened."

"I'm so glad you got away from him," said Charlotte. She squeezed Dora's arm and said, "And so thankful that you were saved from his clutches."

"Thanks to my mom and to Sherry," said Dora with a nod in Sherry's direction.

Charlotte looked over her shoulder to make sure the guys were keeping up. Marcus noticed and waved. Charlotte waved back and sighed happily. She turned to Sherry. "Now that Abe is gone, who looks after your apartment building?"

"I don't know, but the rent keeps going up. I think someone must have decided to line their own pocket..."

Dora interrupted Sherry, "And that someone is the building superintendent, isn't it? He always has that greedy look when you hand over the rent money."

"Probably because no one's checking up on him," said Charlotte with furrowed brow. "With Abe gone; who would he be accountable to?"

Sherry shook her head and shrugged, "I don't know. I guess he'll keep collecting the rent until someone of authority shows up."

"Well, if he gets out of hand, you let me know. We'll get my lawyer, Mr. Rand, to recommend someone local who can look into it."

Zach's Diner was the first stop on their way home. "You're all coming in for a cup of hot chocolate to warm up before you go the rest of the way home," said Charlotte as she unlocked the front door.

No one argued the order. They piled their coats and scarves on the first table and made their way to the back. Everyone pitched in and in short order they were seated with a mug and spoon in front of them.

In the midst of the clinking sound of stirring spoons, Marcus leaned toward Sherry who was sitting beside him. "I couldn't help but overhear you guys talking about the high cost of rent." He grinned and whispered, "Marry me and then you can move in with us."

He waggled his eyebrows at her as she blushed. The look in her eyes was filled with longing but she shook her head and said, "I can't, Marcus. We'll manage somehow." She reached across the table and squeezed Charlotte's hand, "Especially now that I have such a good-paying job."

"Hear! Hear!" shouted Davy. Dora sent a grateful smile at Charlotte.

Ted got up to retrieve a container of shortbread cookies. "To celebrate God's goodness to all of us I think these have aged long enough to merit a sampling."

Laughter echoed around the table. They shouted, "As if we need any excuse to sample your cooking, Ted!"

Chapter Fifty-Three

The rest of the gang left for their homes. It was only 9:30 and Marcus wasn't ready to go to bed yet. He felt restless. He selected his sister's favorite Christmas movie, Miracle on 34th Street, while she locked up for the night.

Soon Charlotte seemed settled for the duration of the movie but Marcus couldn't keep focused on it. He kept shifting around on the couch; He coughed; He got up to get a drink of water.

"What is it, Marcus? Are you in pain?"

He shook his head. Charlotte's kind sympathy brought the moisture to his eyes.

"I can't get over how much you care about me when all I've ever done is caused you pain and heartache." His voice trembled, "I wanted so much to be with you and Edith but wouldn't let myself."

Charlotte picked up the remote and aimed it at the VCR. When silence filled the room she turned to him and said, "Oh, Marcus, please, it's all behind us now. Don't even think about it anymore."

"I have to." His voice, harsh with emotion, wouldn't be stopped. "I was so angry because of all my resentment. I felt mean and miserable and there you two were; so at peace; so loveable; caring about others... and I couldn't let myself be a part of it. It was like an iron grip held me back."

Both were quiet. Then Charlotte reached over and cupped Marcus' face in both her hands. "God loves you, Marcus. Actually God likes you!"

She leaned closer until their foreheads touched. "Marcus, what else can I say? You are so dear to me, and to Jesus. Why don't you just say yes to Him?"

Marcus pulled away from Charlotte as once again his thoughts wandered to the past. He couldn't help but remember Edith's admonition and the truck driver's words.

He turned to face Charlotte and took courage from the genuine caring he saw in her eyes. Tears spilled over as he finally gave in. "I can't fight God anymore."

He dropped his head into his hands. The tears seeped out from between his fingers. He cried out in anguish, "Oh God, I come to you as Charlotte suggested. I know that I'm an awful sinner and I'm not ready to meet you. I don't know why you should want to waste a minute on my miserable person...but I...but I...give up. I can't go on by myself. I hope your forgiveness is really available for someone like me. Please be merciful to me. Forgive me; clean up my heart and make me your child. The Bible says that you love me and that Jesus died to pay for my sin. I accept your offer of eternal life." A brief pause and he added softly, "Thank you, Jesus."

There was a hush in the room. When Marcus looked up, Charlotte's eyes were filled with tears. He could tell that they were glad tears. He reached out a hand and said, "Hello sister."

Charlotte burst into sobs and threw herself into his arms, knocking the breath out of him. "Oh Marcus, it's finally happened! What I've longed for and prayed for, for so long. Now we're a for-real family."

He grinned and awkwardly patted her back. "Well, I'm just glad that I was sitting on the couch when you decided to attack me. Otherwise we'd both be on the floor."

She started to pull away but Marcus tightened his arms around her and held her close. She murmured against his chest, "Sorry, brother, I should have been more careful."

"Don't worry about it. Hopefully soon I won't be such a weakling." He felt her nod.

"God is just going to have to make you all better now. We have so much living to catch up on," said Charlotte with a starry-eyed smile.

Marcus sat back contentedly as she stood up and stretched. Her hand came up to cover a yawn. Before she could comment he said, "I agree. I'm emotionally exhausted after that, even though my heart is at peace. For the first time in all my life I feel freed of the tightness around my heart."

Charlotte reached down and gently pulled him to his feet. With arms threaded around his waist for a goodnight hug she murmured, "I am so glad for you, Marcus. And I know the others will be delighted to hear that their prayers have been answered."

"I must remember to thank them," he said as he made his way to his bedroom.

The last thought to crowd through his mind was *I must tell Sherry. Maybe now she'll take me serious when I ask her to marry me.*

Charlotte's Reward – Book 4 of the Series, coming soon.

Other Novels

By

Violet Moore

Whimsical Edna

Violet Moore

Whimsical
A biographical novel of the author's mother.

Edna chose to find delight in every situation, whether it was being relegated to her in-law's kitchen to eat with the servants, or sleeping under the stars with her husband on one of their moves.

She shares her simple faith with her children, by actions and by words. She refuses to allow a spirit of bitterness put a crimp in her days.

Charlotte's Rescue
An Inspirational Novel
First in a series of four

     Charlotte White was rescued as a baby and then again as a teenager. Her nemesis, Marcus, does his best to make life miserable for her. Despite being rejected time and again, she continues to hope that things will be different.

     "It's been three years, Charlotte. You are going to have to accept the fact that he is not coming back." Charlotte sagged against the wall and swallowed hard. "I'm sorry, Kay. All I've ever wanted is for us to be a real family. You know - do brother and sister stuff – like fight and then forgive and laugh together about it."

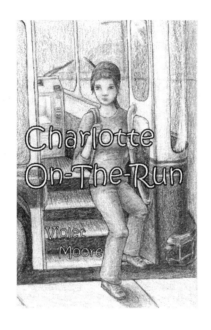

Charlotte's On-The-Run
An Inspirational Novel
Second in a series of four

Will Charlotte ever realize her dream of having a family? Or will distrust and pain from the past be too great to overcome.

Robbed while on the run, penniless and friendless in a strange city, thrown in jail… does God even care?

Find out as you walk with her, cry with her and maybe even laugh with her.